The Womanizers

A novel

Dwayne S. Joseph

URBAN BOOKS LLC
www.urbanbooks.net

Urban Books
6 Vanderbilt Parkway
Dix Hills, NY

Copyright © 2004 Dwayne S. Joseph

ISBN 09743636-8-5

First printing September 2004

10 9 8 7 6 5 4 3 2 1

Distributed by Kensington Publishing
850 Third Ave
New York, NY 10022
For store orders call 1 (800) 221- 2647 ext 527

Printed in Canada

Dedication

I dedicate this book to my wife Windalisa. Wendy, thank you for helping me make this book what it is. Are you ready? The next one's coming.

I also dedicate this to my daughters, Tatiana Marie & Natalia Simone. Daddy loves watching you grow, learn and explore. I promise that I will always be there for you.

Acknowledgments

It's 11:43 at night, and all's quiet in the Joseph household—a big deal with two little ones! Time to count my blessings while I have the silence.

First—as always I have to thank God for all of the obstacles that He puts in my path. With each one that I overcome, I grow as a man and a person. I know that is His intention and I am grateful.

Next—to my beautiful wife, Windalisa, and our two little princesas, Tatiana & Natalia. This truly is for you three and our future. Wendy, this was a fun story, wasn't it? I love you. Your support means everything to me, and to hear you say that you are proud of me, means more to me than you realize. Next year's going to be interesting with two little chatter boxes running around, huh? I can't wait!

To my family—Mom, Dad, Teyana & Vaughan, Daren, Granny and Grandmother—I thank you guys for the love and support. Granny, you are an angel. Thank you for saving us tons of money on babysitting! Vanessa Gray—thank you for being a good friend!

To Chris, Lisa, Jessie & Jasmine, Gregg, Kristi, Brian Keister & Mia, Mariana, Julian—thank you for the support, friendship and for keeping in touch. Lives change and get hectic, but no matter what, you guys are always a phone call or an e-mail away. That's what friendship is about. To say I have some of the best friends in the world would be an understatement. To my extended family—Lourdes, Russell, Ivan, Grace, Prianna, Leila—always there, always a phone call away. Thank you for adapting to the change. I love you guys.

To my friends within the industry—Carl Weber—I'm still rolling with you, man. I have nothing but the highest amount of respect for what you represent, what you do, and the opportunity that you've given me. This is round two—it's time now. Martha—damn—thank you isn't even enough for what you've done and shown me. You bring it all together and make sure that everything is as tight as it could be, and that is priceless. I know it's not enough, but THANK YOU! La Jill Hunt—my twin. It is truly a blessing to call you one of my best friends. I am so happy for you and proud of your accomplishments. You bolted from the gate when that bell went off and made your mark. Some people were, but I wasn't surprised. I knew you would! Now please get going on your next novel! People are going to be feenin' for more after *No More Drama* drops. Eric E. Pete, man...move the family to MD already! Bruh, the connection—it's real. We must have known each other before. It's our time, man. *The Womanizers* and *Gets No Love* in 2004! Can you say can't stop...won't stop. Believe that. Marsha, thank you for your feedback, the conversations, for doing what Wendy does for me, and making sure that your husband is one of the best. Suzette D. Harrison—I keep telling you I'm waiting for that next book. Thank you for the confidence, support and friendship. You know I have your back just the same. Congrats also to you and your husband on your new home. Angel Hunter, doing your thing day in and day out. I am blessed to know you. Riding the wave you, La Jill and I have been riding wouldn't have been the same with anyone else. I'm waiting for your book to drop.

To the Urban Books family: Roy Glenn, Thomas Long, Thomas Green, Stephanie Johnson, Jihad, Chunichi, Felicia Madlock and the rest of the crew. What's our anthem? We ain't goin' nowhere. We can't be stopped now. It's Urban for life! Congrats to all of us on making our marks.

To Ms. Robilyn Heath—Mother Hen—where would myself and the rest of the family be without you? You keep us focused, grounded & determined. You truly have been a blessing to all of us. I appreciate EVERYTHING you do, and I appreciate those phone calls just to say hello. I know I speak for everybody when I say that we love you.

Thank you also to Cydney Rax of Book-Remarks.com, Cheryl Robinson of Avid-Readers.com, Karen E. Quinones Miller, Mark Anthony, Anthony Whyte, Alex Hairston, Marcus Major, RM Johnson, Richard Holland from Sepia, Sand and Sable, Yasmin Coleman from APOOO, Charles Kumbersmart, and Yvette Estrelda.

To Portia Cannon—thank you, thank you, thank you, thank you, THANK YOU! You told me once to just write and to let you do the stressing. Portia, the stress you lifted from my shoulders, I will always be grateful for. I am so, so glad to have you in my corner. Thank you for being accessible whenever I need you. When we first spoke I said I had big plans. Well, now it's time to go to work.

To my special readers—Heather Seegel, Julie May, Joy Young, Lourdes Trevino, Tania Johnson, Marsha Pete,

Quaasmirah Baten, Monte Hanes, Granny, Grandmother—thank you for the feedback. It made a difference!

A special thank you to the USF crew—James Scott(much thanks and appreciated friendship), Crystal Underwood (I got you), Sheanea Powell, Jenaye Dickerson, Amy Santa, Nakyia Savoy, Amber Kerr, Tanyen Kerr, Lisa Purkey, Shantel Boykin, LaKeysha Glenn, Felicia Johnson, Kirsten McCree, Kara Taylor, Mahlon Adams, Brandee Izquierdo, Kenneth Frazier, Diane Richardson, Charles Inokon, James Brown, Hedy Dieso—thank you all for supporting a brother the way you did that last round.

Finally, to my readers: For those of you that enjoyed *The Choices Men Make*, "One Night, Six Dreams" in *A Dollar And A Dream*, and "Played" in *Around The Way Girls*, I present to you *The Womanizers*. Read, laugh and enjoy. I gave this one my all, and I will continue to do that for the ones that follow. Keep those e-mails and reviews coming! You know I'll respond! Jocelyn Lawson—I think you'll be proud!

And of course: To my New York Giants. New coach, new quarterback, a whole new look. I'm ready for the new season. It's our time!!!!

Dwayne S. Joseph - 5/14/04

www.DwayneSJoseph.com

Djoseph21044@yahoo.com

Mike
Smooth Operator

My cell phone was ringing. No doubt it was Mya looking for my ass. I was supposed to be at the grocery store getting a few things before the anticipated snowstorm came. The trip should have taken me about forty minutes tops; it was now going on an hour and a half. If I were my wife, I'd be looking for my ass too.

But I couldn't take the blame for my lateness. Let's look at the facts, shall we? I didn't tell the cashier, a 5-foot 9-inch darker version of Tyra Banks who I'd been flirting with for the past week, to give me an erotic glare, lick her full lips in a way that let me know it was on, and slip me a note saying she would be off in ten minutes and wouldn't mind a "ride." Those are the facts, and nothing but the facts. Now, having said all of that, do you really think I could have gone home right away? I mean, what kind of man would I have been to leave a woman stranded? A fool, that's what kind. And I am certainly not that.

So after making sure that she reached her desired destination, I moved back up to the front seat of my Durango, dropped ole girl off, and headed back home. I didn't mean to take so long, but Tyra's twin insisted on thanking me deeply before the ride began. Again, I didn't want to be rude, so I sat back and accepted her slow . . . gratitude.

So you see, I was being a stand-up cat. A respectful guy. I should not be chastised for my acts of chivalry. I laughed at that last thought then answered my cell. "Hey, baby," I said evenly.

"Mike," my wife said with agitation running rampant in her tone. "Where are you?"

"I'm sorry, baby. There was drama down here. Two guys tried to rip off an elderly couple. Unfortunately for them though, I happened to be walking out of the grocery store when it all happened. I ended up chasing them around Owen Brown before I caught them."

Mya sighed. "Can't you ever just be off duty, Mike? You don't have to be Super Cop all the time."

"Baby, would you rather that I just let them get away with what they did?"

"No, but it would be nice if we could spend some quality time together. I swear I feel like I'm last on the list sometimes."

"Come on, Mya. You know you're not last."

"No I don't, Mike. If you're not at work doing double-time or you're not at the gym, then you're out with Ahmad and Max. I come somewhere after that. I don't feel like I come first at all."

"I'm sorry, baby. I didn't know you felt like that. How can I make it up to you? I don't want my baby feeling last ever," I said as genuinely as I could.

"Well you can start by getting your behind home. I want to cuddle up with you."

I smiled. "Is that all you want to do?"

"Get home and find out."

"I'll be there soon." I hit the end button then turned on the radio. Ironically, Sade's song "Smooth Operator" was playing. I couldn't help but laugh. Sade must have had me on her mind when she wrote the song because I was certainly that.

Now, I know what some of you all must be thinking, especially the women, but believe me, I'm a good ass husband, and I love my wife. She's attractive. She has feline eyes that speak, lips that whisper seduction even when they don't move, a body made from the mold of an hourglass, an ass that won't quit, firm, smooth breasts, and golden, flawless skin that smells like sweet chocolate. She's all that. But there's more.

She's also stylish, intelligent, witty, funny, and passionate. She loves life and that is what I love about her. She knows how to have a good time. She's exactly the type of woman that I need to complement me and my style.

I'm sure you're all asking the same question right about now: If she's so fine, why do I cheat on her?

Well, the answer is one that most men will be able to relate to and most women will probably hate. But hey, I'm keeping it real. Quite simply, I fool around on Mya because there is just too much ass out there in the world to let it go to waste. I mean let's look at the ratio here. For every male, there are what—four to five females? As men we are outnumbered. Hell, we have to keep swimming in the pond, but we also have to make sure that we find that one special female to carry our seeds. And that's what I've done. There's Mya, my wife, my partner, my child-bearer, and then there's everyone else.

Brothers, holla if you hear me. Women, if you don't like my answer—tough. That's the way it is. I didn't make the rules; I just joined the game. But like I said, I'm a good husband, and when the time comes, I know I'm going to be a good father too.

I turned up the volume on the radio and sang along with Sade. No doubt, I am a smooth operator.

Ahmad
Mr. Commitment

"Ahmad, I don't want to have sex. I'm not in the mood."

Not in the mood. Goddamn. That's all I'd been hearing for the past six months.

"Come on, Shay. Nicole is actually asleep. Let's take advantage of the moment." I put my hand on my wife's thigh and caressed it gently. She pushed it off.

"Ahmad, I told you I'm not in the mood." She turned over on her side for me to stare at her back.

"Shay, it's been six months. How the hell can you not be in the mood?"

"Because I'm not."

I tossed the covers off of me in frustration and got up from the bed. "I'm tired of this shit, Shay. You're never in the goddamned mood. I could understand when you were pregnant, and I could even understand after you had Nicole, but that was six months ago. I've been a patient man, Shay. Damn patient."

"What are you trying to say, Ahmad?" Shay asked, her back still my only point of focus in the moonlit room.

"I'm saying that your husband is sexually starved and would like to have some sex."

"So, it's all about you, is that it?"

I shook my head and clenched my jaws. "Shay, this is about us. We are married and we should be having sex. Why aren't we having sex, Shay? We're both able to."

Finally turning to face me, Shay said, "We're both able to? So, I guess since *you* say that we are, I should just lie on my back, spread my legs, and have sex like a good wife. Is that what you want Ahmad? Will that make you happy? Here." Shay did just as she said; she lay on her back and opened her legs. "Take it, Ahmad. Take what you're starving for. Let's do what we should be doing."

I slammed my hand against the dressing table. "Why do you make it seem like having sex with me is a bad thing? Like it's the worst thing in the world?"

"Ahmad, why does this have to be about you?"

"It has to be about me because you don't tell me anything. I try to talk to you to find out what's going on with you and all you do is close up on me. What am I supposed to think, Shay? How can I not think you not wanting to have sex with me isn't about me?"

"Ahmad, for the last time, this has nothing to do with you. This is about me. Me, okay?"

"Then talk to me, damn it. Tell me what's going on with you."

Shay gave me her back again. "I don't want to talk about it," she said softly.

I threw my hands in the air. "Fine, Shay. You don't want to talk about it. You don't want to have sex with me because it's about you and not me, and you don't want to talk. Fine." I snatched my pillow from the bed and stormed out of the bedroom.

"Where are you going?" Shay asked as I walked down the hallway to the living room. I never answered her. I was too pissed. I'd heard people talk about how the sex stopped after marriage and kids, but I never thought that would happen to us. I mean, before we got married it was sex, sex, sex. We were like rabbits in heat on speed—day and night, night and day. Then became pregnant, and that's when my boys started talking.

Be ready for a lifetime of celibacy.
The only way you'll get sex is by paying for it.

Better get acquainted with your hands.

I hope you saved that black book for the rainy days because it's about to flood in your world.

Comment after comment, that's all I heard, but I never sweated it. Her not wanting sex during the pregnancy never made me worry. I figured that once she had the baby things would go back to being semi-normal. I knew, of course, that we weren't going to have as much sex as we used to; that's how it is with kids, but damn—to get none and not know why?

I groaned as I stretched out on the couch and grabbed the remote control. I was too agitated to fall asleep. I know sex isn't everything, but hell, it's a big part of a relationship. A couple has to be compatible sexually if they're going to last. Let's face it—good to great sex will keep a marriage above water, but bad to no sex? That's a problem, because then there's a good chance a couple will be headed down a road that dead ends with only two possibilities: divorce or infidelity. Those were the roads I'd seen friends in the past take, and they were roads that I wanted to avoid. But how much longer could this go on? How much longer could I deny the fact that the tension in my household was getting thicker by the minute and my relationship with my wife was slowly deteriorating? Worst of all, how much longer could I deny that my eyes were beginning to wander?

I tried to exhale away frustration as the television watched me, but it didn't do much good. If anything, I became even more frustrated. I stared at the television screen but didn't really see anything at all.

Six months. Six months without sex. Damn. I didn't remember signing up for the celibacy ride when I said, "I do." I loved my wife and thought she was as beautiful as ever, even with the baby weight she'd gained, but something had to change and change fast.

Max
Family Man

"That's it! Right there! Don't stop!"

"You like it?"

"Oh yeah!"

"Am I working it right?"

"Right on point, baby!"

"Is it mine?"

"It's yours!"

"Say it again!"

"It's yours!"

"Again."

"Oh shit. It's yours, baby. It's all fucking yours! Oh shit, here I come! Don't stop. Don't stop. Oh yesssssss!"

It was a good thing Sharon came when she did because I couldn't hold back any longer. I quickly pulled out and released into my condom while I leaned on her ass. Sharon looked at me over her shoulder.

"Why don't you just come inside of me, Max?"

I shook my head and peeled off the rubber. "I told you before, Sharon, I ain't takin' no chances."

Sharon chuckled. "I'm not going to get pregnant."

"No chances," I said again.

"But you wear a damn condom."

"That shit ain't foolproof. Quit asking me to stay inside of you, 'cause it's not gonna happen. Now hurry up and get dressed. Trina'll be home in a half hour." I got off the bed as Sharon sucked her teeth and stretched out.

"Let her come home. Bitch. She ain't all that with her stuck-up ass. I don't know how or why you put up with her. Besides, I'm all the woman you really need."

"First of all, I'm with her stuck-up ass because she's the one with the money and the high-salaried job. Second of all, you ain't got shit but good pussy. Now get your ass out of my bed. I gotta change the sheets."

I went to flush the condom down the toilet. When I came back, just like a good girl, Sharon was getting out of bed. I stared at her naked rear end as she bent over to grab her clothing from the floor. Goddamn. I couldn't lie—for an older woman, Sharon had a fine ass. And it was soft as shit too. For some women, having babies is murder on their bodies, but for Sharon, having babies had the opposite effect. She was thick in all the right places. I considered hitting it from the back one more time. Shit, I know she wanted me to. That's why she was taking her sweet time to grab her shit. But damn, I couldn't blow up what I had with my wife, Trina. Anything and everything I wanted, Trina gave me. All I had to do was take care of shit around the house and keep laying the pipe in the bedroom. As good as Sharon's pussy was, I couldn't let my wife come home and find me in bed tapping her mother's ass.

"Yo, Sharon," I said, ignoring my stiffening penis. "Stop playing around and pick your shit up."

Sharon stood up and walked toward me, twirling her thong. "You sure you don't want to have me one more time?" She passed her thong beneath my nose for me to sniff and grabbed my crotch. I looked down at her. For a forty-six year old woman, she was sexy as hell. Her breasts were full and firm, her body was toned and didn't have an ounce of cellulite, and her ass—well, you already know about the ass. Shit, to be honest, she looked better than Trina. There was just one problem. Sharon was as ghetto as a two-dollar crack ho is nasty. And what I said was true—she didn't have shit but good pussy. Pussy that she was willing to give up like Halloween candy.

I had started messing with Sharon two months after Trina and I got married. I didn't make the first move. I mean, I always thought she was attractive, even with her ghetto mentality, but Trina was my golden queen. Trina clocks big dough as a finance director. She and I met at a party that a mutual friend of ours threw. From the moment I laid my eyes on her I knew that she had a thing for bad boys. I could tell by the way she carried herself. She had this I-like-to-keep-my-nose-in-the-air-and-perpertrate-like-I'm-above-everyone-else attitude, but I'm a pro at spotting out the fakers, and it wasn't hard to see through her façade. She was the type of female who had dough but didn't want a man with dough because she liked being the top dog. I had no problem with a woman taking care of me. That's why I stepped to her and gave her what she was looking for.

I didn't meet Sharon until two months after Trina and I started seeing each other, and that was only because we bumped into her at the store. Sharon and I clicked instantly because we come from the same place—the gutter. Trina couldn't stand that we got along, because she couldn't stand her mother. She hated that Sharon was ghettofied and never tried to get out of the projects, while Trina had worked hard to get as far away from them as she could. Sharon couldn't deal with her daughter's bourgeoisie attitude and she never let an opportunity go by without letting her know that.

I knew from that first meeting that they had issues between them, but I didn't know how bad they were until Sharon showed up at the house out of the blue one day. I was at home conducting some business—and if you must know, my business ain't no illegal shit. I'm in the process of trying to get a few of my cousin's boys signed to this major record label. I'm their manager. Anyway, like I said, I was conducting business when the doorbell rang. I was shocked when I opened the door and saw Sharon standing there looking phat to death in a black mini-skirt that barely covered her ass, a silver V-neck top showing me nothing but cleavage, and some black pumps. Like I said, she's ghetto.

"What's goin' on, Sharon?"

"Is Miss Priss here?" Sharon asked with heavy attitude.

"Nah, she's still at work. She ain't gonna be home for another two hours."

"What are you doing?"

"I'm working. I got some dudes here talking business."

"Well, tell your dudes to leave," she said, stepping past me.

I grabbed her by the arm. "Sharon, I told you I'm conducting business."

Sharon looked me up and down with a devilish smirk. I always knew she was attracted to me. I knew that the first moment we met. "If you want to feel this ass, you better tell your dudes to leave." She walked away toward the living room, and I swear she hiked that skirt up a notch for me. I didn't know what was going on, but I went into the living room to get rid of the group.

"Yo, dawgs, y'all gotta jet. I gotta talk to my mother-in-law."

After they left, I went back into the living room where Sharon was sitting on the couch, legs crossed, pumps off. She was sipping on a glass of wine.

"What's going on, Sharon? Why you come in here talking all that shit?"

Sharon laughed, took another sip, then put the glass down and walked towards me. "You know I always thought you were fine, Max," she said, standing in front of me.

I nodded. "Is that right?"

Passing her hands over my cornrows, she said "On some men the cornrow look don't work, but on you it sure does."

I slipped my hand up her skirt. She wasn't wearing panties.

"I know you always thought I was sexy, Max. I knew it when I met you. I saw the way you looked at me." She moved from my hair to my chest then down to my crotch. "You want to fuck me. I know that."

Playing with her clit, I said, "How you know?"

Sharon pulled down my zipper. "Because we come from the same place, Maximillian."

While she stroked the shit out of my manhood she rammed her tongue into my mouth. I was confused and shocked by what was going down, but I didn't stop her. I mean let's face it—she was right, I was always turned on by her. Besides, how could I turn down an opportunity to tap my mother-in-law's ass? And a fine mother-in-law at that.

We fucked right there in the living room and when I say fuck, I'm talking about some no holds barred, yoga-type fucking. When we were done I said, "You're my mother-in-law."

Sharon adjusted her mini-skirt. "And you were just inside of me."

"You hate Trina that much?"

"Just as much as you love her."

"Why'd you come onto me?"

Sharon grabbed her purse from the couch and stepped to me. "Don't worry about why. I have my reasons."

"So when are you gonna tell me the reasons?"

Sharon grabbed my crotch. "Don't worry about my reasons, Max. Just know that you have free ass whenever you want it."

I watched her with a scrutinizing eye. "You tryin' to set me up?"

Sharon laughed. "If I were setting you up, I would have stopped before I let you have me. No, Max, this isn't a set up. I'll see you later." She squeezed my crotch one last time then left.

Since that first time we'd fucked at least once a week. She still hadn't told me her reason for sleeping with me, and I didn't really care. As long as she kept her mouth shut and her ass in the air, I was cool.

I pushed the thong away from my face. "Get dressed, Sharon." I walked out of the room and went downstairs to get a fresh set of the same black satin sheets that were on the bed. When I came back, Sharon was gone. I changed the sheets, threw the ones we'd used in a plastic bag, and put it in the garbage outside. Before Trina made it home, I made sure the room was clean and funk-free.

Mike

"Fellas, it's official." I paused to take a sip of my rum and Coke. "It is absolutely, positively impossible for me to remain faithful to Mya." Even though my eyes were glued on a gorgeous sister with honey-brown skin who'd been staring at me as she danced with her man on the dance floor, I could see my boys Max and Ahmad shaking their heads. I turned towards them. "Yo, I'm telling y'all, I can't do it. There are just too many women out there in the world."

Max laughed and swallowed some of his Corona. "So why'd you marry Mya if you knew you couldn't be faithful to her?"

I cut my eye at my boy who I'd known, along with Ahmad, since the sixth grade. "Nigga, I know you're not about to preach to me with your mother-in-law fuckin' ass."

"Nah, I ain't gonna preach shit. All I'm sayin' is if you knew you couldn't be true, why'd you make the ultimate sacrifice and commit?"

"Man, for the same reason you're ass is with Trina. I gotta have a good woman to go home to. And I gotta have a good woman to give me some sons."

"Right, right," Max said, giving me a pound.

I looked at Ahmad. "So how come you didn't say anything, Mr. Commitment?"

Ahmad shook his head. "Man, I'm not even gonna waste my breath on you two fools."

Max and I gave each other a look of pure skepticism then leaned against the bar counter and waited. We knew what was coming next.

"I just don't understand you guys," Ahmad said, sipping on his bitch drink—an Amaretto Sour. "You guys are married to two beautiful, intelligent sisters, yet that's not enough. I mean come on. Mike, you have Mya, who's easily one of the baddest women out here. A woman who loves and puts up with your ass like ninety percent of the sisters in this world wouldn't, yet you fuck around with freak after freak like it's a sport. Why, man? It ain't like you can't get the sex at home, because you already told us how Mya loves to give it to you. So why risk losing that?"

I shook my head. I loved Ahmad to death, but sometimes he could really get on my nerves with his non-understanding ass. "Nigga, do I need to explain the ratio to you again?"

"Man, that ratio doesn't mean squat when you have a woman like Mya."

"Damn, man," Max interjected. "You act like you want to fuck Mya."

"Shut up, fool," Ahmad said. "Anyway, all I'm saying is that when you've found the right woman, you should forget about the rest. And Max, you need to heed my advice. Shit, I don't agree with fucking around on your woman, but if you're gonna do it, you don't sleep with your mother-in-law. You keep fucking around with her and see what happens to your ass."

I had to laugh at that. I remember the day Max told us what he was doing with his mother-in-law, Sharon. Ahmad and I couldn't believe it. I've fucked around with a lot of women, but I don't know if I'd ever go there.

"Yo, you guys have seen the titties and ass that Sharon got. Don't tell me if your mother-in-laws were stacked like that and wanted to give you the pussy that you wouldn't take it."

"Hell no, I wouldn't take it," Ahmad said.

I had to think for a minute, then shrugged. "Yo, Sharon's body is off the meter. If Mya's mom were put together like that and wanted to give me some, shit, I might have to consider it."

"Of course you would," Max said. "Most normal men would. Only the choirboy here would turn down pussy like that."

I laughed out loud and gave Max some dap. "Choirboy . . . that's a good one."

"Yeah, real funny. Ha ha," Ahmad said. "You guys go ahead and crack jokes all you want. Messing around on your ladies may be fun now, but in the long run that shit'll come back to haunt you."

I set my drink down on the counter. I was used to his preaching, but I was tired of hearing it. "Says who?"

"Come on, man. It always happens to fools who take things too far. I'm saying if you guys don't chill, Mya and Trina are going to find out. Mark my words on that."

"Mark your word? What the fuck does that mean? What are you gonna do, tell them?" I took a step toward him.

"Chill out, man," Max said, grabbing my shoulder. "You know he wouldn't do that. Right, Ahmad?"

I pushed Max's hand off of me and stared at Ahmad. "I ain't chillin' nothin' out, man. So, what do you mean, mark your words?"

Ahmad stared back at me but didn't say anything. Any time we started talking about women, this always happened. This was the only topic that could make us come to blows. While I admittedly couldn't stop cheating, Ahmad was Mr. Faithful with a capital F. Even when we were teenagers he never cheated. That's why his heart had been broken more than once.

Ahmad had always given all of himself to a woman, even if she's not treating him right. He claimed it took a strong man to give his heart and be true. I say a man who passes up ass is one of two things: Either he's gay or he's a fool. Since I knew Ahmad wasn't gay, he was a stupid-ass fool. All it took was getting my heart broken once for me to learn my lesson about how much to give to a woman. I wouldn't do that shit again.

"So what's up, man? You planning on telling our wives?"

Ahmad kept his eyes locked on mine. He must have been on some shit, because I know he didn't want to go at it with me.

"Nah, man, you know I'm not gonna do that. I'm just saying don't risk losing a good thing at home."

"Look, man, I ain't risking nothing. If Shay is the perfect woman for you and you don't want to fuck around on her, then don't. But don't sit there and tell my ass what I should and shouldn't be doing. Talking about mark your words. Nigga, I been with Mya since I was eighteen and she was seventeen. You think she's going anywhere now? I don't think so. I may mess around on her, but I treat her like a queen. Anything she wants I provide—the house, the car, anything. She ain't gonna give that up."

"How do you know that?" Ahmad asked.

"Because I know." Ahmad and I were silent as we stared at one another. I watched my boy intensely. I couldn't believe he was coming at me like that.

"Yo, will you two chill the fuck out?" Max said, breaking the tense silence. "We came to throw back some drinks and look at the ladies, not argue. Shit. Now, I see this shorty over there that I want to step to, but I won't be able to do that if you two idiots are planning on having a rumble up in here. So what's up? You guys gonna chill so I can snatch that honey up, or you gonna make me baby-sit your asses and watch another dude get her?"

I kept my eyes locked on Ahmad. "Can we chill so this fool can go?" I put out my hand for dap.

"Yeah." Ahmad dapped me then turned to Max. "You sure Sharon won't get mad?"

"Whatever, man," Mike said, heading for the floor.

As he stepped, I turned back to Ahmad. "Yo, what's eating you, man? I mean, I know we go at it about that sometimes, but you ain't never tried to commit suicide. What's troubling you?"

Ahmad sipped his drink and shook his head. "Nothing much, man. I just have some stress on my mind."

I ordered another rum and Coke for me and another bitch drink for Ahmad. "Speak, man. What's up?"

Ahmad opened his mouth to speak but then closed it. "Nah, it's nothing, man. Just some stress about school."

"That's it? That's what's got you all wound up?"

"Yeah, man. That's it."

I shrugged. It was obvious that something other than school was stressing him out, but if he didn't want to talk about it, that was his prerogative. "Alright, man. Whatever you say. But don't say I didn't offer."

"Nah, everything's cool, man."

"That's cool. So how're Shay and my goddaughter doing?"

With a proud smile, Ahmad said, "Man, Nicole is doing great. She speed crawls. She's standing up all the time. She's holding her own bottle, and she loves the hell out of Elmo."

"Damn, she's doing a lot."

"Yeah. The doctor says she's advanced for her age."

"Good deal. So, what about Shay?" As soon as I asked that, the smile that had been plastered on his face quickly disappeared.

"She's cool," he said bluntly. Nothing more. It didn't take a genius to know where the real stress in his life was coming from.

"That's good to hear. So, other than the job things are going alright?"

"Yeah, everything's cool."

"Alright."

We didn't say anything for a few minutes after that. We just chilled out, drank our drinks, and enjoyed the hip-hop being played. Five minutes later, Ahmad threw some dollar bills on the bar counter. "Yo, I think I'm gonna jet."

"You sure? Max and I might head to a strip club after this."

"Nah. That's the last place I need to be right now."

"You sure?"

"I'm sure. I'll catch you guys later."

"Alright, man. Yo, before you go . . . you still have my back, right?" After the way he'd come at me, I had to know if I could still trust him.

Ahmad put his hand out. "Come on, man. I've been covering for your ass all these years. You think I'm gonna stop now?"

"My nigga."

"Yeah, yeah. Just make sure I don't get any speeding tickets. Talk to you later. Tell Max I said peace."

"Alright, man."

After Ahmad left I hung by the bar by myself for a few minutes. I hoped Ahmad and Shay would be able to work through whatever it was they were going through because they made a decent couple, even though I personally didn't like Shay too much. I thought she was annoying as hell and her mouth was too damned big sometimes. If it weren't for being Nicole's godfather, I'd probably just tell Ahmad to come and chill out by my place when the games were on TV, just so I wouldn't have to deal with her nasty looks and not-so-subtle comments. But whether or not I liked Shay made no difference because Ahmad loved the hell out of his woman. Hey, to each his own. I wasn't the one sleeping with her at night.

I swallowed the rest of my drink and smiled. The cutie with the honey-brown skin had been arguing with her man and he'd just walked off, leaving her alone on the dance floor. Idiot. I ordered two more drinks then made my move.

Ahmad

When the school bell rang, I let out a slow sigh of relief. Midterm week had finally come to a close. As my students rushed out to enjoy their hard- earned weekends, I gathered the pile of exams on my desk to take home to grade.

"Mr. Jefferson?"

I looked up; I hadn't even noticed that my top student, Maxine, had still been in the room with me.

"Hey, what's going on, Maxine? I didn't realize you were there. I'm surprised you didn't race out to get the weekend started like everyone else."

Maxine shrugged her shoulders. "I don't have anything big planned."

"I got you. So what's up?" I went back to gathering my things.

"Not much. I just figured I'd hang around and walk out with you."

I paused for a second, raised an eyebrow an then looked up at my student. It was no secret that she had a crush on me. It was actually a long-running joke in the teachers' lounge. For a while people actually thought she had been getting A's in my class because of "extra-curricular" work she'd been doing. But even though Maxine was a drop-dead gorgeous young woman with Pocahontas-like features and a body criminally mature for her age, she was still only a teenager and a student who earned her A's the old fashioned way—studying.

"Um, that's really nice of you, Maxine, but you really don't have to do that."

"Are you sure, Mr. Jefferson? I don't mind waiting. I can help you clean up or something."

I smiled and shook my head. "No, that's okay, Maxine. There's not much here for me to clean up, but thanks anyway."

Maxine smiled at me, stood up and grabbed her backpack and purse. I let out a slow breath. It was flattering that she had a crush on me, but I was relieved that she was going.

Maxine walked up to the desk. "Mr. Jefferson, can I ask you something?"

I continued with my clean up. "Sure. Go ahead."

"Do you think you'd ever have sex with me?"

I nearly choked on the piece of gum I'd been chewing. As I gagged I said, "What?"

Maxine leaned forward on the desk. "Mr. Jefferson, I think you are fine as hell. I know I'm your student, but I'm eighteen, so legally we could have sex and it'd be no problem."

I didn't know what to say. I opened my mouth then closed it. I did that two more times before backing two steps away from the desk. "Uh, Maxine, it's really flattering that you, uh . . . like me, but you're my student."

Maxine put her hands on her hips and gave me attitude that I never knew she had. "I'm eighteen. I'm legal."

"Uh, yes, but . . . uh . . . that wouldn't be right. Besides, I'm a married man."

"I won't tell your wife."

I took another step back while the sweet, reserved Maxine I'd always known disappeared right before my eyes. I couldn't believe this was happening. Maxine watched me with eager eyes. She was dead serious.

"Maxine, look. You're a beautiful, intelligent young woman who's got the world waiting to be conquered. You also have the right guy waiting for you."

"But you're the right guy, Mr. Jefferson."

"For my wife I am."

"I promise not to tell her.

"Maxine, you don't have to promise anything because nothing's going to happen between us." I gave Maxine a serious stare. Although the flattery was nice, I had to put a stop to her advances because I wasn't trying to have anyone accuse me of sexual misconduct. "Do you understand what I'm saying to you, Maxine?" I asked sternly. She didn't answer me right away, and for a second I wondered if I had been too firm.

Finally she said, "I understand."

"Good. Believe me, Maxine, I'm truly honored that you find me attractive. If this was ten years ago and I wasn't your teacher, maybe we could talk about going out. But for now, why don't we just stick to Algebra?"

"Okay, Mr. Jefferson." Maxine adjusted her bag on her shoulder then came around the desk with her hand extended. "I just want to apologize," she said as I took a step back.

I took her hand. "No need to apologize, Maxine. Nothing happened. I'm just glad we're still cool."

Maxine smiled. "We're definitely cool." She let go of my hand.

"Good. Well, enjoy your weekend," I said, relieved. Just when I thought I was safe, catastrophe happened.

"One more thing before I go, Mr. Jefferson."

"What's that?"

Maxine took a step toward me. I wanted to back up again, but my back was already against the wall. "You know how you said if you were ten years younger we could talk about dating?"

"Yes," I said hesitantly.

"What if I were ten years older? Could we still talk about it?"

"Maxine . . . " I started.

"Don't worry, Mr. Jefferson, you don't have to answer that now. But just so you know, this is what you could get ten years from now."

Before I realized what was happening, Maxine
lunged forward, wrapped her arms around my neck, and
planted her lips against mine. Her tongue was in my
mouth, checking around for cavities when the school
principal walked into the room.

"Mr. Jefferson!"

I quickly pushed Maxine off of me. "Mrs. Baker!" I
said.

"Mr. Jefferson, what is going on here?"

I looked from the principal to Maxine. "Ah . . .
nothing is going on. Maxine and I were just . . . talking."

"That's not what I saw," Mrs. Baker snapped.
"What I saw—"

"Was a misunderstanding," I said, cutting her off
and cutting my eyes at Maxine. "Isn't that right,
Maxine?"

Maxine wiped her mouth and smiled at me slyly.
"That's right, Mr. Jefferson."

"I think you better go home now, Maxine," Mrs.
Baker said. "Mr. Jefferson and I need to talk."

Maxine nodded, looked at me, then walked out of
the room. When she was gone, Mrs. Baker closed the
door. "What the hell did I just walk in on, Ahmad?"

"Irene, believe me. What you saw wasn't real."

Irene folded her arms. "Oh, it wasn't? So, what was
it then, my imagination?"

"Yes—I mean no! Look, what I meant was that kiss
wasn't real." Irene gave me a cross look. "I mean she
kissed me."

"And what were you doing?"

I groaned. "Look, Irene, you know that Maxine has
a crush on me. Everyone does. But what you saw wasn't
real. I had just turned down an advance by her when,
out of nowhere, she kissed me. You walked in a second
after that happened."

"Ahmad, she's your student, for Christ's sake!"

"I know that."

"And you're a married man!"

"I know that too. Believe me, I did not intend, want, or ask for that to happen."

Irene shook her head. She'd been the school principal for the past year and a half, although she rarely left her office. Irene was a short, big-boned white woman in her mid-fifties with iron-gray hair kept up in a bun. There was a rumor that she used to be a popular stripper in a high-priced club way back in the day. With her slightly crossed eyes, big beaked nose, and lips that looked like they'd sucked on one too many lemons, it was hard for me to imagine her as a woman who commanded top dollar.

"Look, Irene, I promise you—no, I swear to you that Maxine took it upon herself to come on to me." I wasn't trying to lose my job or go to jail.

"Well, you must have said or done something to instigate her actions."

I shook my head. "No! I swear I didn't do anything. I just turned her down."

Irene stared at me silently for a few seconds then said, "I believe you, Ahmad."

I breathed out a sigh of relief. "Thank you."

"Of course," she said, walking toward me, "I would believe you a lot more if I could feel those lips of yours like Maxine did."

I stared at her. Was she serious? "Uh . . . come again?"

Irene smiled. "And again and again. I'd like that."

"Uh, Irene, what are you saying?" *Lord, please let me wake up now,* I thought.

Irene stood just inches away from me. "I'm saying that my husband will be away next weekend and if you want what happened with Maxine to become a memory that I can't recall, you'll be at my place next Friday night at six."

I stood in complete shock as she laid her chapped lips against mine and squeezed my behind. When she pulled away, she was smiling. "Of course, if you'd rather not come over, I'll understand, although I don't think the school board or your wife will understand why you were in here practically having sex with your student."

"That's not what happened!"

Irene backed away. "Hey, I'm just the principal who walked in on it. They don't have to believe me. Six p.m.—sharp." Irene walked out of the room with a chuckle.

I sat down—or maybe collapsed would be a better word—into my chair and threw my hands on top of my head. I couldn't believe what had just happened. I couldn't get sex at home from my wife, but my student, whose soft lips I didn't think I could forget, and my boss, whose lips I didn't think I could forget either, were both willing and eager to sleep with me. Sex with Maxine was impossible; I knew that. But sex with Irene? She threatened my job and my marriage. She said ten p.m. Damn. What the hell was I going to do?

Shay

I stood in front of the mirror disgusted from head to toe by what I saw. My cheeks were round like I had cotton stuffed into my mouth. My chin had a new friend that I hadn't invited. My breasts were sagging as though weights were hanging from my nipples. My stomach was bulging. My hips were wide as though they were running away from my waistline, which was doing its best to catch up to them. And my thighs were thick, and stingy with the air in between them.

I frowned at my naked self. My mirror image was the only person I'd allowed to see me completely undressed since giving birth. Not even my own husband had seen me this way. I just didn't feel comfortable with my body anymore. Okay, I'll be straight up—I hated it. I hated the way my body shape had changed and I hated the weight I'd gained. I was so unhappy with my appearance that I'd started doing some things differently. I got dressed in the bathroom whenever Ahmad was around, I wore clothes to bed, and worst of all, I'd stopped having sex with my husband. I knew that it was a cruel thing to do to a man who had been nothing but an angel and damn near perfect, a man who loved me and loved the body I wouldn't let him touch. I knew it was wrong of me not to talk to him about how terrible I felt about myself, leaving him to wonder if he'd done something wrong. I just couldn't talk to him. I couldn't talk to anyone. This was something I had to deal with on my own, and until I did, the changes I'd made in my life would just have to stay.

I moved away from the mirror and sat on the bed with my face in my hands. I was so happy yet so depressed at the same time. The birth of our daughter Nicole was one of the most special moments in my life. I loved being a mother. It's almost impossible to put into words the incredible feeling of devotion I had for my little angel. The love I had for her was everlasting. I would do anything and sacrifice anything for her wellbeing. When I held her, I could completely forget about the awful nine months I suffered through to bring her into this world.

But then Ahmad would come with his love and affection and touch me, and bring back to my mind just how hard carrying Nicole had been. I threw up almost every day for six months. I couldn't stand the scent of anything. Ahmad had to change his deodorant just so he could be next to me. He had to spend incredible amounts of money on fast food because I couldn't stand the scent of food being cooked in the house. Hell, I couldn't even stand the scent of my own house.

I was miserable.

To make things worse, giving birth was one of the most painful experiences I'd ever gone through, one that I didn't know if I wanted to endure again. That was one of the main reasons I wouldn't let Ahmad touch me. Honestly, I was scared to get pregnant again. Even though I was on the pill and the chances were slim, becoming pregnant was still possible.

I hated what my fear and lack of self-esteem was doing to my marriage. I mean, he was such a damn good black man. I loved his gray eyes and the shoulder-length dreads he wore. I loved his toned upper body and scrawny legs. I adored the affection he had for me and our little girl. Excluding my daddy, he was by far the most loving, respectful, self-giving man I'd ever known. Of course, he had ways that got on my nerves, but all of them combined couldn't taint the beautiful man that he was. On top of all that, Ahmad was also the best lover I'd ever had. Now, I'm not a ho or anything, but I'd had some experience with men, and believe me, none of them could match my husband's deft skills in the bedroom.

Before I became pregnant I used to have sex with him like my life depended on it. I couldn't keep my hands off him. Now it was a challenge for me just to lie beside him. I knew that if I didn't find a way to change what was going on inside of me, I could wind up losing him. He loved me and would do just about anything for me, but let's face it—he's a man. A good one, but he's a man nonetheless. If I didn't find a way to start having sex with him again, he was going to go looking for it somewhere else.

As I slipped into my underwear, the phone rang. I ran and grabbed it before its noise could wake Nicole. "Hello?"

"Hey, Shay."

"Hey, Mya! What's going on, girl?"

"Not much. I'm just looking for my husband, Robocop."

I laughed. "Sorry, girl, but he's not here."

"He's not?" Mya asked, her voice full of surprise.

"Nope."

"Well, is Ahmad there?"

"He hasn't come home from work yet."

"You mean he wasn't off today?"

"Off? Oh no. He had midterms this week."

"Humph," Mya said. I didn't even have to ask why she thought Mike would be at my house now or why she thought Ahmad was home, because I already knew the answer.

"Did you call Mike's cell?"

"Five times," she said angrily.

I shook my head. There was no doubt in my mind that my husband's friend of sixteen years was out somewhere cheating on his wife again. I didn't know why Mya put up with his unfaithful ass. He may have dimples and be Morris Chestnut fine, but the way he ho'd around made him one ugly dark-skinned brother. Everyone knew that he was unfaithful to Mya and I know that she knew it too.

There was an uneasy silence over the phone. I wanted to say something about how I felt, but I couldn't do that for two reasons. One, I didn't want to get involved in any of their drama. Their life was their life, and how they chose to live it was up to them. If she wanted to be disrespected, that was her prerogative. The second reason I didn't say anything, and this was the major reason, was because Mike was Ahmad's lifelong friend, and putting my two cents in would be disrespectful to my husband. As much as I wanted to, I couldn't.

"Hey, girl, don't worry about Mike. He's probably on the job somewhere and can't answer his phone." I knew it was a weak ass lie, but I had to say something to get rid of the negative silence.

"Why did he tell me that Ahmad was off today, Shay?" Mya asked me. I could tell by the quivering in her voice that she was about to cry.

"I don't know, girl. Maybe he thought Ahmad was off. It could just be an honest misunderstanding. Hey, why don't you come over? It's Friday and Ahmad will be home soon. We can send him out for some take-out and movies and we can all just hang out. Mike will probably show up here later anyway, and when he does, you can ask him all the questions you want."

Shay sniffled. "You sure you and Ahmad wouldn't rather be alone?"

"Girl, please. Alone is the last thing we need to be right now."

"Okay, but I won't stay too long. I'll just watch one movie."

"Just come on over, Mya."

"Okay, but I'll bring the movies. What do you want to see?"

"Girl, bring that new movie with the Rock, *The Rundown*. That man is just too fine."

Mya laughed. "You ain't lying. What other movies?"

"You can bring whatever you want. Just make sure you bring me the Rock."

"How about an old one—*Two Can Play That Game*?"

"Oh, we have that one. But bring *Barbershop*."

"Will do. What time should I come over?"

"Make it seven. That'll give Ahmad some time to wind down before you get here, and it'll give you about two hours with Nicole before she falls asleep. She's usually out by nine."

"Sounds good. Your little girl is so precious. You know she's gonna be a heartbreaker, don't you?"

"I know that's right."

"Ahmad buy a shotgun yet?"

"Not yet, but he will soon."

We laughed, which was a good thing because I didn't want her to ask me any more questions about Mike. "Anyway, girl, Nicole's stirring in the crib, which means I need to get a bottle ready. I also need to get some clothes on."

"Okay, Shay. You go on and handle your business. I'll see you at seven."

"Alright, girl. I'll see you." I hung up the phone, threw on a bra and some sweats then went to prepare a bottle for Nicole. Ahmad came home while I was in the kitchen.

"Hey," he said softly, walking straight to the refrigerator. No kiss hello, no hug. We'd barely been talking since he slept on the couch a few nights ago. I turned and looked at him. He was looking so sexy in his light blue shirt, black pants and yellow tie. Damn this lack of a sex drive.

"How was your day?" I asked.

Ahmad cracked open a beer and took one long gulp. "Um . . . it was uneventful," he said. It sounded like there was something he wasn't telling me, but I let it go. "How was Nicole today?"

"She was in one of her clingy moods today. She should be awake soon."

"Okay."

"I just got off the phone with Mya."

"Oh yeah?"

"Yeah. She was looking for Mike, and she was under the impression that you were off today."

"I see," Ahmad said, taking another long swallow. "Well, I wasn't. I'm gonna go and get changed."

"Mya's coming over at seven with some movies. I told her you'd go and get some take out for the three of us. I'm in the mood for some Chinese."

Ahmad finished his beer. "Whatever. I'm going to check on Nicole."

He walked out without saying anything else to me. I hated the tension between us.

Mya

I didn't know why the hell I was crying over Mike's ass. It wasn't like that was the first time I'd ever caught him in a lie. There'd been many other times. He just didn't know that I knew about them. Damn it. Why did I have to fall so head over heels for him? I'd known him since I was fifteen years old and started dating him when I was seventeen. He was my first and the only lover I've ever had, and he hadn't changed at all.

Mike had always been a womanizer. I knew that before we started dating. Women could never resist his dark chocolate skin, his dimples, his intense brown eyes, or his pretty boy smile. Mike always had an inflated ego, and the attention women gave him made him weak when it came to temptation. If a woman wanted to give him the booty, he took it without hesitation. I knew all of this and I still fell for him. But it wasn't only looks. He was also a very smooth brother. He knew the right things to say and the right things to do at the right times. He was blessed with the skills of a ladies' man.

My husband wasn't all bad, though. He was actually a very sincere, caring man, and he never hesitated to make me feel special. I couldn't be faulted for falling for his looks or the way he treated me, but I could be blamed for one thing—I was a fool to ever think that I could change him.

I grabbed the phone and dialed his cell again, and as expected, I got his voice mail. I threw the phone across the room in frustration and wiped my eyes. I deserved better.

Mike

My cell phone went off again just as I finished getting my freak on with this fine-ass Asian chick named Ming, who I'd pulled over earlier for speeding. I was sure it was Mya calling for me again. I knew I needed to call her quick because this would be the fifth time she'd called, but I was busy cleaning myself up. Ming had been true to her word. She said she could easily work off the $120 speeding ticket that I was going to give, and she certainly did that. Ming was one of those petite, Asian females who loved brothers. I could tell that the minute I walked up to her car to get her license and registration. She was lucky I was down for her brand of payment, because bribing an officer is a serious offense.

"So, did I work off that ticket?" Ming asked with a sweet smile. She was on the bed still, naked, with her slender legs open for my pleasure. After we had agreed on the method of payment, I had her follow me over to an out of the way motel that I liked to use. The owners gave me free use of the rooms since I kept my eyes closed to any illegal activities that went on there.

"What ticket?" I asked, wiping myself down with a washcloth. When I was finished, I grabbed my cell. I looked at the caller ID and saw that the last call had been from Ahmad. I hadn't spoken to him since he left the club a few nights ago. I dialed him back. "What's up?" I asked when he answered.

"Yo, where are you, man?"

I could tell by the tone in his voice that this wasn't a social call. "Man, I'm at my spot."

"Yeah well, next time you decide to use me for an excuse, how about letting a brother know?"

"Oh, damn. My bad, man."

"Yeah, your bad. Man, I had midterms this week. You told Mya I was home sick?"

"Man, I completely forgot. I was supposed to meet up with my captain's secretary, Reina, but her husband fucked things up by showing up at the station to take her to lunch. Since my plans were screwed I just went out on the road and pulled Ming here over for speeding." I turned and looked at Ming, who was climbing out of the bed to get dressed. "Damn, my bad for real. So, was Mya mad? She's been blowing my cell up."

"Man, I don't know. Shay talked to her."

I shook my head. "Shay? Man, I know that's your wife and everything, but man, she has a big ass mouth. She didn't blow my shit up by saying some shit to Mya, did she?" Damn, I couldn't stand her.

"Man, I don't know. I don't think so, though, because Mya's coming over here tonight to watch some movies with us. I doubt she'd be coming over if Shay said something."

"Yeah, yeah. Maybe she did keep her mouth shut. So, Mya's gonna be over there. That means I don't have to rush home."

"Man, what are you gonna tell Mya?"

"I'll think of something. You know I'll cover that shit up. But if she asks or says anything to you, just tell her you had mentioned to me that you were thinking about taking the day off because you weren't feeling well yesterday. I'll take care of the rest."

"Whatever, man. Just remember what I said about shit coming back on you."

"Man, not now. We went through this already."

"Alright, man. Anyway, I'm gonna hop off. I have to go and get some take out for tonight."

"Alright, man. Good lookin' out on the call."

"Yeah, yeah."

Ahmad hung up and I turned to Ming, who was slipping her thong on. "Guess what, Ming?" I asked, getting up from the bed.

Ming looked at me. "What?"

"I forgot that you were speeding in a construction zone."

"I was?"

"Yeah. That means your fine was doubled."

"So, I guess I'm not done, huh?" Ming asked with a knowing smile.

"Nah. Looks like you're gonna have to work out that other half too."

Ming let the thong fall to the ground and giggled. I'd take care of Mya later.

Trina

I was only too happy to walk into my house. Work had been hell. It had been one of those days where everything that could have gone wrong did, and anyone who could have been a royal pain in my fine, honey-roasted ass was. This was one of those times when I wished that Max's career in the music business would take off so I could quit working and do the fun things in life like sit around and watch TV all day long and eat bon-bons like Peg Bundy. But I only wished that for a second. I could never really do what Peg did, because I'd be bored to death. The truth is, I loved what I did, even with the stress. I loved that people looked to me for all of the answers. I'd worked hard to be where I was. From the bottom floor of the projects to the top floor of the penthouse, I'd made it.

Ever since I was a little girl I'd always wanted to succeed. I guess that was because of my humble beginnings. Okay, humble is the wrong word. I was poor. No, not even poor. I was po'. I'm talking cheese and crackers for dinner with roaches as daily guests, wearing the same clothes three days out of the week, no heat for the winter, five people sleeping in onc bed po'.

I came up in the projects, but unlike my mother and my little brother Jamal, I made it my mission to claw and scratch my way out of there and never go back. I followed my older sister, Nikita, as she set the example and became a doctor. Sharon and my brother, on the other hand, were still living in the very same projects where I grew up. Jamal wouldn't climb out because he was working on his pharmaceutical degree. For those who don't know, that's code for 'he was a drug dealer.' From what Sharon told me, he was a good one.

I didn't speak to my brother too often. I understand the concept of doing what you have to do to survive, but Jamal had always been smarter than my sister and I, and if we made it out, then he damn sure should have. His problem was that he was lazy. He got that quality from Sharon, the one person I absolutely couldn't get along with.

If you haven't guessed by now, Sharon's my mother. She and I had always had a strained relationship. She thought that just because I liked the finer things in life, I was stuck up, but let me tell you, I'm not. I just didn't think there was any reason to grow up in the ghetto, have kids in the ghetto, and stay in the ghetto after her kids had up and gone.

There was absolutely no excuse for Sharon's desire to stay at the bottom. What bothered me the most was that she didn't just live in the projects physically, she was a permanent resident mentally too. My mother was so ghettofied she should have been the ghetto spokeswoman. She belonged in a damn rap video the way she dressed. She had absolutely no class at all.

I wished my husband wasn't such damn good friends with her. That bothered the hell out of me. Even though he had climbed out of there, he still had a slight project mentality.

Max was a bad boy, and I'd always had a thing for bad boys. The first time I saw him, I knew I wanted him. He had hair that he wore in a blowout like Maxwell or sometimes cornrows like D'Angelo. If I had to compare Max to anyone, it would be the guy with the gun in his locker in the movie *Barbershop*. I don't remember his name, but Max looks like him only taller. Rent the movie if you don't know who I mean.

Most of my friends disagreed with my choice of a man. They felt that I was selling myself short because he didn't make enough money and his career hadn't taken off. I didn't care about what they thought. What he made didn't bother me, because he treated me right. His only flaw was his relationship with my mother. I swear, the older I got, the more I disliked her. And I knew she felt the same way.

I kicked off my shoes by the front door and went upstairs to change into my workout clothes. I was about to get my *Power 90* workout on. I was surprised to see that Max wasn't home. Usually he was handling business with his groups. If he wasn't doing that, then he was cleaning up. I swear he was one of the neatest men I knew. After slipping into my Spandex and Nike sports bra, I bent down to grab my sneakers from under the bed. "What the hell?" I said, seeing not the sneakers, but something entirely different.

I stood up and held in my hand my mother's earring. I knew it was hers because I'd seen her wearing it before. Besides, it was too damn big and gaudy to be mine. "What the hell is this doing here?" I asked myself out loud.

"What's what doing here?"

I jumped and spun around. "Jesus, Max! You scared the hell out of me. Don't you know not to come sneaking up on a woman like that? Damn."

"I'm sorry, baby," Max said, giving me a kiss. He started to laugh.

"That wasn't funny. My heart's beating like wild drums."

He kissed me again. "I'm sorry," he said. "But that shit was funny."

I tapped him on his arm.

"So, what were you talking to yourself about? Or do you have some nigga in our bathroom?"

"Oh yeah. He's right in there naked and shaking. Anyway," I held up the earring. "I found this under the bed. It belongs to my mother." I noticed a slight lift in Max's eyes. "You seem surprised."

Max turned away from me. "Yeah, yeah. I am surprised. I'd forgotten all about it."

"You knew it was here?"

"Yeah. I found it in the living room by the sofa the other day."

"Hold on a second. The living room? Sharon was here?"

"Yeah. She came by to see you one day, but of course you weren't here. She ended up hanging around for a few, listening to my female group practice and then she left."

"Why didn't you tell me?" I asked, getting irritated. I didn't like her being there when I wasn't around.

"Aw, baby. I was busy. Besides, the last person on my mind is Sharon."

"So how'd her earring end up on the floor?"

Stripping down to his boxers, Max shrugged. "Baby, I don't know. It must have fallen out. All I know is I found it and brought it upstairs to give to you. But like I said, she ain't important to me and I forgot."

I sucked my teeth and threw the earring in the garbage. "What did she want? She knows I work, unlike her welfare check-cashing ass."

"I don't know, baby. She wouldn't tell me."

"Humph. Wouldn't tell you? She probably came over to beg for some money to buy some more hoochified clothing. I don't know why, though. She knows I wouldn't give her shit."

"Baby, honestly, she'd ask your brother for dough before she asked you."

I curled my lips. "Oh yeah, my brother the kingpin. Well, if it wasn't money then what did she want?" I was feeling warm beneath my skin. I was gonna have to pull out the free weights today. "Well, since she didn't tell you what she wanted it must not have been important, so whatever. Her earring's in the garbage where it belongs." I grabbed my sneakers. "I'm going downstairs to work out."

"Alright, baby. I'm gonna take a nap. I had a rough day."

"How's it going getting your new girl group signed?"

Max sighed. "Rough. The people like their songs, but they don't like their image."

"What's wrong with it?"

"They say they're too innocent looking."

"But they're only twelve."

"I know, baby, but you know how the industry is now."

I shook my head. "So what, they don't want to give them a deal unless they act like little hoochie mamas, like ninety percent of these other groups out here?"

"Basically."

"Humph. Are you going to let the industry pimp them like that?"

"Baby, I don't know. Put it like this: If the execs don't like the image, they ain't putting together no contract. So what am I gonna do?"

"But those girls have real talent."

"I know that, but this is about money, not talent. It's all about how much they think they can make off of them with the right image."

I *humph*'d again and headed to the door. "That's why I don't like half of the music that's out today. Everything is about sex, sex, sex."

From under the covers, Max said, "Sex sells, baby."

"Whatever. Maybe you could hire Sharon to teach them all about being ghetto fabulous and hoochied out." I closed the door behind me and went down to work out. I was only too irritated now. I've heard his girl group, 4A. For twelve year-old girls, they were extremely blessed with the gift of song. I'd hate to see them get pimped and turned into grown women before their time. I popped in the *Power90* DVD and hit play. "Bring it on,"

I said as I stretched. Finding Sharon's earring irked the hell out of me.

Max

Shit. When Trina showed me Sharon's earring I nearly lost it. I'd told Sharon's ass to make sure she took all her shit with her when she left. Damn. How the hell could she forget her fucking earring? I knew she had to miss it. I swear to God, it almost seemed like she left it on purpose. I mean, how else did it end up under the bed? I swear that better not be the case, because Sharon didn't want to play those kinds of games with me.

I had to wait until the next day when Trina left for work to call Sharon about it. Trina was barely out the door before I had the phone in my hand and was dialing Sharon's number. "Sharon, what the fuck is your problem?"

"Hello to you too," Sharon said.

"Fuck hello," I snapped. "What the hell is up with forgetting your earring here? I told you to make you sure you leave with all of your shit."

Sharon chuckled. "Who found it?"

"Why you laughing like that? You left that shit here on purpose, didn't you? What the fuck is wrong with you?"

"Calm down, Max. I was just having a little fun. Besides, I'm sure you came up with something to tell her ass."

"Having a little fun? This isn't some fucking game, Sharon. I'm warning you, whatever beef you have with Trina, you keep that shit between you two. Don't be fucking up shit for me."

"Or else what, Max? What the fuck are you gonna do?"

I gritted my teeth and clenched my jaws. I knew she was waiting for me to threaten her, just so she could threaten me right back about bringing Jamal to come and shoot my ass. I wasn't afraid of nobody, but I wasn't stupid. Jamal was gully and would shoot a nigga in a heartbeat.

Sharon laughed at my silence. "That's what I thought. You ain't gonna do shit."

"Why you wanna fuck around like that, Sharon?"

"Like I said, I was havin' some fun."

"Yeah well, enough of the playtime."

"Whatever. So you ready to take it again?"

I shook my head. Damn, if her pussy wasn't so good . . .

"Trina just left."

"I'll be over in an hour."

"Make it two. I need a nap." I hung up the phone and lay down in the bed. Sharon's idea of fun and games bothered the shit out of me. I had a bad feeling that if I didn't quit fucking with her, something was gonna come back to bite me hard. I started to doze for a while when the phone rang. I prayed it wasn't Sharon looking to bother my ass. I looked at the ID. It was Mike. "What's up, man?" I asked, breathing heavily into the phone.

"Not much, man. What's going on with you? Why you sound all stressed and shit?"

"Man, because I am. Sharon is trippin'"

"Oh yeah? How?"

"Man, that bitch left her earring here for Trina to be found on purpose."

"Damn. For real? So what happened?"

"Just like the bitch wanted, Trina found it. Luckily I was able to think on my feet and come up with an excuse, but man, I was heated."

"Damn."

"Yo, I called Sharon's ass this morning and let her know that I didn't appreciate her games."

"What'd she say?"

I groaned. "She told me to relax."

"Relax?" Mike said.

"Yeah, I know. I started to rip into her about that, but then she threatened to get Jamal on me."

"What? Max, man, I told you before I could take care of Jamal's ass. I could easily set that fool up."

"Nah, man. The minute you do that, Sharon'll go straight to Trina."

"But she won't know that you or I had anything to do with it. He's a fucking drug dealer. You and the cops aren't the only enemies he has. You follow me?"

"I follow you, man, but it won't matter. Jamal's been doing his thing for a good couple of years now with no flack. If some shit went down on him now, whether she could prove it or not, Sharon would blame me and open her mouth to Trina."

"Damn, man. You got yourself in a bind."

"Yeah," I said, exhaling. "Anyway, man, I'm about to catch some Z's for a few. What'd you need?"

"Oh, yo, I'm throwing a surprise birthday party for Mya next weekend, so make sure that you and Trina keep your calendars clear."

"No problem. How you gonna get her out of the house?"

"I might need Trina's help on that one. I would ask Shay, but she don't like my ass and would probably tell Mya just to spite me."

I laughed. "You're probably right about that, man. Aw'ight, so next weekend. Cool. I'll give Trina the 4-1-1."

"Cool. Well, go catch your Z's. I'm about to hit the road. I'll call you later this week to give you the details. Peace."

I clicked the end button on the phone and took a glance at the clock. Sharon would be over in another hour. I felt like calling her and telling her not to come over, but by the tone in her voice I knew that she was horny. And when she was horny, the sex was right. I closed my eyes and fell asleep.

Ahmad

I walked into the house with a paper bag filled with Chinese food and found Shay and Mya sitting at the kitchen table, laughing up a storm. "I hope you're not laughing at me," I said, setting the bag on the counter. "I'm not that funny looking." I kissed Mya on her cheek. "What's goin' on, Mya?"

"Not much, Ahmad. Shay and I were just tripping over this week's episode of *Hey Monie* on B.E.T."

"Oh yeah. I watch that. It's pretty funny."

"That show is the truth," Shay said.

"You ain't lyin', girl," Mya said, giving her a high five.

"So where's my little girl?"

"Would you believe she's asleep already?" Shay asked.

"Really? That's a surprise."

"Yeah. She wore herself out climbing up the stairs today."

"Well, that's cool. If we're lucky, maybe we'll be able to get through a whole movie before she wakes up. Speaking of which," I turned to Mya, who was looking especially sexy in a white button down top and navy blue jeans that fit her just right, "what movies did you bring? I hope they're not some movies that'll piss you sistahs off. If that's the case, I'll save myself the aggravation and flee for my life now."

Mya and Shay laughed. "No," Mya said. "There's no *Waiting To Exhale* in there. I brought *The Rundown*, *Barbershop 2*, and *The Wood*."

"That's cool. I could use a laugh right about now." My eyes lingered on Mya for a moment. I knew she was my boy's wife and I really shouldn't have noticed, but she was looking exceptionally attractive. I looked away before she caught me staring. "So, are we gonna eat first?"

After throwing down the Chinese food, Shay and Mya cleaned the kitchen while I hooked up the new DVD player. Not one time had Mya mentioned Mike, and I was glad because I didn't feel like having to lie to her. Shay and I had barely spoken a word to one another, and that was fine with me because I really wasn't in the mood to talk to her. I was just fed up with not getting any sex and not knowing the reason why. And having my student and boss come on to me didn't help.

I still didn't know what I was going to do about Irene's "invitation." I knew I didn't want to have sex with her, but she'd seen Maxine's lips on mine. Would she really go through with her threat and tell the faculty or Shay? More importantly, was I willing to chance it by not going to her house next Friday? Damn. Why did I have to be the one going through all of the stress and drama? Max was messing around and fucking his mother-in-law and what did he get? Ass and no headaches. Mike's mission was to break Wilt Chamberlain's record, and what did he get? Ass and no headaches. Me, I tried to be as good a husband as I could, and all I got was involuntary celibacy, an attraction that could get me thrown in jail, and another that I'd go to jail to avoid.

As I was making sure all of the connections between the DVD, television set and cable box were straight, Mya walked into the living room. "Is everything ready?"

I looked up at her. "Almost. I just have to make a final connection and we'll be ready for business."

Mya smiled and sat down on the sofa. I took a moment to let my eyes enjoy the sight of her again. I'd known Mya for as long as Mike had. Actually, I'd met her first. It was in high school and Mya and I had the same art class. I was immediately attracted to her, but because I was a senior and was getting ready to go off to college, I didn't want to hook up with anyone. Mya and I became good friends, though, and eventually I didn't care about the girls that I'd meet away at school. Mya was always classy and always ahead of the game. College or no college, I wanted to date her. But before I had the chance, Mya asked me in class one day if I could introduce her to Mike. Back then Mike was the star point guard on the high school basketball team. He was also on all of the girls' most wanted lists. I didn't know that he was on Mya's until that day. As much as I wanted to, I couldn't say no. I introduced them after school one day and the rest, as they say, is history. They were married after Mya graduated from college.

Mike had always messed around on Mya. I never understood why or liked it, but what could I do? He was like my brother, and because of that, my loyalty was to our friendship.

I watched Mya as she flipped through a magazine. Shay was attractive, but didn't have the stunning beauty that Mya had. Mike was a fool. "So how's work going, Mya?"

"Work is going well, but I'm thinking of going back to school."

"Really?"

"Yeah. Even though I make a decent salary with the bank, I'm unhappy doing what I do. Honestly, being a loan officer is not what I've always dreamed of doing."

"Oh yeah. So what do you want to do?"

"I want to become an interior decorator."

"Really?"

"Yes, really. Why do you say it like that?"

"No reason. I'm just surprised. What brought this on?"

"It's just something I've always wanted to do. I just never thought that I could. Honestly, I just want a change. And what better change than to go after your passion?"

"Hey, I can't argue with that. Besides, you definitely know a lot about style. I'm sure you'll be the bomb decorator."

"Thank you."

"So what did Mike have to say about your decision?" I didn't want to mention Mike's name, but it really couldn't be avoided.

"He didn't say anything."

"He didn't?"

"No. He doesn't know."

"Oh."

"I think I want to change more than my profession, Ahmad." Mya looked at me with sadness and hurt in her glistening eyes. It was obvious that Mike's disrespect had taken its toll on her heart. I was about to say something when Shay came into the living room with a couple of drinks.

"So, did you guys decide which movie we're watching first?"

With her back to Shay, Mya wiped her eyes with the back of her hands. I looked at Shay. "Why don't you pick?" I suggested, turning on the TV.

We sat through the entire showing of *The Rundown* and half of *Barbershop 2* before Nicole started to cry from her crib. Shay, who'd been drifting in and out of sleep the whole time, stood up quickly. "I'll get her."

"I'll pause the movie," I said.

"No, don't pause it. I shouldn't be gone too long. I won't miss much."

"Maybe I should get going," Mya said. "You guys are probably tired anyway."

Shay sucked her teeth. "Girl, please, keep your butt in that sofa and enjoy the movie. I'll be back."

Mya smiled and sat back in the sofa. We were sitting at opposite ends. Shay had been in between us. I was glad Shay convinced Mya to stay. I didn't want to see her leave for a number of reasons. One, because I was enjoying her company and the faint scent of perfume that she was wearing. And two, because her company was keeping me from having to be alone with my wife.

We continued to watch the movie in silence, until thirty minutes later Mya said, "Ahmad, what happened to Shay?"

I wanted to say that I didn't know and didn't care, but instead said, "I'll go and check." I got up and went to the bedroom. When I peeked in, Shay was fast asleep with Nicole on the bed. I closed the door softly and went back to the living room. "She's asleep with Nicole on the bed."

"Aw, how sweet. I'm sure you want to join them. I think I'll get going."

Mya started to get up when I took hold of her hand. "Don't leave, Mya. Please?"

Mya closed her eyes a fraction at me then sighed. "Ahmad, I'm not trying to get in your business, and if you want to tell me to butt out that's fine, but what's going on between you and Shay? You guys have hardly spoken a word to each other tonight, and you were miles apart watching the movie."

I clenched my jaws and blinked my eyes slowly. "We're having some problems right now, and I don't know why."

"What's wrong?" Mya asked softly.

I took a deep breath and held it as I stared at Mya, who was watching me with genuine concern. I exhaled and spoke.

"We haven't had sex in over six months."

Mya's eyes widened. "What did you just say?"

"Shay hasn't had sex with me in over six months and I don't know why."

"What do you mean you don't know?"

"I mean that Shay refuses to tell me her reason for not wanting me to touch her."

"Are you serious?"

"Mya, I wish I wasn't, but I am dead serious. This shit is just damn frustrating. I've tried to talk to her about it, but nothing I say or do will get her to open up. The only thing she says to me is that whatever her problem is, it has nothing to do with me."

Edging a little closer to me, Mya said, "Well, maybe it doesn't. I mean, she did just have a baby. Maybe she just needs more time to recover from that."

I shook my head. I wasn't buying that logic. "Nicole is six months old, Mya. Besides, if it has nothing to do with me, why can't she open up to me? I mean, damn, I am her husband, right? We are supposed to be able to confide in and lean on each other, right?"

"Yeah."

"Then what the hell is her problem? Six months, going on seven in a couple of days. Mya, I'm a married man and can't get any damn sex. What does she want me to do, go and get it somewhere else?"

"Ahmad, don't you dare."

"Don't worry. I'm not gonna do that. I'm just saying that I should be able to get it at home. Six damn months, Mya," I said holding up six fingers for extra emphasis. "I'm frustrated and angry and I just don't care if she knows it." I grabbed the remote, turned off the DVD player and switched back to cable.

"I don't know what to say, Ahmad."

"There's nothing to say. It's pathetic. I mean, I know sex isn't everything, but come on." I stopped talking finally. It felt good to vent that way.

Mya took my hand. "I'm really sorry that you and Shay are having intimacy problems. Believe me, if anyone deserves to be happy and stress-free it's you. Try to think positive if you can. Maybe whatever is bothering

Shay will go away soon and you two can get back to being normal."

"Yeah. Or maybe things won't change," I said in an aggravated tone.

"Ahmad, try to think positive."

I sighed. "Positive," I repeated. "We'll see. Anyway, I'm sorry to have vented like that. It's funny, the other night Mike asked me what was bugging me, and I didn't tell him anything. That's my boy, my brother, but I couldn't open up to him. And now here I am spilling my guts out to you."

Mya slid closer to me and touched my cheek. "That's what friends are for." Her palm lingered on my cheek for a second before she pulled it away. I didn't know what was happening, but there was definitely a charge in the air around us.

I cleared my throat. "Anyway, new topic. Or better yet, let's pop in that last movie." I got up and went to the television to put in the DVD.

"Ahmad, why hasn't Mike called or come over yet?"

I froze. I'd been wondering the same thing. "I don't know," I said, glad that she couldn't see my face. "He probably got caught up in the job somehow. You know how he likes to play Robocop." I tried to laugh, but stopped when I heard Mya crying. I sank back into the couch and took her in my arms, letting her rest her head on my shoulders. I wiped her falling tears away. "Don't cry, Mya. I'm sure he's okay."

Sniffling, Mya said, "I'm not crying because I'm worried about him. I'm crying because I know you're lying."

I didn't know what to say. I shook my head and cursed Mike for having me in this regretful predicament. "Mya," I started, but she cut me off.

"Don't worry, Ahmad. I'm not mad at you. He's your boy. You don't have to tell me that my husband is out there somewhere with some other bitch, because I already know. I've always known. Why do I put up with it, Ahmad? Why do I let him disrespect me that way?"

I clenched my jaws. "Mya, I . . ." I paused. What the hell was I supposed to say? Thankfully, Mya went on.

Burrowing her head into my neck, she said, "I deserve better. I know that. I want better Ahmad. I want to be treated the way a woman should be treated. I want to be loved the way a husband is supposed to love his wife. I want a man. I'm so tired of being with a boy."

I breathed in and out slowly as I caressed Mya's cheek. This was the closest we'd ever been. Mya's hand slowly traveled from her side to my chest then from there to my neck. I knew that what was happening was wrong. We were both about to commit ultimate acts of betrayal. One to marriage, and the other to friendship. "Mya," I said softly as my manhood throbbed beneath my sweats.

"Shay's lucky to have a man like you, Ahmad. You are everything a woman needs." Her hand was caressing my cheek now, my hand on her waist. "You're intelligent, handsome and genuine. Most of all, you're a real man." Her fingers were by my mouth now; my hands traveled up her side and rested just beneath her breast.

"Mya," I said again, my manhood standing erect now, my skin feeling warm.

"I've always been attracted to you, Ahmad," she said. Her fingers were inside of my mouth now for me to suck; my hand was cupping and massaging her breasts. "I would never let six months go by." Her hand was touching my member above my pants; my tongue danced in between her fingers as I squeezed her nipple through her bra.

This was wrong, so wrong, yet I couldn't stop. I put my finger beneath her chin and raised her head until we were staring at each other eye to eye. "This is wrong," I said.

Then our lips met. Slowly at first, feverishly seconds later as our tongues caressed. My penis throbbed with a force it hadn't had in a long while. I moved from Mya's lips to her neck. Mya moaned in pleasure and slid her hand beneath my shirt. As she played with the hairs on my chest with one hand, she slid her other hand beneath my sweats and wrapped her fingers around me. I exhaled from the sheer pleasure of her touch, from the pleasure of being touched. I took my turn and undid several of her buttons, slid my hand beneath the cotton and unsnapped her bra. Mya stroked me gently as I enjoyed the feel and fullness of her breasts. She moaned as I bent forward and took one into my mouth. I nibbled and sucked on her while letting my tongue apply its own massage. My heart was racing as Mya continued to stroke me, bringing me closer and closer to explosion.

And then we heard Nicole cry.

Mya and I stopped immediately and stared at one another. "Oh my God," Mya said, removing her hand from beneath my pants and rushing to fix her bra and button her shirt. I wiped my mouth and tried to hide my erection as best as I could. Mya quickly slid to the other end of the sofa while I grabbed the remote and changed the channels. Neither one of us spoke as Shay came into the living room.

"Hey, you're still here," she said to Mya.

"Um, yeah," Mya answered. "We both dozed off."

"Well, Mya, it's two o'clock in the morning. You're welcome to stay the night."

Mya shook her head and stood up. "No, that's okay. I've got a lot to do tomorrow morning. I'm just gonna go ahead home."

"Are you sure, girl? You know you're more than welcome to stay."

"I'm sure. I'm going to go home."

"I thought I heard Nicole," I said. My erection had finally gone down.

"She was dreaming. She's back asleep now."

"Well, let me get out of here. Thanks, guys, for letting me hang out with you two tonight."

"Anytime, girl," Shay said, kissing Mya on her cheek. "Ahmad, why don't you walk her out? I'm gonna get a bottle in case Nicole wakes up again."

I didn't say anything as I stood up. When Shay disappeared, Mya and I looked at each other with guilt in our eyes. We headed to the door without a word. When I opened the front door we once again shared a look of shame. Mya left without saying goodbye. When she pulled off, I closed the door, went back to the living room and sat down in front of the television. Shay appeared from the kitchen with a bottle in hand. "You're not coming to bed?"

I shook my head. "No."

"Okay." Shay walked off, leaving me alone to replay what had just happened with Mya. I couldn't believe it. That was my boy's wife I'd just gotten hot and heavy with, while my wife and daughter were in the other room. I slumped into the sofa feeling terrible.

Mya

What the hell just happened? That's all I'd been asking my self since driving away from Ahmad and Shay's house. What the hell just happened? I couldn't believe that Ahmad and I had just done what we did. If Shay hadn't woken up and come out of the room when she did, there was no doubt in my mind that Ahmad and I would have had sex.

Damn.

As guilty as I felt, and as much as I tried not to, I couldn't stop thinking about how good it felt to be in Ahmad's arms. I was serious when I told him that I'd always found him attractive. If I wouldn't have been so caught up, like all the other girls, by Mike's basketball letters, I probably would have become Ahmad's girlfriend instead of friend. But no, I ended up with Mike's ass and now instead of a good man, I had a husband who'd cheated on me more times than I wanted to remember.

I never intended to talk about my feelings about my marriage to Ahmad, but after he told me about the problems he and Shay were having, I realized if there was any one person I could talk to, it was him. I knew he would understand my desire to be happy.

I slammed my hand on the steering wheel. We were only supposed to be talking, but when I broke down and started to cry and he took me in his arms...I don't exactly know what it was, but something happened. Something that just felt so right. Too right. How was I supposed to look Shay in the eyes now? She welcomed me into her home, she trusted me. There are certain lines that are just never crossed, no matter the circumstances. I'd always felt that the only deceit worse than infidelity was betrayal of friendship. Boyfriends and husbands come and go, but friends are forever, and I'd always felt even if our marriages didn't last, the bond and comradeship that Shay and I had developed would. From the first moment we met, it was like we'd known each other forever. I knew that if she wasn't having sex with Ahmad, it was because she was battling with something inside of her. Knowing that made me ask one thing: How could I have done that to her?

I pulled into my driveway feeling worse than when I'd left Ahmad's place. I shut off the engine and looked around; Mike's car was nowhere to be found. Damn him. Even though I'd had plenty of reasons, I'd never fooled around on him. I took the vows I made on our wedding day very seriously. Now here I was sitting in my car, still feeling one of my husband's best friends' lips on mine.

I went into the house and went straight to bed. I thought about calling Mike to see where his ass was, but changed my mind. I didn't feel like listening to another one of his lies. I was dreaming that Shay was chasing me down with a butcher knife when I awoke to the feel of Mike slipping into the bed beside me.

"Baby?" he said, slipping his arm around me.

I didn't answer him. I didn't want to give him the satisfaction of giving me another lie for me to pretend to believe. I wanted to throw his arm off of me and throw him out of the bed, but I wasn't in the mood to argue. I kept my eyes closed and ignored him as he called my name again. Eventually he turned on his side. When I finally fell back to sleep, I dreamt that I was the one with the butcher's knife, and Mike was the one being chased.

Ahmad

I got in my Camry, closed my eyes, massaged my temples, and sighed. My extremely long and frustrating day had finally come to an end. From the moment I walked into the teacher's lounge I knew my day was going to be hell, because the normally busy lounge, was empty save for one person. "Good morning, Ahmad," Irene said in a singsong voice as I walked to the coffee machine.

"Morning," I said. After what happened between Mya and me on Friday night, Irene and her blackmail was the last thing I felt like dealing with.

"Did you have a good weekend?"

"It was fine." I was trying to make the coffee as fast as I could. I just wanted to get the hell out of there.

Irene got up from the round table in the center of the room and walked over to me with a smile. "So, should I expect you on Friday, Ahmad?"

I stared down at the black coffee as it swirled inside my *#1 Teacher* mug given to me by a few students the year before. "Why are you doing this, Irene?"

"Why did you come on to Maxine?"

"Come on, Irene. Stop playing games with me."

"I'm not playing games with you yet, Ahmad, although I'd like to on Friday."

"So, what if I don't give in to your shit? What if I don't come?" I asked defiantly.

"Then that means you'd rather I tell the faculty and your wife about your meeting with your student."

I folded my arms across my chest. "You can't prove that anything happened."

"I don't have to prove anything," Irene said with a sneer. "Not after Maxine files her complaint."

"Her complaint? What complaint?"

"The one about you coming on to her and forcing yourself on her."

"That's bullshit. Nobody will believe that."

"Hey, maybe not, Ahmad. All I can tell them is what I saw after *I* walked in on you with your tongue down the throat of your young and easily manipulated student, who'd been told that her 3.7 GPA would be sorely affected if she *didn't give it up.*"

"What? I never said that shit and I know Maxine didn't either."

"Are you calling me a liar?"

I nodded. "Damn right I am."

"So then I didn't catch you kissing Maxine?"

"I didn't kiss her."

"And I guess you didn't threaten her GPA either?"

"Hell no."

Irene pulled out a folded slip of notebook paper from the pocket of her blazer. "Then Maxine didn't write this letter to me?"

I looked at the piece of paper. "What the hell is that? That's not real."

"Are you sure about that?"

"Let me see it."

Irene laughed and slid the paper back into her pocket. "I paid a nice little visit to Maxine's house this weekend. I happened to be in the neighborhood and I wanted to see how my student was. I also wanted to discuss what actually happened last Friday." Irene leaned toward me. "I think you should know that she is willing to corroborate anything I say. Believe me, this letter is *very* real, and unless you want me to present it to the board, you'll show up Friday." Irene walked off, leaving me alone to fume in silence. Damn, if she wasn't a woman . . . She had my balls in one tight and painful grip and she knew it. It was my word against last year's principal of the year. She was well liked and highly respected by the board, and there was absolutely no way they would believe me over her. What the hell had she told Maxine?

Unfortunately, that wasn't the last time I had to deal with Irene that day. During my lunch break, she sat in the teachers' lounge with me and a few other teachers. I wanted to jump across the table and smack the shit out of her as she smiled at me every so often while making small talk with the other teachers.

The icing on the bitter cake she was serving me came during my last period class, which was the same one Maxine was in. She came to the class and sat in the back of the room for an "observation." All period long I had to keep my composure while she kept her eyes locked on me. It was obvious the only reason she came to the class was to make sure I wouldn't have a chance to speak with Maxine, who did her best to avoid looking at me. When the period mercifully ended, Irene made sure that she was the last to leave.

I sat at my desk with my head bowed for a few minutes before going to my car. *Why me?* I wondered, slipping my key into the ignition. I couldn't get sex at home, I was being blackmailed by my very unattractive boss, and worse than all of that, I'd committed the ultimate act of betrayal by nearly sleeping with my best friend's wife, who I still couldn't get off my mind. I didn't think my life could get any worse until my cell phone went off.

"Hello?"

"What's going on, Ahmad?" Mike said.

My heart beat heavily. Had Mya said something? I did my best to sound normal, although I was nervous as hell. "Not much, man. What's up with you?"

"Nothing good."

"What's wrong?"

"I heard what happened, man."

"You did?"

"I didn't want to believe it when I heard it, man."

Damn. I took a deep breath. "Look, man, I don't know what happened—"

"I don't either!" Mike yelled, cutting me off. "I mean, how the hell could the Giants get rid of Sehorn before Ron Dayne? That shit just doesn't make sense."

"Huh?" was all I could say.

"What do you mean huh? Didn't you watch *Sports Center* this morning?"

I let out a slow sigh of relief. I'd come damn close to blowing up my spot. "No, man, I didn't watch it. So they traded Sehorn?" We were both big New York Giants fans even though we lived in Maryland.

"Yeah, man. How the hell could they do that and keep Ron Dayne? He hasn't done shit for us."

"I don't know," I said, my heart rate returning to normal.

"I don't know either. I swear I don't understand the coaches and the owners sometimes. Why get rid of a guy who could help us? Anyway, man, enough about that shit. I'm starting to get pissed off. I need to chill before I take my frustration out on a jaywalker. Yo, I wanted to call you this past weekend but I was working some real overtime. So, how was Friday?"

"Friday?"

"Yeah. How was it? Did Mya complain about me all night long?"

I frowned and shook my head as I thought back to Mya in tears on my couch. "Mya didn't mention you at all, man," I said.

"Really?"

"Yeah. Why do you seem so surprised?"

"She hardly spoke to me over the weekend. I figured it was because she went over by you and complained until she had no complaint left."

"Nope. She didn't say a word."

"That's cool."

That's cool? I couldn't believe he was acting like his not being there was no big deal. "Man, where were you Friday night? I thought you were going to come by after you finished with that girl you pulled over."

"Ahmad, man, I was planning on coming over, but I got tied up—literally."

"What do you mean you got tied up?"

"Man, that girl Sally was off the hook. After I hit it for the second time I was gonna go home, shower and change, and swing by you, but before I could make moves, Sally started talking about how she had another two friends who were into brothers in uniform. Man, she called her friends up, they came over and it was on. I'm talking ménage a trois and then some." Mike laughed while I once again recalled the sight of Mya crying on my shoulder. I couldn't believe him.

"Yo, can I ask you something?"

"What's up?"

"I know we've talked about this before, but are you happy with Mya? I mean, have you ever been happy with her? Truly happy."

Mike sighed. "Man, you're not about to preach to me again, are you?"

"I'm not trying to preach. I'm just trying to figure out why you can't stop stepping out on Mya."

"I've explained this to you before man . . . "

"Yeah, yeah. I know. The ratio."

"Alright then. Why are you bugging me?"

"Man, if that's the real reason, why did you take a good woman like Mya and slip a ring on her finger? Why didn't you just stay single? At least then you could do whatever you want without having a chain around your ankle."

"Look Ahmad, we've been boys for a long time, right?"

"Yeah."

"And for as long as you've known me, I've never changed, right?"

"Yeah, and that's the problem. You got married and didn't change."

"Ahmad, why the fuck do you insist on going down this road with me? Yo, I love Mya, plain and simple. That's why I put that ring on her finger. But as far as why I keep stepping out on her, man, I do that for my marriage."

"For your marriage?"

"Look, you may not understand this, but my stepping out keeps my sex life with Mya fresh because I don't have to have sex with her all the time."

"Mike, you're not making any sense."

"I'm making perfect sense. My sex life with Mya is sweet because we only have sex like once or twice a week. It doesn't get boring. But if she was the only woman I was sleeping with, I'd be frustrated as hell because the sex would be so routine and scripted that I probably wouldn't even want to have sex with her."

"Come on, man." I couldn't believe what I was hearing.

"What I'm saying is the truth," Mike said. "Your faithful ass should try fooling around. Then you'll get what I'm saying."

"Man, don't you ever worry about what it would do to Mya if she caught you? Shit, she's not a stupid woman. How do you know that she doesn't already know?" I was really staring to get angry. I wanted to talk about the way Mya had cried and just how much she was hurting, but I didn't because I wanted to stay as far away from talking about Friday night as I could.

"Man, first of all, I don't worry about getting caught because that ain't gonna happen. Not unless you or Max plan on blowing up my spot, which I know neither one of you will do. So that takes care of what it would do to her. And as far as her already knowing, like I've said before, she ain't going nowhere. Anymore questions, or have I made my case yet?"

"Just one."

Mike sighed. "What, man?"

"What if Mya stepped out on you? How would you feel?"

There was a short moment of silence before Mike answered. "You know, I'll be honest with you," he said finally. "That shit would bother the hell out of me."

"Alright then."

"But your question is irrelevant, because that would never happen."

"You sure about that?" I asked.

"You know something I don't know?" Mike asked.

"Nah. I'm just playing devil's advocate."

"Man, why are you always on my back about this shit? You're supposed to be my boy, not my fucking momma."

"I care, man, that's all. Like you said, we're boys, and I'd hate to see some ugly shit happen and you end up losing a good woman."

"Yeah well, thanks for worrying, but you can stop now. Mya and I are cool and will remain that way. Anyway, man, I didn't call you to talk about this shit. I called because I need your help. Well, actually I need Shay's help."

"Shay? What's up?"

"Remember when I was talking about doing something special for Mya's birthday next week?"

"Yeah."

"Well, I'm throwing a surprise party for her next weekend, and I need Shay to keep her occupied for the day. I asked Max if Trina could do it, but she can't. Besides, having Shay do it makes sense because she's closer to Mya. She gonna be able to?"

"This is kind of short notice, isn't it?"

"Yeah, I know, but Max just got back to me with Trina's answer. What's up? You guys have plans?

"Nah. We just have to make sure my parents can watch Nicole. I'll tell Shay about it tonight and get back to you."

"Alright, cool. Anyway, man, let me hop off this phone. I gotta get back to work. I'll give you all the details later this week. I would say to tell Shay I said thank you, but she don't like me."

"It's not you she doesn't like; it's the choices you make."

"Yeah well, they're my choices. I'm out."

I hit the end button and leaned my head against the headrest. A surprise party for Mya. I shook my head. How could he disrespect her so much? I closed my eyes again and in the darkness behind my eyelids I saw Mya crying once again. I thought back to how I had taken her in my arms and given her my shoulder for support. I felt so bad for her. She was too beautiful a woman, both inside and out, to be hurt like that. I exhaled slowly. She'd felt so good in my arms; so right. Suddenly, the image of her crying on my shoulder faded away and a new one took its place. She wasn't crying now. She was breathing heavily as I kissed her softly, moving from her neck to her lips. She moaned and whispered my name as my hand enjoyed the curves of her breasts. She reached her hand down to feel me.

I opened my eyes quickly to make the pictures go away. With everything else going on in my life, fantasizing about something that should never have happened and could never happen again was not what I needed to be doing. I started the car and pulled off, wishing for the days when all I had to worry about was not getting any sex.

Trina

"Baby, can't you just buy that and call it a day?"

I looked at my husband from the corner of my eye. I should have just come to mall by my damn self. "Max, you know how I am when I shop. I have to browse around before I settle on what I'm going to buy."

"Browsing is one thing, Trina, but I'm saying, do you have to browse in every single store in the mall?"

I shook my head and put down the mocha-colored silk top I was looking at. "Shut up and stop exaggerating. We've only been to a couple stores and you're screaming bloody murder. If we were shopping for a big screen or a stereo you'd be just fine."

"Of course I would. That's something I could enjoy. I don't care about silk tops and matching whatevers."

I put my hand on my hips. "Max, why don't you stop thinking about yourself for a little while? We're here trying to find a gift for Mya. Now, if you don't want to help me then why don't you go to the food court or Circuit City or wherever, so I can shop in peace?" I turned away from him and went back to looking at blouses. If there was one thing that Mya loved, it was blouses. She had a ton of them in her closet, and she always said she could never have enough. I figured a slamming blouse and a sexy skirt with a slit up the side would help her feel sexy and take her mind off of turning thirty.

"You sure you won't mind me going?" Max asked. It was obvious by his tone he wasn't really concerned with whether I minded or not. Plus, he was already turning around to go.

"Just go. I'll call you when I'm done." I was actually anxious for him to go because after the little speech I gave about not worrying about himself, I saw some tops and bottoms that I wanted for myself and I didn't want him to see me buy them.

"Aw'ight baby. I'll be waiting for your call."

"Yeah, sure you will."

Once Max left, I was able to relax and do some serious shopping. If there was one thing I loved to do it was shop. Growing up, I'd never been able to indulge in the glory of having new clothes like a lot of the kids in school. After landing my first high-paying job, the first thing I did was take myself on an expensive shopping spree. I bought pumps, skirts, blouses, sexy bras and panties, suits, jewelry and perfume. I wanted to have all the things I never could have but wanted so badly. I was admiring a sheer mauve V-neck when I heard a voice I didn't want to hear.

"Well, well, well. If it isn't my high-class daughter."

I turned around and was greeted by the sight of Sharon. I put a scowl on my face. "Looking as good as ever, Sharon," I said, frowning at her ensemble: a leopard skirt so short it looked like it was afraid of her thighs, a too-tight white tank-top with the word *Bitch* going across her breasts, and a pair of sandals with straps wrapping around her calves.

"What are you doin' here? Shouldn't you be in Nordstrom's or one of them expensive-ass stores?"

I sucked my teeth. "The real question, Sharon, is what are you doing here? They don't have hoochie clothes here."

Sharon and I stared each other down. I swear it was hard to believe she gave birth to me. If I didn't look exactly like her, you'd never know we were related. When I was a little girl, I wanted to get plastic surgery to change that.

I curled my lips and turned my back to her. "What do you want?" I asked, looking at the clothing again, although all my desire to shop was now gone. "I hope you didn't track me down so you could ask for money, because you know I'm not giving you any."

"Bitch, please," Sharon said for everyone to hear. "I wouldn't ask your stuck-up ass for shit."

I turned around quickly. She was making my blood boil. "Well, if you don't want money, then why don't you get the hell out of my face?" Usually I was able to stay calm and deal with her vulgar attitude, but I was still bothered by her coming over to my house when I wasn't there.

"Who the hell do you think you're talkin' to? Bitch, I will knock that weave right the hell out of your head."

I smirked and shook my head as people around us watched eagerly. I'm sure they were anticipating a catfight, and I can't say that I wasn't about to give them one. I took a step toward her. "For your information, this is all my hair. I don't wear nasty, fake-ass weaves like you do."

"Bitch, you better step back before you get slapped."

"You need to stop calling me a bitch," I said, pointing my finger in her face.

"If you don't get that finger out of my face, *bitch*, I will beat your ass right here for everyone to see."

"You know, you need to stop making threats that your old ass won't be able to back up. I may not be ghettofied like you, but I do know how to throw down."

My mother put up her fists. "Well, bring it on, then."

I threw up my hands while the spectators watched. I knew that I was wrong for acting the way I was. I knew that I was being the very thing I couldn't stand about my mother—ghetto. But you know what? At that particular moment I didn't care. I was tired of her attitude, tired of her disrespect; I was just tired of her shit. I was about to haul off and lay a smack into her when Max came barreling between us.

"Whoa, whoa, what the hell's going on? Sharon, what the fuck are you doing here?"

"Fucking up my day!" I yelled.

"Fuck you, Trina."

"No, fuck you, Sharon." I charged toward her but Max held me back.

"Trina, what the hell is your problem? Why are you causing a scene like this?"

"I don't care if I'm causing a damn scene," I yelled. "She gets on my damn nerves and I'm tired of her shit."

"Yeah well, I'm tired of your bourgie ass too. You're lucky your husband is here."

"Shut up, Sharon," Max said.

"Yeah, you heifer, shut your ass up!"

"Trina, calm the fuck down," Max said sternly.

Just then, a mall security guard appeared. He was a 6-foot 5-inch tower of muscle. "Sir," he said, staring at Max. "I'm going to have to ask you and your girlfriends to leave."

"Excuse me," I said, catching immediate attitude with him. "I am his wife, not his girlfriend. And that one over there is a trifling excuse for a woman, so you better be careful. She may try to take you home."

As people around us laughed, the guard said, "You all are going to have to leave. Now."

"No problem, dude," Max said, grabbing Sharon and me by our arms. "We were just leaving."

He dragged us out of the store and all the way outside the mall like two rag dolls. When he was satisfied that we wouldn't draw an audience, he let us go. "What the fuck is wrong with you two? Shit. Acting like a bunch of hood rats. Sharon I could understand, but you, Trina?"

I folded my arms across my chest and twisted my lips into a sneer while I cut my eyes at Sharon. "She started it," I said.

"I don't believe you just said that," Max said. "She started it," he mocked like a little kid, which was how I'm sure I sounded. "You are not a little girl. I mean damn, you were just about to beat down your own mother."

"She wasn't about to beat down shit, thank you very much," Sharon interjected. That only got my blood boiling.

"Why don't you come over here and find out?" I threatened.

"Trina, will you chill the fuck out?" Max said, grabbing Sharon when she started to charge toward me.

"Let me go!" Sharon yelled, trying to remove Max's arms from around her waist. "I wanna beat her ass!"

"Sharon, shut the fuck up!" Max yelled. "Shit, both of you shut your fucking mouths."

I stood silent and stared Sharon down. My heart was beating in triplets, my hands shaking. I'd really lost my cool. No one said a word for a minute. Sharon and I stared each other down like boxing opponents waiting for the bell to ring, while Max played the role of referee and kept us apart.

"You two have some real fucking issues. Damn, y'all are supposed to be some grown-ass women, not little schoolgirls. If y'all hate each other, that's cool, but just hate each other silently and move the fuck on. How the hell did this start, anyway?"

Sharon and I started to talk at the same time. Max cut us off. "Trina, you first."

I gave a smirk to Sharon. "Baby, I was just shopping for Mya's gift when she came and started blabbing her mouth and talking shit. She knows I can't stand her, and that's the only reason why she did that. She probably came to the mall just to harass me."

"Bitch, please. My world don't revolve around your ass."

"Whatever," I said, sucking my teeth.

"Yeah, whatever."

Max sighed and turned to face her. "Sharon, why don't you take your ass and get the fuck out of here before some more unnecessary shit happens?"

I was surprised by the hostility in his tone. I'd never heard him talk to her that way. I agreed with him one hundred percent. "Yeah, Sharon," I said, "be gone. And don't be coming by my house when I'm not there, either." I just had to get that off my chest.

"Don't be coming by your house?"

"Leave, Sharon," Max said, pushing her back.

"Bitch, I gave birth to your ass. I'll come over when I damn well feel like it. Oh, and you're lucky I got my earring back."

"Sharon!" Max yelled. "This is the last time I'm gonna tell your ass to leave."

"Got your earring back?" I asked. I looked at Max. "What does she mean got her earring back?" I looked at Max. "What does she mean got her earring back?"

"I mean I got my earring that you—."

"Bitch, I'm not talking to you!" I snapped as a small crowd started to gather around us. I put my attention back on Max. "Max, I threw that earring in the garbage. How did she get it back?"

"Baby, let's not talk about this right now," Max said, staring down at Sharon.

"Don't baby me. And look at me, not her."

"Humph, you let her talk to you like that?" Sharon said.

I looked at her. "Shut up, bitch!" I looked back at Max. "How the hell did she get her earring, Max?"

"Trina, what's the big deal about the earring?" Max asked. It was obvious that he had something to hide.

"The big deal is that I threw that shit away, which means the only way she could have gotten it is if you took it out and gave it to her. And if that's the case, that means that she was in my damn house again. Max, I swear you better give me another scenario." I watched Max with a deadpan glare. I'm sure if looks could kill, mine would have had him on the ground, dead to the world. Max looked from me to Sharon then back to me. "Well?" I asked, folding my arms across my chest. "How did she get the earring back?"

"What do you want me to say, Trina?"

"I don't care what you say, Max, just so long as you tell me how she got her fucking earring."

Max sighed. "I gave it to her."

"Yes, he certainly did," Sharon said with a chuckle. There was something about the way she said it that gave me an ill feeling. I was about to ask her what she meant when Max spoke.

"Sharon, take your old ass the fuck outta here. Trust me, that's the last warning you're gonna get."

"Oh, so my ass is old now?" Sharon yelled, twisting her neck. "That's not what your ass said about it the other day."

"The other day?" I asked, looking at Max, whose eyes remained glued on Sharon. "You saw her the other day?"

"Damn right he did," Sharon said. "He saw a whole lot of me, too. And my ass wasn't old then."

"What! What do you mean by that?" I turned and faced her.

"Why don't you ask your husband?"

I turned back to Max, who stood with his fists clenched, his jaws tight, and his eyes dark. I shook my head. I didn't want to believe that Sharon was implying what I had no doubt she was implying. "Max, what's she talking about?"

"Don't pay attention to her, Trina. She's fucking lying."

"Lying about what?" I yelled. I shook my head again. "Did you fuck her?"

"Come on, Trina," Max said, looking at me. "How are you gonna ask me that?"

I looked from him to Sharon, who stood with a smile that begged to be smacked off. "Did you fuck him?" I asked her.

"I didn't fuck her, Trina," Max said. I could hear guilt in his voice.

I didn't acknowledge him. My attention was solely on Sharon. "What the fuck happened the other day? Did you sleep with my husband?"

Sharon smiled wider. "Twice. And in your fucking bed, too."

"Bitch!" Max yelled. Suddenly, before I could even react, Max slapped the hell out of Sharon. I stood in complete shock as Sharon cried out and fell to the ground. Standing above her, Max yelled, "You stupid-ass bitch! I told you to keep your fucking mouth shut. I told you to leave."

I stared down at Sharon, who was licking blood away from the corner of her mouth. I didn't know what to say.

"Baby," Max said, turning toward me. "Don't listen to her shit. She's just trying to instigate problems."

"Why did you hit her?" I asked.

"Because she has a big fucking mouth and I was tired of hearing it."

"Did you fuck her, Max?" I asked, tears welling in my eyes. I didn't wait for him to answer me. I turned to Sharon. "Did you fuck my husband?" She didn't answer, but instead started to laugh. "I asked you a fucking question!" I raged. By this time, the small crowd had become a large one, but I didn't care. "Did you sleep with my goddamned husband?"

Sharon continued to laugh and didn't answer. By then she didn't have to, because I could see the answer in the look of hatred she gave me.

"You low-life motherfucker!" I yelled, turning back to Max. "You fucked that bitch!"

"Baby, that didn't happen."

"Then how'd she end up at the house to get the earring?"

"She came by."

"Why?"

Max hesitated before he said, "I don't know. She just showed up."

I turned to Sharon. "Why were you in my damn house?"

"Because your husband wanted some ass," she said coolly.

"Baby, don't listen to her."

"Are you lying?" I asked, locking my eyes on her.

"What the fuck do you think?"

"Baby, she's fucking lying! Bitch, I'm gonna kill your ass."

He started to charge Sharon, but before he could get to her, I stepped in his way. I wasn't trying to protect the bitch. I just wanted to smack the shit out of Max. "You asshole!" I yelled, smacking him across his face. "You slept with my mother. You fucking asshole!"

I slapped him again and then started swinging wildly, hitting him with everything I had. I didn't stop until a police officer grabbed me by my arms.

Max

An officer was twisting my arm behind my back while another one pulled Trina away from me. I couldn't believe this shit was happening. "Get the fuck off of me!" I yelled, trying to pull my arm away. I should have known better than to do that, because the next thing I knew, I was being wrestled to the ground. "I didn't do anything!"

"Sir, calm down," the officer said. "Don't make this any worse on yourself."

"Worse? What are you gonna do, Rodney King my ass?"

The officer pressed his knee deep into the small of my back and leaned down close to my ear. "No," he whispered slowly, "but if you don't calm down, we'll take a little trip to the police bathroom and take a broomstick with us." I didn't say a word as he slapped handcuffs around my wrists and hoisted me from the ground.

"Why you got me in handcuffs?" I asked, looking over at Trina as she stood with tears in her eyes, talking to a female officer who was writing notes on a pad. "She's the one who needs cuffs, not me."

"Sir, if you know what's good for you, you'll quiet down."

I wanted to say something else in protest, but his comment about the broomstick shut me up. I gritted my teeth and shook my head instead. I looked around to see Sharon staring hard at me while she talked to another officer, who was also busy writing things down. Trina started yelling obscenities at me while the female officer gave me evil glances. I looked back at Sharon, who now had a paramedic examining her lip.

The cop tugged on my arm and dragged me away to his police car, shoving me into the back seat. He went to join Trina and her officer. As they talked, he pulled out his own notepad and started writing. When he came back ten minutes later, he got in the front seat.

"Hey," I said. "Where are you taking me?"

"We're going for a little ride to the station."

"The station? What the hell for? I didn't do anything but have an argument with my wife and mother-in-law. That's not illegal."

The cop snickered a few times and pulled away from the curb. "Yeah, I know all about you and mommy dearest."

I sighed and sat back in the seat.

Four hours later I was sitting in the front seat of Mike's Jeep, fuming. I'd called him right after the cops let me go, and that only happened because he came down and vouched for me. I told him all about what went down with Trina and Sharon. I normally don't make it a habit to hit women, but when Sharon opened her mouth and told Trina about us, I couldn't help myself. My hand just flew. Mike spoke to his buddies at the station and found out that despite their attempts to get her to press charges against me, Sharon refused. I knew that only meant one thing. She was gonna get her son to come after my ass. Fuck it. Let her do what she had to do. I had other, more important things to worry about—like my marriage.

While I was in jail I had time to calm down and realize what I'd done. I'd betrayed the one woman who had truly loved me for who I was. It didn't matter that I was rough around the edges. It didn't matter that I wasn't the most successful brother, or the brother with the largest bank. Trina loved me regardless. Not only that, but she supported my dreams. I wanted to be the biggest manager in the music business; I wanted to launch and sustain careers, and as long as that was what I wanted, Trina wanted it too. For the first time, I truly understood what Ahmad had been talking about when he said that what Mike and I had been doing would come back to bite us in the ass. I shifted in my seat; my ass was hurting like a motherfucker right now.

"Yo, I should have stopped fucking with Sharon," I said, dialing my home number and getting no response for the fourth time. I knew Trina was home because the answering machine didn't come on, which meant that she'd turned it off.

"You just now realizing that, man?" Mike asked. I'd always been a little tighter with him than I was with Ahmad, but that was primarily because we were both the same kind of dog. "Stepping out is one thing, bruh, but stepping out with your mother-in-law was kind of crazy."

"Yeah, I know," I said solemnly.

"I mean, I know Sharon's body begged to be fucked, but man, she's as ghetto as ghetto gets."

"Yeah, I know," I said again, reclining in the seat and closing my eyes. "Man, you think Trina'll be willing to hear me out?"

"Man, what are you gonna say? Shit, what can you say?"

"I don't know, man. I gotta try something, though."

Mike suddenly laughed out loud.

"What are you laughing at?" I asked, opening my eyes and looking at him.

Mike laughed harder.

"What's so funny?"

"My bad, man. It's just that this shit is hilarious."

"Hilarious?"

Mike chuckled again. "Man, your mother-in-law, who's been serving you ass like ice cream sundaes, just blew up your whole spot."

I closed my eyes. "Nigga, I don't see the humor in that."

"Bruh, you let her play your ass like a PlayStation game."

"What are you talking about?"

"Man, I don't know why, but Sharon was out to hurt Trina. That's why she let you hit it like that and then let the cat out of the bag. For whatever reason, she wanted to bring some grief into Trina's world."

I thought about what he was saying. Could he have been right? "Man, what would she want to hurt her like that for?"

"I don't know, bruh. All I know is you thought you were the mack, when all you were was a pawn. And guess what?"

"What?" I asked, sighing.

"You can forget about trying to get Trina to listen to your ass. Take a look."

I opened my eyes and looked out the window as he pulled to a stop in front of my house. I frowned as Mike started to laugh again. Littered across the front yard was everything I owned. I'm talking everything: my clothes, my shoes, my CDs, my stereo and TV, now broken into pieces. All of it there for the entire neighborhood to see. "Shit," I whispered as I got out of the car.

"Yo, I think I'll wait here where it's safe," Mike said. "You want my gun?"

I ignored him and closed the door then walked slowly past my belongings. I stopped momentarily to look down at one of my most prized possessions: a gold record earned by a rapper I managed before he'd been shot and killed. He had been my only success story, and every day I would plant a kiss on the album with the hopes of managing another act that would surpass him. I had the record encased in an expensive lacquer frame. It was now on the ground—broken. Trina knew how much that record meant to me, so for her to ruin it meant that I'd hurt her damn bad.

I sighed, took my keys out and stepped to the door. I never got to slide my key in the lock, though. "What the—"

I tried to push the key inside again and just like seconds before, it didn't fit. "This can't be happening." I rang the doorbell. When I didn't get a response, I pressed it again, several times. I finally had to resort to banging on the door. "Trina!" I yelled. "Trina, open the door!" I stopped banging for a few seconds as my neighbor, Ms. Reinsdorf, opened her door and stepped outside. She looked at me and shook her head disapprovingly then stepped back inside. I flipped her the finger and went back to banging on the door. "Trina! I know you're in there. Come on, baby. Open the door."

"Get the fuck away from here, Max!" Trina yelled from behind the door.

"Baby, open the door. Let me just explain some things to you."

"Explain? What the fuck could you possibly say to me, Max? That you didn't mean to fuck Sharon? Or do you want to tell me how it never happened? You make me sick!"

I pounded on the door again. "Baby, please. I'm sorry."

"Fuck you and your sorry ass."

"Open the damn door, Trina!"

"Go to hell, Max!"

"Open the fucking door!"

"Max, trust me. You don't want me to open this door."

"Yes I do, Trina. Open the door. I wanna talk to you."

"Get your black ass away from here, Max!" Trina yelled, her voice full of hostility and pain.

I didn't back down, though. I hit the door with my fist again. "Don't make me break this door down, Trina. I swear I will." I banged on it and then kicked it to stress how serious I was. I thought I was really going to have to break it down until I heard the locks click. "About time," I said to show that I was the man.

But when the door swung open, I nearly pissed on myself. Standing in the doorway with tears and mascara streaking down her face was Trina, my gun in her hand, aimed right at my head. I never even knew she knew I had a gun. I backed up a step. "Trina, what the fuck are you doing?"

Sobbing and shaking, Trina said, "I told you, you didn't want me to open the door."

"Trina, baby, please put that gun down," I begged slowly.

From behind me, I heard Mike yell, "Trina, put the gun down! Now!"

I took a quick peek over my shoulder. Mike was leaning over the hood of his car with his police issued .45 pointing toward us. "Mike, what the fuck are you doing man?" I screamed out.

"Saving your ass!" Mike yelled back. "Trina, put the gun down."

"I'm gonna shoot his ass, Mike," Trina screamed. "You hear me, Max? I'm gonna shoot your filthy ass."

My legs wobbled as I took another cautious step back with my hands in the air. "Trina, please. I'm sorry, baby. Please put the gun down."

"Fuck you, Max. I'm gonna shoot you. Right here, right now."

"Put it down, Trina!" Mike yelled. "He's not worth it."

"Damn right he's not worth it!" Trina yelled back, burning holes into me with her eyes. "He's not worth living."

"Come on, Trina. Don't do this," Mike said, softening his tone. "Don't waste your time on him."

I tried to take another step back as my heart beat like thunderous drums, but my legs wouldn't move. "Trina . . . don't shoot me . . . please."

"Why, Max?" Trina asked vehemently. "Why the fuck shouldn't I shoot you? That's what you did to me. You shot me right in the heart, you no-good piece of shit."

"I know, baby, and I'm sorry. You got to believe me. I regret what I did."

"You regret it? Why? Because my ho of a mother won't be there to give up the ass anymore? My mother, Max. You fucked my mother. In our goddamned bed!" Trina stiffened her arm. "I hate you for that, Max. I fucking hate you!"

"Baby," I said weakly.

"Trina, if you shoot him I'm gonna have to shoot you, and I don't want to do that," Mike said.

"Baby, listen to him," I pleaded. "Put the gun down, okay? I'll leave. I promise."

Trina stood in front of the door with tears dripping from her chin. To say that I felt like an ass would have been an understatement. I hated to see her in such pain. "Trina, please. I'll leave. I swear."

"You swear? Just like you swore on our wedding day right?"

"Baby . . . "

"Fuck you, Max," Trina said, throwing the gun at me suddenly. As it fell at my feet, she went back inside and slammed the door shut. When I heard the locks click, I bent down and picked up my gun. Mike came running up beside me.

"Yo, you okay?"

I shook my head. "Nah, man." I turned and walked to his car, pocketing my unloaded firearm.

Trina

I should have shot him. Goddammit, I should have shot his pathetic ass. I couldn't believe he had the nerve to come here trying to talk to me. I couldn't believe he thought I'd be willing to listen to what he had to say. Goddammit. I hated him. Cheating was one thing, but what he did . . . I leaned against the door and slid down to the ground.

Sharon.

Of all of the nasty ass bitches in this world, he had to go and fuck the one bitch I truly couldn't stand. I slammed my palm on the ground. I was so angry—angry at Sharon, angry at Max, angry that my heart was hurting. I loved Max like I'd never loved any man before. I gave him a chance and let him in when others told me not to. I slammed my palm down again. I should have listened when people said he was no-good.

Sharon.

If she thought she got the last laugh, she had better think again. She was lucky that I'd been in shock when she let the cat out of the bag about her and Max, or else it would have been my smack she felt instead of Max's. I closed my eyes tightly and balled my hands into tight fists.

Sharon.

I stayed on the ground crying for several minutes until I got a sick feeling in my stomach. I got up quickly and ran to the bathroom. I just managed to get the toilet cover up before I started to throw up. When I was finished, I flushed the toilet, washed out my mouth, lowered the seat cover, sat down and stared at the floor. I had found out I was pregnant three days earlier. Actually, I knew before then because I was a month late with my period and my stomach had been feeling queasy. The doctor just confirmed what I knew. This was the first night I hadn't been able to keep myself from vomiting. I was going to tell Max the news before everything happened. Tears began to fall from my eyes again.

Sharon.

Max.

My baby.

My life was falling apart.

I slept on the floor that night because I couldn't stand the thought of lying in the bed knowing that Max and Sharon had sex in it. I was going to sleep on the couch but changed my mind. Who knew where else they got it on? The next morning, I woke up, called in sick then called my sister and told her what happened. She came over right away and lent me her shoulder. Later that afternoon, she and I went to a furniture store to pick out new sofas and a new mattress and box spring. I also bought a new TV and stereo to replace the ones I'd thrown in the yard. I didn't know what time he did it, but some time in the middle of the night, Max came and got his shit out of the yard. I was glad he didn't ring the bell and beg to come inside. I must have really scared the shit out of him with that gun. I didn't even know he had it. I found it by accident when I was grabbing up all his shit to throw outside. I found the bullets too. Damn, I should have loaded the thing.

After my sister left, I opened the windows, cleaned the entire house and sprayed it down with Lysol. The house smelled like Max, and I just wanted that scent gone. After I finished cleaning, I went through my albums and got rid of any and all pictures with Max in them. I ripped some and I burned others. I felt like Angela Bassett in *Waiting to Exhale*. I really should have reenacted that scene.

When I was done getting rid of Max's presence, I sat on my brand new beige leather sofa, contemplating one of two actions. One, I wanted to grab my car keys, take a trip down to Sharon's house and beat her ass. Two, I wanted to grab my car keys, take a trip down to the gun shop then find Max's ass. Ultimately, I ended up throwing up then crying again.

I was pregnant, and like my mother, I had no man, because as far as I was concerned, Max and I were finished. I swore I'd never be in that position. I never wanted to have a baby daddy. Of course, Max being the baby daddy was all dependent on whether or not I kept the baby. I still wasn't sure what I was going to do about that. That's why I never told my sister about being pregnant.

I never wanted to be like my mother. I never wanted there to be a chance for any type of comparison other than looks. The fact that I was considering having an abortion only made my tears fall harder. I cried until I fell asleep.

Ahmad

The N.C.A.A. championship basketball tournament between Syracuse and Kansas was on. Mike, Max and I had been looking forward to the game. We'd all bet in basketball pools on-line, with some of the guys from Mike's station, and amongst the three of us. We'd all picked both teams that were now set to tip-off, so there was a nice pot of change at stake. Our moods should have reflected the moods of everyone else around us in the ESPN Zone—festive and hyped. But while everyone else laughed, drank, and had a good time, Mike, Max and I sat at our round table, solemn and quiet. The game was the last thing we cared about.

Mike had called and told me all about what happened with Max and Trina. I couldn't say that I was surprised, because I wasn't, but I promised Mike I wouldn't give any speeches that night. Max sat with his hand clasped around a bottle of Heineken that he was barely drinking. Since getting kicked out of his home, he'd been crashing on Mike's couch. He looked worn out with heavy bags under his eyes. It was obvious that he wasn't sleeping right. He needed to shave; his usually wild and unkempt but always groomed hair was looking exceptionally wild and unkempt, and nowhere close to being groomed. I felt bad for him, but he did deserve what he'd gotten.

I looked from him to Mike. Mike was his usual self, checking out the women around us. After what happened with Mya, it had become so hard not to feel anger toward him. The more Mya appeared in my thoughts, the more difficult it became to deal with his disrespect. I was his boy, but I didn't know how much longer I could go on covering for him.

I looked away from Mike. I had to stop thinking about him and I damn sure had to stop thinking about Mya, especially with all of the shit going on in my world. Shay and I were still barely speaking. If it weren't for Nicole, we probably wouldn't be speaking at all. I'd come close to spending a couple of nights on the couch because it was just getting more and more difficult to lie next to a woman who refused to have sex, refused to be touched, and wouldn't explain why. With Shay and me not communicating and me getting hornier and hornier, it had become impossible not to think about Mya's lips or her breasts or the way she'd touched me. It had been even harder not to let my mind go further and imagine us having sex.

Someone walked by and bumped into my chair. I was glad that they had, because my mind had begun to drift to a place it didn't need to be. I sighed. Shit was just so complicated. There was Shay and the celibacy she'd forced me into, my ever-growing attraction towards my best friend's wife, and last but not least, my dilemma with Irene at school. I still didn't know what the hell to do about that. Irene had made it her point to remind me constantly about Friday. I tried to talk to Maxine once in between classes about what happened when Irene had paid her a visit, but before I could, Irene appeared, causing Maxine to disappear quickly down the hall. Friday was coming and I didn't know if there was a way to avoid having to give her what she wanted. I needed advice.

"Yo, guys," I said, sipping on my Amaretto Sour. "I have a dilemma that I need your help on."

Max barely looked up as Mike said, "What's up?"

"I'm being blackmailed."

At the same time, the fellas said, "What?"

"What do you mean you're being blackmailed?" Mike asked.

I sighed and recounted the entire story from Maxine's advance to Irene's discovery and proposition. When I was finished, both Max and Mike were laughing. I frowned. "Glad to see I lifted your spirits," I said to Max. That only made them laugh harder. "Yo, this is serious. It's not funny."

"Ahmad, man," Mike said, wiping tears from the corners of his eyes. "That is probably the funniest shit I've heard in a long time."

Max agreed. "It is funny, man."

"Alright, alright. You guys had your laugh. Now help me figure out what to do."

"What's there to figure out?" Mike asked.

I looked at him. "What do you mean? There's a lot to figure out, like how I can get out of this and keep my job and marriage."

"Man, just go over to your boss's house, hit that old ass and call it a day."

Mike broke down laughing again while Max struggled to keep from spitting out his beer.

"Whatever, man," I said, laughing with them this time.

"Whatever nothing," Mike said. "You better hit that shit and keep stepping."

I shook my head. "Trust me, Mike; you wouldn't be saying that if you saw Irene." Images of her wrinkled skin, brown age spots and dull yellow teeth from an overdose of nicotine popped in my mind and made my face scowl. "Believe me, not even you would hit it."

"Ahmad, bruh, unless you plan on getting freaky with the bitch, you're not gonna fuck her face. Just keep the lights off and do what you gotta do."

I shook my head again. "No way, man. I'm not sleeping with her."

"It's just pussy, man," Mike said.

"Yeah well, it's pussy I don't want."

"So, what are you gonna do? Let her spread some lies and have you fired?"

"I don't know what I'm gonna do. That's what I'm asking you two fools to help me figure out."

Mike swallowed some of his beer. "I don't know what to tell you, bruh."

No one said anything for a few minutes. Mike went back to looking at women around us, while I stared up at the screen, not really watching the game.

"I have an idea," Max said suddenly.

I looked at him. He was looking pretty rough. The turmoil going on with Trina and Sharon was really taking its toll on him. "Yeah?" I asked.

"Yeah," he said, nodding. "It'll keep you from having to sleep with your boss and it'll put some leverage in your pocket. Shit, you'll probably get a raise after this."

I was all ears. I ordered another round of drinks for the three of us and got real comfortable. Two hours later Syracuse won the championship and I had a foolproof plan to get out of the situation with Irene. We grabbed our coats to leave.

"Yo, I'll catch up to you guys outside. I wanna holler at this honey over there." Mike walked off. All I could do was shake my head.

As we stepped outside, Max said, "He's gonna lose Mya if he doesn't stop fucking around."

I zipped up my coat but didn't say anything because I could see that he had more to say.

"Man, I should have listened to you. I really miss the shit out of Trina." He paused and shook his head. The pain was heavy in his voice. I felt for him; nobody liked learning lessons the hard way. "I knew that I loved her, but I didn't realize how much until this shit happened. Man, all the times I fucked with Sharon's ass I never stopped to think how it would hurt Trina. I can't believe I let that bitch play me like that."

"It never occurred to you that's what she was doing?" I asked.

"Nah, man. Never. About the closest I came to thinking she was trying to game me was when she would try to get me to stay inside of her when I busted my nut. She would always tell me how she couldn't get pregnant and shit."

"You didn't do it, did you?"

"Hell no! Even with a damn condom on I wasn't trying to take no chances." Max sighed. "Ahmad, man, Trina won't even give me the time of day. What the hell am I gonna do?"

"You're just gonna have to give her time, man."

"That's about all I got now. So, with all of the speeches you give, how come you never gave me the I-told-you-so speech?"

"No need for that," I said. "Plus, Mike asked me not to."

As we laughed, Mike came running up beside us with a big grin on his face. Max and I shook our head at him. "Don't go joining this fool's side," Mike said to Max.

"Man, you're gonna lose Mya if you keep it up," Max said.

"Whatever, man. I didn't tell you to bang your mother-in-law. Anyway, before we get into some big argument, Ahmad, what's the word on Shay picking Mya up?"

"She can do it."

"Cool. How early can she come and get her?"

"I think she's supposed to be getting her at one."

"One won't work. I need her to get Mya out of the house by twelve because the DJ's coming over around one to start setting up his equipment."

"I'll let her know."

"Cool."

We switched topics and started talking about the game that we had barely paid attention to. That night in bed, I flip-flopped between thoughts of Irene and Mya. I was sure that the plan Max had come up with would get Irene off my back for good. As for Mya, I just couldn't get her off my mind. I didn't know what her feelings or thoughts were. Did she regret what happened between us? Would she still be the same around me? Did she spend as much time fantasizing as I did? I fell asleep with Mya on my brain.

Mya

I picked up the phone and put it back down. This made three times in the past half hour that I'd done that. I shook my head slowly. I was certifiable. I had to be. That's the only explanation I could come up with for even entertaining the idea of calling Shay to see if she was up for spending another Friday evening watching movies, just so I could see Ahmad again. Crazy. Definitely.

That's why I picked up the phone, dialed the first four digits of their phone number then put the phone back in its base again. I sighed. Ahmad had been on my mind all week long, refusing to leave. No matter how hard I beat up my conscience for thinking about my husband's best friend, I couldn't stop going back to the night we'd kissed. Mike was a great kisser, but I had to admit he'd never kissed me so gently or so sensually. Ahmad's kiss was a lover's kiss, not just a man's.

There are two types of kisses that a man can give. There's a man's kiss, which is straight and to the point, often greedy and a little overpowering. And then there's a lover's kiss, which is gentle and slow, patient and generous. A lover's kiss is given more for the woman's pleasure than the man's. It is impossible to forget. That's why I could still feel Ahmad's full lips. That's why I couldn't let go of the way his tongue danced with my own. He kissed me in a way that made me want to lose control, made me want to forget my inhibitions.

I stared at the phone. I'd wanted to call Ahmad all week to talk about what happened between us. I wanted to know how he felt, or if he felt anything. I didn't call because I knew that was the wrong thing to do. I sighed again and reached for the phone, deciding to call just to talk to Shay instead. Maybe hearing her voice would be the best thing for me. Maybe it would work on my conscience just enough to let go of any ill-advised thoughts of romance and bliss between Ahmad and me. The phone rang before I could pick it up. "Hello?"

"Hey, Mya. What's going on, girl?"

My heart beat heavily for an instant. "Hey, Shay. Girl, you must be psychic. I was just getting ready to call you."

"Really?" Shay laughed. "Well, having a baby *has* changed me. What did you want?"

I hesitated for a second, contemplating my movie idea. "Oh, nothing much. I was just going to call to see how you and the baby were doing."

"Nicole is as precious as ever and looking more and more like her father every day. Her first tooth finally came in this week. She looks adorable."

"I bet she does," I said with a smile. There was once a time when talking about kids would make me happy. Being a mother was something I'd always wanted, and I'd hoped to have some with Mike some day. Now I wasn't so sure about kids because I wasn't even sure about how much longer I could put up with him. "Hey, what did you call me for, Shay?"

Shay sighed. "Girl, I'm gonna have to cancel tomorrow afternoon's outing. My mother called and she needs me to take her into DC to see her friend, Mrs. Alice, who's in the hospital suffering with cancer."

"Oh, I'm so sorry," I said sympathetically.

"I'm the one who's sorry. I know you must have rearranged your day to go shopping with me."

"It's no big deal, Shay. Believe me, my shopping for clothes is nowhere near as important as taking your mother to see her friend. I guess Ahmad will have babysitting duties tomorrow."

"Actually, he's going to be busy tomorrow, so I'm taking Nicole with me. That'll actually be a good thing.

She'll help lift my mother's spirits. Mrs. Alice is one of her dearest friends. Anyway, girl, enough about that. I'm starting to get sad. What are you doing tonight?"

"Nothing much," I said after hesitating for a brief second. "I have some cleaning up to do."

"On a Friday?"

"Yeah. Mike's still at work. Besides, it's Friday and I know he won't be home any time soon. I'll be here alone, and tomorrow's going to be a nice day, and the last thing I'm gonna feel like doing is cleaning."

"Why don't you come over a watch some movies again?" Shay suggested, making my heart beat even harder. "We can send Ahmad out for Chinese again and I promise not fall asleep on you two this time."

I was silent for a few seconds. I thought about Ahmad's hands caressing me, his lips on mine, his tongue licking around my breast. I shook my head; I couldn't go there again. But God, did I want to. "I'm gonna have to pass tonight, girl," I said reluctantly.

"Are you sure? We wouldn't mind the company."

Hearing the tension she tried to mask in her voice made me think about my conversation with Ahmad. I knew she must have had her reasons for not wanting to be intimate with him, but after last Friday I didn't see how she could turn him down. I thought about asking her what was wrong, but I didn't want her to know that Ahmad had confided in me. "I'm sure, girl," I said, wanting more than anything to say yes. "I'm just gonna clean and then make it an early night. I'm kind of tired anyway."

"Okay, but you know you can call and change your mind."

"Thanks, girl."

"Hey, is Max still staying with you and Mike?"

I frowned. "Yeah."

"I'm gonna be honest, girl, I don't know how you can stand him being there after what he did to Trina."

"Believe me, Shay," I said. "I didn't want him here, but you know he's Mike's boy, so I couldn't say anything."

Shay sucked her teeth. "Shit, let him try and stay here and see what happens. You're a better person than I am. His mother-in-law, Mya. How could he do that? First of all, other than her body, there is nothing attractive about her. Sharon has no class. Max is damn trifling to ever choose her over Trina."

"I agree with you there," I said.

"Have you spoken to her?"

"Once. I called her the day after Mike told me what happened."

"How is she? I've been meaning to call her, but with Nicole it's hard."

"She's holding up as best as she can. Max hurt her bad, but I think she'll be okay. It's just going to take some time."

"I hope she doesn't take his ass back," Shay said.

"I don't think she will."

"Good. I swear if Ahmad ever fooled around on me, I'd never forgive him. I'd divorce his black ass in a heartbeat."

"What about Nicole? Would you want to put her through the pain of divorce?"

"It's not an easy thing to deal with, but eventually she'd cope."

"Well, as long as you're keeping Ahmad happy, I guess you won't have to worry about that, right?" I just had to put it out there. I wanted to see what her reaction would be. There was a short moment of silence and when Shay said, "Yeah, that's true," there was a definite difference in her tone.

"So, Ahmad is still at work?"

"Yeah. He should be home in a little while, though." I heard my call waiting beep. "Hold on a second, Mya. I have another call."

Shay clicked over and while I waited, I gave some serious thought to going over to watch the movies. A few minutes later, Shay came back on. "Speak of the devil," she said. "That was Ahmad."

"It was?"

"Yeah. He has a few things to do after work and then he said he might meet Mike and Max out for a drink."

"Oh," I said, letting go of any thought of going over.

"So, if you decide to change your mind, it'll just be you, me and the baby. Not the wildest girls' night out, but it's something."

"I'll think about it."

"Hey, maybe next week you and I can swing by Trina to see how she's doing."

"Sounds like a plan."

"Oh, before I forget, Ahmad said to tell you hi, and that the last movie you guys watched was better than he thought it would be."

I smiled as a hot flash came over me. "Well, tell him I said hi back. Anyway, girlfriend, I'm gonna get going. I want to get started on this cleaning."

"You sure you don't want to come over?"

"I'm sure, but thanks anyway. Besides, when Ahmad comes home he may want a little somethin'-somethin', and the last thing you want is me there messing up your flow."

I noticed another drop in pitch as Shay said, "Yeah."

"I'll talk to you later, Shay." I hung up the phone and closed my eyes. I no longer had to wonder if Ahmad had been thinking about last Friday. I smiled. I thought the movie was better too.

Ahmad

I got in my Camry and checked the time. I still had some time before I had to head over to Irene's. I frowned and shook my head, thinking about how she was probably at home setting things up for the night, which I was going to do my best to ruin. Hopefully when I was through with her, the last thing she would be thinking of was sex with me.

I thought I was going to have to deal with her during school, but she was absent, so instead of facing off with her, I took advantage of her absence and spoke to Maxine after class. This was the first time I'd gotten to do that because for the entire week, Irene had made it a point to "observe" my last period class. Maxine was walking out when I stopped her.

"Maxine, could you hold on a second?"

She said goodbye to a few of her classmates then turned around. "Yes, Mr. Jefferson?"

I could hear the apprehension in her voice. I waited until the final student walked out. "Hey, Maxine, I just wanted to talk to you. I know we haven't really had a chance since last Friday."

Maxine nodded her head slowly and before I knew it was happening, tears welled in her eyes and then ran down her cheeks. "Mr. Jefferson, I'm so sorry. I didn't want to lie on you, but Mrs. Baker said that if I didn't she would expel me from school for being involved with you."

I stood and walked over to her, but made sure to keep my distance. I wasn't trying to have someone walk in on another misunderstanding. "It's okay, Maxine," I said, feeling regretful that I couldn't comfort her.

"At first I told her I wouldn't lie. I told her I would tell everyone that she was the one lying, but then she said that no one would believe me because she was the principal. I can't afford to be expelled, Mr. Jefferson. I'm trying to go to MIT." She covered her face with her hands, dropped her chin to her chest, and cried heavily. Making sure to keep a very safe distance, I patted her shoulder. Once.

"Don't worry, Maxine. Everything's going to be okay."

"How, Mr. Jefferson? Mrs. Baker still has the letter I wrote."

"I'll take care of the letter. You don't have to worry about anything but getting into MIT."

"Why is she doing this, Mr. Jefferson? What did you do to her?"

"I didn't do anything to her. We just had a difference of opinion about something."

"She's an ugly bitch," Maxine said.

I smiled. "I have to agree with you there. So, are you okay now?" I backed away and went to my desk, grabbed a couple of Kleenex, and handed them to her. She wiped her nose and patted her eyes.

"I'm fine. I just don't want you to get fired because of me."

"Don't worry, Maxine. I won't be getting fired. Now go study for that test I'm giving you guys next week."

Maxine gave me a half smile. "Okay, Mr. Jefferson. I'll see you later."

"Take it easy."

Maxine walked to the door, but instead of leaving, she stopped and turned around. "Mr. Jefferson, before I forget, I wanted to let you know that the next time I decide to kiss you, I'll make sure no one is around."

Before I could respond to her comment, Maxine waved and walked off. I shook my head. If there was one thing I would do the remainder of the school year, it would be to make sure that Maxine and I were never alone again. I'd had all the drama I needed.

Since I had some time to spare, I sat down and caught up on some paperwork that I'd been neglecting. Two hours and forty-five minutes later I was ringing Irene's doorbell.

"You're early. I said six o'clock," Irene said, swinging the door open.

She'd tried to make herself look sexy by putting on eyeliner and lipstick, but her attempts were all in vain. I shuddered at the sight of her as I noticed the silk robe tied loosely around her overweight body, revealing a touch of lace underneath.

"I came, didn't I?" I said coldly.

"So you did," Irene said. She stepped back. "Come inside."

I stepped past her.

"Do you want something to drink?" Irene asked as she closed the door.

"No. I don't plan on being here that long."

Irene stepped behind me and wrapped her arms around my waist. "Are you sure about that?" she asked, her hand slinking down to my crotch.

I quickly unwrapped her hands and stepped away from her. "Very sure."

Irene purred.

"Whatever," I said. "Look, there's just something I don't understand," I started, but before I could say anything else, Irene put her pudgy finger to my lips.

"Shh. Not now. We'll talk later. Right now I'm horny and I want some." She moved to kiss me on the lips, but I quickly turned my head, giving her only my cheek.

"Come on, Ahmad, don't be like that. Give me those lips," Irene said, placing her hands on my cheeks, trying to force me to kiss her.

I wasn't having it. I moved her hands away and took a step back. "No kisses, Irene. Not until we talk about the lies you've made up."

"Ahmad, Ahmad, Ahmad," she said, stepping forward and wrapping her hand around my bicep, giving it a squeeze. "Are you trying to trick me into confessing about lies that don't exist?" She leaned toward me in an attempt to kiss me again, but before her leather-like lips could touch my skin, I pushed her back.

"So you admit that you're lying?"

"I don't admit to anything."

"Drop the act, Irene."

"This is no act, Ahmad," she said, reaching out to grab my crotch. "Now give me what I want."

"Or what? You'll smear my reputation?"

"I don't know what you're talking about."

I nodded. "I had a talk with Maxine after class today. She told me all about how you threatened to expel her if she didn't lie and write up that note of yours."

"Where's the proof, Ahmad?" Irene asked, putting her hands on her wide waist. "How are you possibly going to prove that Maxine was telling the truth? Do you want to come with me and my note and meet with the school board? Would you like to see whose words they believe?" Irene watched me with a smirk on her face. She just knew she had my back pinned against the wall.

I looked at her and shook my head. "You know, I became a teacher to make a difference. To influence kids, especially minority kids. I lived in a rough neighborhood when I was growing up. Drug dealers, gang bangers, prostitutes . . . These were the people around me. Had it not been for my parents' tough discipline, my nosey neighbors, and a couple of my teachers, I might have ended up like a lot of my friends—hustling or even dead.

"Kids today don't have the same type of examples I had. Many of them don't have both parents in the home. Neighbors don't say shit nowadays, and teachers—well, a lot of teachers are underpaid, disrespected and just don't seem to care, so they don't give their students their all.

"But I'm one teacher that does care, and I thought you were too. Obviously I was wrong. You don't have the integrity I thought you had. If you did, you'd never be blackmailing me and threatening to ruin Maxine's chances of getting into MIT."

"Oh please, spare me the long-winded speech, Ahmad. Why don't you grow up and come to grips with what's going on around you? The world isn't what it used to be. Times are tough and to survive in these times, you have to be tougher. Be an example? Please. I don't get paid enough to be an example. I'll let the rappers and sports figures do that. The only thing I'm concerned about is making sure I get mine. And right now, I want you. So, if that means I have to blackmail you to get what I want, then so be it."

I looked at her and shook my head with disdain. "So basically, unless I have sex with you, you'll continue with your lies and make sure my job's taken away and my marriage destroyed? You'll expel a top student for having a crush on her teacher and ruin her chances for furthering her education? That's what you're willing to do for sex? Are you really willing to lie and cause all of that damage?"

I held my breath as Irene smiled, giving me a dull yellow spectacle to view, and untied the belt of her robe. As it fell to the carpet, she said in the most confident tone, "That's exactly what I'm willing to do, Ahmad. Now bring your black ass over here and save your job."

It was my turn to smile. I reached in my pants pocket and removed the micro-cassette recorder that had been taping our entire conversation. I held it in the air for Irene to see. "Any last words?"

Irene stared at me wide eyed. "What the hell is that?"

"This," I said hitting the stop button, "is what's going to make you hand me the note Maxine wrote. This is what's going to shut your fucking mouth and forget all about trying to blackmail me or Maxine. And this is what's going to make your fat ass give me all of the perks I want. Days off, no cafeteria duty, whatever."

"I . . . I can't do that!" Irene yelled.

"Are you sure? Maybe I should let the school board determine that. The note, Irene. Get it."

Irene glared at me for a few seconds then bent down to pick up her robe and cover the disgusting body I had tried my best to avoid seeing. "You're an asshole, you know that?"

"Yeah, and now I'm an asshole with privileges. Get the note."

Irene walked over to the coffee table and fished the note out of her purse. She threw it at me with a curse.

"Thank you," I said, picking it up. I opened the folded piece of paper, read what Maxine had been forced to write, and then ripped the paper into pieces.

"Okay, so you got your note. Are you going to destroy that tape now?" Irene asked.

I raised an eyebrow at her. "Destroy this? Are you kidding me? Think of this as your lifeline. As long as you keep that mouth closed, your life can go on business as usual. The minute you even make an attempt to fuck with my life or Maxine's, not only will the school board hear this, I'll make sure the faculty, the students and your husband hear it too." I gave Irene a wicked smile and walked out of her home.

Max's plan had been too perfect. I laughed, got in my car and raised the volume on the radio after I started the car. Usher's new song, "Yeah" was playing, and that was one of my favorites. I tapped on the steering wheel and drove away while Irene stood at her door looking defeated.

Shay

"Girl, I don't even know how to tell you this."

I closed my eyes and frowned. I should have never answered the phonc. My former co-worker was such a gossip queen.

"What is it, Rosette?" I asked reluctantly. People like her were one of the main reasons I decided not to go back to work and became a stay at home mother instead.

I had slaved my hours away in the purchasing department at US Foodsupply for three years. Rosette joined the company during my second year. We were the only minorities in our department, so naturally we hung together. Rosette and I were good friends in the beginning. We'd talk over e-mail and trip out during lunch, and sometimes after work we'd go out for some drinks to bitch and complain about the job and the low salaries we were making. Because I usually don't trust them, I don't have too many girlfriends, but in Rosette I thought I'd found one. One night, though, Ahmad and I had a big argument over an ex-girlfriend he dated for three years, who'd called him up out of the blue to invite him to dinner. I'd seen pictures of her before, so I knew that she wasn't some unattractive woman that I didn't have to worry about.

"Baby, it's just an innocent dinner. There's nothing to worry about. She knows I'm married."

"If she knows you're married, why is she asking you out to dinner?"

"She's in town for a few nights and she just wants to catch up with old friends."

"If that's the case then why are you the only friend going out to dinner with her?"

"Like I said, baby, it's an innocent dinner."

"I bet she wants to catch up," I snapped.

"Shay, why are you flipping out over this? I'm married to you. She's nothing but my ex."

"Exactly. She's your ex. That means she's in the past and should stay there."

"She's a friend, Shay."

"Who you haven't spoken to in two years. So, why now?"

"Baby, like I said, you have nothing to worry about."

"So, what are you saying? That you're going to go out with her even though I'm against it?"

"Shay, did I trip out when Anthony asked you out?"

"No, but that was different."

"Different how? He was an ex, wasn't he?"

"Anthony asked me out because he was going through a divorce and he needed a friend to talk to. He didn't want to 'catch up.' He didn't want to reminisce about old times and how good we used to be together."

"Who says that's what we're going to talk about?"

"What other kind of catching up is there between old lovers, Ahmad?"

"Whatever, Shay. Stop being so insecure."

"So, you're going?"

"Yeah, I'm going."

"Even though I, your wife, don't want you to?"

"It's an innocent dinner, Shay."

After Ahmad left I called Rosette and asked her if she wanted to go out. I was angry and I needed to vent. This was the first time that I'd ever confided in her. I told her all about my argument with Ahmad, and told her how attractive the ex-girlfriend was. Rosette sided with me and together we got tipsy off of one too many Long Island Iced Teas. I went to work the following week thinking I had a real confidante, but I was wrong. I found out that as nice as she was, Rosette also had a big mouth. Different women were coming up to me saying how sorry they were to hear that Ahmad had been cheating on me with his ex. Some couldn't believe he had the nerve to go and get her pregnant. My supervisor even asked me if I wanted to take some time off to deal with Ahmad, since he heard we were on the verge of getting a divorce.

After putting the rumors to rest, I tracked Rosette down and ripped into her for putting my business out there for everyone to talk about. She was lucky I couldn't wait until we got out of work, or else I would have done more than curse her out. Rosette apologized over and over but needless to say, I never trusted her again. I got over her making me front page news for a day at the office, but since then, the only time I really talked to her was when I needed something for work.

"So, what is it, Rosette?" I asked again. I had just finished fighting a long, hard battle to get Nicole to sleep and I really didn't feel like dealing with her.

"Shay, I don't even know how to say this."

"Just say it, Rosette."

"Your husband drives a black Toyota Camry, right?"

"Yeah. What about it?"

"Shay, your man is fooling around on you."

I shook my head. "Rosette, what did I tell you about making up lies?"

"Shay, I'm not lying. I swear."

"Whatever, Rosette. I let you off the hook easy last time, but I'm warning you, don't be spreading any more rumors about me or my husband."

"Shay, I told you I'm not lying," she insisted. "Just hear me out at least."

I rolled my eyes. I couldn't believe I was about to entertain her. "What, Rosette?"

"Girl, you know the principal that lives in the house across the street from me?"

"Who? Irene Baker?"

"Yeah, that's her. Well anyway, I'm sorry to tell you this, but I just saw your husband driving away from her place."

I sighed. "I can't believe I just let you waste my time, Rosette. Irene is my husband's boss. If that was him, he probably stopped by to pick something up or drop something off. You have some fucking nerve coming to me with this bullshit, especially after the lies you told before." I was so pissed off.

"Shay, I'd be crazy to call you to tell you a lie like this. I'm telling you I saw him leave with my own eyes, and I don't think it had anything to do with business. Not unless Irene always handles her business in a silk robe with lingerie underneath."

"Rosette, what are you talking about?" I didn't want to give her the time of day, but she had a point—it would have been stupid to call me to lie. "What do you mean lingerie?"

"Shay, she was standing at the door looking all sad with her robe halfway off her shoulders."

"There's no way," I said, shaking my head. "First of all, Ahmad wouldn't cheat on me. And you know what, even if he did, trust me, it would not be with Irene. My husband's not desperate." *Is he?* I wondered as my words slipped from my lips. I knew we weren't having sex, but he wouldn't sink that low, would he? I shook my head to get rid of that thought. Rosette was probably wrong. It was probably just a case of mistaken identity. I mean, what reason would Ahmad have to go over to Irene's house, anyway? I couldn't think of one. "Rosette, look, I got to go."

"Well, what are you gonna do, girl?" Rosette asked, much too interested in my business.

"Look, Rosette, the person you saw was probably not even my husband. I mean, he's not the only person in the world with a black Toyota Camry."

"Shay, the license plate said *Ahmad*."

I pulled the phone away from my ear and stared at it. Was she standing at her door with a set of binoculars? I put the phone back to my ear. "Rosette, I'm going now," I said with a lot of attitude.

"But what are you gonna do?" she asked again, her insistence getting on my last nerve.

"Don't worry about what I'm gonna do," I snapped.

"But girl, he's messing around on you. You have to do something."

No longer able to keep my cool, I snapped. "Look, I know your nosy ass wants more information, but let me warn you, I better not find out that you're telling people my damn business again. I may not work at US Foodsupply, but I still speak with people who do. Stay the hell out of my business, Rosette." I slammed the phone down, angry that she might be telling me the truth.

Ahmad wouldn't cheat on me. No way. And like I said, he wouldn't be that desperate for some ass. I paced back and forth in the living room a few times and then went to check on Nicole. I'd been a little loud on the phone. Luckily, she was still sleeping soundlessly. I adjusted the blanket covering her and then stepped out of the room. As I did, I heard the front door open then close. I walked into the living room to see Ahmad walk in with a box of pizza and some Blockbuster movies. He had a big smile on his face. Too big.

"Where have you been?" I asked.

"Hey, Shay," he said, putting the pizza down. "I had some things to take care of."

"What things?"

"Nothing big. Just a couple of errands."

"Like what?" I asked, watching him closely and not liking the way he was tiptoeing around my questions.

"Damn. Hello to you too, Shay. Yeah, I had a good day. Thanks for asking."

I put my index finger in the air. "Don't get smart with me, Ahmad. I asked what errands did you have to run and where were you?"

Ahmad looked at me. "Shay, what the hell is your problem? I walk in the door and you're grilling me like I did something. What's up with that?"

"The only problem I have is you not telling me where you've been," I said, my blood boiling more and more. I watched his body language. I could tell that he was hiding something. Rosette's voice popped into my head.

"Why do you want to know where I've been?"

"Because I want to know."

"Errands. I had to run some," Ahmad said, walking past me.

I turned and faced him. "Mm-hmm," I said, curling my lips and folding my arms across my chest. "Did these errands require going to your boss's house?"

Ahmad stopped dead in his tracks and turned around. "What?"

"What?" I mocked. "Oh, you want to talk now, huh? So, it's true, isn't it?"

"What's true?"

"You were over at Irene Baker's house fucking her, weren't you?"

"What?"

"Don't what me," I yelled. "I heard all about your fucking visit. I can't believe you, Ahmad. I can't fucking believe you would stoop so low to go and fuck Irene. You asshole."

"Shay, what are you talking about?" Ahmad asked. I could see the shock in his eyes. He'd been cold busted. "Where are you getting all of this?"

"Don't worry about where I get my information, you ass," I said harshly. "The only thing you better worry about is the divorce that I want."

"Divorce?"

"Yes, divorce. If you think I'm gonna stay with your ass after you went and fucked Irene, you've got another thing coming. You can go to hell, Ahmad."

"Shay, will you quiet down? I don't know where you got your information, but believe me, it's wrong. Very wrong."

"So you weren't at Irene's house?"

Ahmad hesitated for a second before saying, "Yes, I was."

"You ass!" I yelled, swinging at him.

Ahmad grabbed my wrists. "Shay, calm the hell down and let me explain."

"I don't want any damn explanations!" I tried to pull my hands free, but his grip was too strong. "Let me go, Ahmad."

"You gonna let me explain?"

"No. I've heard enough already."

"Well, then I'm not letting you go."

"Asshole!" I screamed, managing to pull one wrist free. Before I could do any damage, Ahmad grabbed it again.

"Shay, believe me, whatever it is that you heard or whatever it is that you're thinking is so far from the truth. Now, I'm gonna ask you one last time to let me explain."

"You're hurting my wrists, damn it!"

"Well, then stop acting like Leila Ali up in here and give me a chance to explain." Ahmad pushed me back away from him. I rubbed my wrists. I wanted to rush at him again, but I knew it would do no good. "Sit down, Shay," he said.

I slit my eyes at him. "Your child is in her crib," I said defiantly.

Ahmad removed a tape recorder from his pocket. "Please sit," he said in a softer tone. There was something in the tone of his voice that made me wonder if I'd been wrong for attacking him. I sat down.

"What, are you going to tape this conversation?" I asked, looking at the recorder.

"No."

"So, what's it for?"

Ahmad sat down beside me and put the recorder on the coffee table. "This is the reason why I was at Irene's house." He hit the play button and sat back in the sofa.

A few minutes later I looked at him as he watched me with *I told you so* written all over his face. "I'm sorry," I said softly. After listening to the taped conversation I felt like a damn fool for listening to Rosette's ass and not trusting my husband. "Forgive me for doubting you."

Ahmad took my hand. "Don't worry about it."

"I can't believe the nerve of that bitch to try and blackmail you. I feel like hopping in the car and going over to her house to give her a piece of my damn mind."

"No need for that, baby. As you can see, I've handled her."

I was relieved, but I still had one thing to clear up. "So, this kiss between you and your student . . ."

"Was completely not instigated, perpetuated, suggested, offered, asked for, or wanted by me," Ahmad said. "One minute she was asking me if I'd go out with her and the next minute she jumped forward and kissed me and that's when Irene walked in."

"And the kiss lasted . . ."

"Less than a second, baby. Believe me."

I looked at my husband and saw in his brown eyes that he was telling the truth. "Okay," I said.

"So, no divorce?"

I smiled. I couldn't believe I'd gone there. "No divorce," I said. "I'm really sorry that I acted like that, Ahmad."

He slid closer, put one hand behind my back and lifted my chin up toward him with the other. "No more apologies," he said just before resting his lips on mine. I was apprehensive about kissing him at first. It had been a while since we'd even done that. I have to be honest, though; it felt good. He kissed me lightly a few times, with me responding in kind. When his tongue knocked on the doors of my lips asking if my tongue could come out to play, I couldn't say no. I enjoyed the feel of my husband's tongue as he gently passed his hand up and down my back. I moaned and as I did, Ahmad gently pushed me back until I was lying on the couch. We kissed like passionate teenagers as our hands intertwined. It felt so good I could have kissed him forever, but then he let go of one of my hands and made his way toward the edge of my shirt to lift it and go under. That's when I tensed up. He noticed my tension.

"What's wrong, baby?"

"Don't stop kissing me, Ahmad." I tried to grab his hand to hold it again, but he pulled it away.

"Baby, I want to feel you. It's been so long since I've felt you." He made an attempt to go under my shirt again, and again I stopped him.

"Stop, Ahmad."

"Stop?"

"Yes. Now."

"But Shay . . ."

"Just get off of me, Ahmad. Please."

"Shay, what's your problem? Why are you stopping this?"

"Because I don't want to. Now get off." I didn't wait for him to move. I pushed him off and stood up.

"What the fuck is your problem, Shay?" Ahmad asked loudly. "We're a fucking married couple."

"I just don't want to have sex, Ahmad. Just leave it at that."

"Here we go again with this bullshit!" Ahmad said, throwing his hands in the air. I felt so bad. I wanted him. I really did. I just didn't want him to touch the fat I was hiding. I didn't want his fingers to go over my stretch marks. I didn't want him to realize how unattractive I was.

"I am fed up with this shit, Shay! You are my damn wife. I'm tired of not getting any damn sex."

"Why does it always have to be about sex, Ahmad? Why can't we just cuddle and kiss?"

"Cuddle and kiss? What, are we in elementary school?"

"I just don't want to have sex." I turned my back to him, angry with myself for not being able to overcome my destroyed self-esteem.

"Why, Shay? Why the fuck don't you want to?"

"Because I don't!"

"Because you don't? Well you know what, Shay? I fucking do. Goddamn. I should have taken Irene up on her damn offer. She's not the prettiest, but at least my dick would have been satisfied."

"Go to hell, Ahmad. Go and fuck her if you want, you insensitive ass."

"Insensitive? How the hell am I being insensitive? All I want is to make love to my wife. What the hell is wrong with that?"

As we yelled back and forth Nicole started to cry from her crib. My back was still to Ahmad, and I was glad, because I didn't want him to see the tears of shame that were falling down my face. I was glad for Nicole's screaming. It gave me an excuse to walk away.

Mike

"What do you mean you're not going out shopping with Shay?"

I was just about to leave to get some things for the surprise party. With my hand on the doorknob, I turned and looked at Mya, who was sitting on the couch in her bathrobe, turning on the TV. She'd just dropped the bomb on me. "I thought the plans were set."

Flipping through the channels and not paying much attention to me, Mya said, "Shay called me yesterday and cancelled. Her mother's friend is in the hospital and she'll be with her all day."

"She called yesterday? Are you sure?"

"What do you mean am I sure?"

"Uh, I mean I just thought you were supposed to go and have a girls' day out kind of thing." I clenched my jaws. I couldn't believe Ahmad hadn't called to tell me.

"Why do you sound so distressed over me not being able to go out and shop?" Mya finally looked up at me.

I put on a quick smile. "Aw, baby, I'm not distressed. Come on. It's just that it's your birthday and with me having to work overtime, I thought it would have been nice for you to have a girls' day out to enjoy. It's your birthday, baby." I walked over and planted a kiss on her lips.

"Mike, it's not a big deal. I'll just enjoy my birthday being a couch potato. I haven't done that in a long time."

"So, you're just going to sit here all day?"

"That's what couch potatoes do, Mike."

I stood up straight. There was no way in hell I could let her stay at home today. "Where's Max?"

"Oh, he stayed out all night. He called around ten last night and said he wouldn't be coming. You know, for a man who swears he loves his wife, he's been staying out a hell of a lot."

"He does love Trina, baby. He's just down in the dumps right now. Besides, most of the time all he does is sit outside the house watching her, hoping she'll give him a chance."

"He has some nerve. I don't care if he's your boy. I hope Trina doesn't take his ass back. He deserves everything he's getting for what he did."

"Yeah well, everyone makes mistakes, baby. Maybe this is the wakeup call he needs."

Mya *humph*'d. "Why is it that you men always need wake up calls to set your asses straight? Y'all ain't shit. Wanna have a good woman sitting at home while you're out there trying to sleep with any skank with breasts. Then you want to stroll in the house all hours of the morning with some lame-ass lie."

I cleared my throat as Mya sucked her teeth. I had a feeling she was talking directly to me. I'd gotten home at three that morning. I had finally hooked up with captain's secretary. "Yeah well, enough about why men are so stupid," I said changing the topic. "Let's talk about you and your thirtieth birthday."

"What's there to talk about? I told you what I'm going to do."

"But it's going to be a nice day out today, baby. It's not supposed to be that cold."

"Mike, don't you have to go to work?"

"Yeah, yeah. I just wanted you to enjoy your day, not sit in the house."

"Believe me, I will enjoy watching the TV."

"Alright, baby, whatever you want. I'll see you later tonight." I kissed her goodbye and hurried out of the house. When I got in the car I grabbed my cell and dialed Ahmad's number. When he answered, I didn't even hesitate to rip into him. "Ahmad, why the fuck didn't you tell me Shay couldn't take Mya out today?"

"What?" Ahmad said groggily. I'd obviously just woken him up.

"Don't what me, man. You could've called my ass to let me know what was up."

"What are you talking about, man?" Ahmad asked. "What do you mean Shay can't take her out?"

"You mean you don't know?"

"Know what?"

"Nigga, Mya just told me that Shay has to go out with your mother-in-law to see some friend of hers. She called Mya yesterday and cancelled. She didn't tell you?"

There was a moment of silence before Ahmad sighed and said, "Nah, man, she didn't."

"Why the hell not?"

"Man, we got into it last night. Shit, I'm out here on the damn couch."

I slammed my hand on the steering wheel. "Well, you know what, bruh? Mya's on the couch too, and she plans on staying there all fucking day. Man, the DJ's gonna show up at my place at one o'clock. Mya can't be there. She's gotta be out of the house all day."

I didn't want my plans to be ruined. I needed this surprise party to jump off. I needed Mya to see that it was all about her, because I had a feeling that she was starting to wonder about my whereabouts. I figured the party was one good way to keep her head filled with nothing but love for me. I needed her to stay naive so that I could continue doing what I was doing.

"Where's Max?"

"That fool's not here. He stayed out all night. His ass is probably camped out in front of his house."

"Well, why don't you try calling Trina?"

"Come on, man. Trina's not gonna help me out."

"So, what are you gonna do?"

"What do you mean what am I gonna do? Man, your wife caused this mess. You need to fix it."

"Me?"

"Hell yeah, you."

"Man, but what about Shay? She's coming too."

"Yo, I'll pick Shay up and have her here before you get back with Mya."

"Man, how am I supposed to pull this off?"

"I don't care how you do it. Just make sure Mya's out of the house by twelve. I'll call you and let you know when to bring her home." I hit the end button and tossed my cell into the passenger seat. I looked at my watch. It was nine in the morning. I didn't know how he was gonna do it, but Ahmad had to get Mya out before I got back.

Max

"You had a week, ma'fucka. I gave your ass a whole week to disappear!"

I grunted in pain as Trina's brother Jamal punched me in my jaw again. He'd been beating me like this for the past twenty minutes. The only reason I hadn't fallen to the ground was because two of his boys were holding me up. I coughed and cringed from the intense pain in my ribs, which I had no doubt were busted. I tried to lift my head but was too weak, so I continued to stare through the one eye that hadn't swollen shut yet. I watched the blood falling from my busted mouth, dropping to the ground. Jamal punched me again, this time in my stomach. This was my payback for having slapped Sharon.

"You a stupid nigga," Jamal said, lifting my chin so that I could look at him. "I mean, did you think you could slap my moms and get away with that shit?" Jamal spit in my face then pulled out a gun from his waistband. "You know you a dead ma'fucka, right?"

I watched Jamal smile as he pointed the gun at my chest. I wanted to do something—fight back or beg for my life, maybe, but I couldn't get my body or mouth to move. I was about to die, but I wasn't scared. As a mater of fact, I wasn't even thinking about death. With death being only seconds away, the only thing I could think about was Trina.

All week long I'd been calling her at home and calling her job, but she never answered the phone. She must have known I was calling, because I'd left countless messages. Along with the calls, I went by the house, but I could never get past the front door. I begged her over and over to let me inside, not even giving a fuck about the neighbors who watched. I just banged on the door and rang the bell non-stop.

When I got nowhere at the house I tried her job, but I only got as far as the security desk in the building. I was miserable without Trina. It was like I couldn't breathe. I never thought I'd feel that way. I never realized what she meant to me until she wasn't there anymore.

I called Sharon once to curse her out for what she did. I was drunk and depressed and didn't give a fuck when she cursed me back and said she was going to get Jamal to come after me. I could have asked Mike to help me out, but I didn't want to get him involved in my drama. Besides, after what I'd done to Trina, I deserved an ass kicking.

Jamal pressed the gun into me. "Any last words, ma'fucka?"

I coughed up blood again and took a labored breath. I looked at Jamal through the blurred vision of my one eye, which was slowly swelling shut. "Trina," I whispered as I exhaled painfully, then I saw nothing but a bright, white light.

Mya

I was all into some Saturday morning cartoons when the doorbell rang. I got up from the sofa but waited before going to see who was at the door. *Osmosis Jones* was at a good part and I didn't want to miss it. When it finally trailed off into a commercial, I went to the door, hoping that whoever it was had gotten tired of waiting and left. I was having fun vegging it up on the couch, and I really wanted to get back to the cartoon. I looked through the peephole and caught my breath when I saw Ahmad standing outside. I took a step back. What was he doing there? The doorbell rang again. I took another couple of steps backwards. "Coming," I said, trying to make it seem like I was farther away.

I looked down at the oversized T-shirt and flannel pants I had on. Damn, I looked like a bum. But it was my birthday, I was home alone, and wasn't expecting any visitors; I was entitled. I wanted to go and change, but that would have been a hassle because I would have taken too much time trying to find the perfect thing to wear. At least I had brushed my teeth. I passed my hand through my hair and sighed. There was only so much I could do. I went back to the door and opened it. "Ahmad?" I said, feigning surprise as best as I could.

"Hey, Mya," Ahmad said, smiling at me. "I hope I didn't interrupt anything."

"No, you didn't. Come in."

I closed the door after he walked past me. "I was just watching some cartoons. Mike had to go into work this morning."

"Yeah, I know."

"You do?"

"Yeah. He called me this morning."

"Really? So . . . then what are you doing here?"

"Well, I can't really tell you why," Ahmad said.

I looked at him like he was crazy. "You can't?"

"No."

"Okay," I said skeptically.

"All I can tell you is that I need to get you out of the house by twelve o'clock, and if my watch is correct, that gives you exactly an hour to get out of that cute outfit." Ahmad smiled at me.

I blushed. "Shut up."

"Hey, it is cute. Especially the hole in the knee."

I turned sideways so he wouldn't see my hole. "Whatever. Anyway, so I *have* to leave my house before twelve?"

"Yup."

"And can I ask why?"

"You can, but I can't tell you."

"Okay. And how long do I have to be out of my house?"

"Pretty much all day."

"Is anyone else with you?"

"No."

"So, it's just you and me?" I asked, my voice softening.

With his eyes locked on mine, Ahmad said. "Yeah. Just us two."

Neither one of us spoke after that. My heart was beating heavily and my palms were getting sweaty with nervous excitement. We hadn't spoken or seen one another since our semi-sexual episode on the couch, but I knew from his comment through Shay that he'd been thinking about that night as much as I had. I cleared my throat. "I guess I better get ready then." I headed to the living room. "You can take over for me and watch cartoons. Or you can change the channel. Doesn't matter to me, really." I was glad I had my back to him. I bit down on my bottom lip; I couldn't believe I was rambling like that.

"Cartoons are fine," Ahmad said.

"Okay. Good. I'm gonna go upstairs and take a hot shower now," I said softly. "Umm, is there anything you want . . . or need?" I watched him remove his coat. He was wearing a cream-colored turtleneck and navy blue jeans. Damn, he was looking good. "I meant like a drink or anything," I said as he gave me a burning gaze. I looked away from him and put my attention on a cushion on the sofa. I needed to get upstairs. More importantly, I needed to get away from him.

"No, I'm good," he said, "but if I need anything, I'll get it. Thanks."

"Okay. I'm going upstairs now."

We stared at each other again for a few seconds. There was something in the air. I knew he could feel it, because I damn sure could. Ahmad shifted and cleared his throat. "Before you go, Mya..." He paused and took a step toward me. I slowed my breathing as he continued. "I just wanted to say, that I—"

Ring.

Ahmad and I both looked at the phone, which had picked a bad time to ring. I looked at Ahmad, who was no longer moving forward, but backing up instead. When he sat down and grabbed the remote, I sighed and grabbed the phone. "Hello?"

"Hey, baby," Mike said.

"Hey, Mike," I answered reluctantly. I looked at Ahmad and I swear it looked like his shoulders dropped. I turned away from him. "I'm surprised you're calling."

"Well, I had a free moment, so I figured I'd call."

"Oh, okay. Well, guess who's here?"

"Who?"

"Ahmad."

"Oh yeah. What's he doing there?"

I looked over at Ahmad, who was doing a terrible job of trying to seem unfazed by Mike's timing. "He came over to see you."

"Oh yeah? Put him on."

I walked over to Ahmad. "He wants to talk to you." I handed him the phone, picked up a bowl I'd had cereal in, and walked into the kitchen. A few minutes later, Ahmad appeared with the phone.

"I told him that you were going to help me find something for Shay. He had to get going."

I took the phone from him. "Okay." Ahmad turned to walk out. "Ahmad," I said softly. He turned around.

"Yeah?"

"Uh . . . what were you going to say before?"

Seconds of silence again passed between us. "I was just going to say don't take too long."

"Oh. That was it?"

"Yeah."

"Okay. Well, I'll be down in a few."

"Alright."

My shoulders were the ones to slump this time as Ahmad walked out of the kitchen. Damn it, this was so wrong.

Ahmad

I wanted to grab her hand. That's all could think about as Mya sat quietly beside me in the car. I took a deep breath and turned up the radio, to drown out how frustrated my exhale had been. Why did Mike have to call when he did? No, I quickly told myself. It was a good thing he'd called. He was my boy. 'Nuff said. I looked at Mya, who was looking so sexy in a pair of light blue jeans and a red sweater that sat perfectly against her mahogany-colored skin. "So, where would you like to go?" I asked.

Mya looked at me. "I don't know. You pick."

"It's your birthday, though."

"I know, and if I had it my way, I'd be on the couch watching cartoons. But since I can't do that and don't know why, you pick. Just make sure it's something fun."

I nodded. "Okay. Have you ever been to Jillian's at the Anne Arundel Mills mall?"

Mya smiled. "That's one place I haven't been to yet."

"Okay, cool. That's our destination then." I headed down I-95 then veered onto route 100 toward Glen Burnie. I took another quick peek at her hand as it lay on her thigh, then looked back to the road. I had a feeling she saw me because out of the corner of my eye I saw her smile.

I turned up the radio another notch, and for the rest of the twenty-minute ride, neither one of us said a word. The silence was awkward and frustrating. As long as we'd known each other, we'd never been unable to communicate. Now here we were, both afraid to bring up what happened, even though we both knew that we eventually had to talk about it.

When we got to Jillian's we continued to avoid the topic and put our focus on all of the video games they had to offer. Jillian's is similar to Dave & Busters and ESPN Zone. In addition to the arcade area, there's a restaurant area with big screens and a bar, another section with pool tables, and one with bowling lanes. There's even a club. I chose Jillian's because I figured with all of the people around there'd be no chance for us to be intimate in any way. Damn, was I wrong. It seemed like no matter what game we played, Mya and I found a way to have some type of physical contact. We started off with a few games of air hockey and after each game, no matter who'd won or lost, we exchanged friendly shoves. After air hockey, we graduated to racing games. We really shouldn't have had contact then because we were each in our own stations, but somehow we found a way to shove and grab each other again.

To the average person, what we were doing would have been no big deal. We knew better, though, especially after we played *House of the Dead*, a game with two guns for two people to stand, aim and shoot as many zombies as possible. This is one of my favorite games to play because it's fast and it's simple.

It doesn't take a rocket scientist to play the game. Hell, ten-year-old kids can and have mastered the game, so when Mya started to complain that she couldn't get the hang of it, I knew what was up. It shouldn't have happened, but I ended up standing behind Mya with my arms around her waist, showing her how to aim the gun properly while I inhaled the intoxicating fragrance of her perfume. If there was any room for doubt about her intentions, it disappeared when Mya made sure to press her behind into my quickly hardening crotch. After a few seconds, the game was the last thing we were paying attention to.

"Do you want to grab something . . . to eat?" I asked, leaning close to her ear.

Mya tipped her head back slightly. "Yes," she whispered. I knew there was a whole lot more to her yes, just like there had been a whole lot more to my question. When Mya stepped away from me, I had to stuff my hand into my pocket quickly to adjust myself before anyone noticed. By the look on the face of one teen who'd been waiting for a turn, I hadn't done a good job.

Mya and I sat in a booth over by the big screens. We were staring at each other silently when our waitress, a short, slightly overweight blond, came to take our orders. We ordered our drinks and food and before the waitress walked off, she smiled and said, "I hope you don't mind me saying, but you two are one of the most attractive couples I've ever seen in here."

Mya and I looked at each other and smiled. Then Mya looked to the girl. "Thank you, but we're just friends."

The waitress looked from Mya to me then down to Mya's hand. "Oh, I saw the rings and just assumed . . . I'm going to get your drinks now." She walked away, her face a shade darker.

Mya and I laughed as she walked away then locked eyes on one another again. "So," I said, forcing myself to look away. "Are you enjoying yourself so far?" I kept my eyes focused on one of the big screens, which was showing a highlight from a football game.

"I'm having a great time," Mya said.

I looked back at her. "Good. Not bad for a birthday outing, right?"

"Not bad at all." Mya stretched her arm across the table and put her hand on mine. "Thank you, Ahmad," she said softly.

"My pleasure."

Mya's hand lingered on mine until the waitress came back with our drinks. She looked down at Mya's hand on mine and her eyes widened just enough to reveal what was going through her mind. Mya quickly removed her hand as the girl left. She grabbed her drink and took a sip. "So," she said, her eyes following the waitress who had hastily pulled one of her co-workers to the side, undoubtedly to gossip about us. "How is Shay?" Mya turned her eyes back to me.

I tightened my jaws as memories of the previous night's unsuccessful attempt at sex came to my mind. "She's fine."

"And how are you two doing?"

"Fine," I said bluntly.

"I don't believe you," Mya said.

I stared at her. With the fire I was feeling for her, and knowing that she was feeling it too—whether she admitted it or not—the last thing I wanted to do was talk about what happened. But I could tell by Mya's body language that the waitress's perceptiveness had gotten to her. I sighed; I knew that talking about Shay was for the best. "I tried to have sex with her last night and she turned me down again."

"Really?" Mya asked sympathetically.

I could feel myself getting angry. "Yeah. And just like all of the other times, she wouldn't give me an explanation as to why. I mean, one minute we're on the damn couch kissing, and the next minute she's telling me to stop."

Mya reached out and touched my hand again. "I'm sorry, Ahmad. I don't know what's wrong with her, and believe me, I've been wondering how she could turn you down."

"Yeah, I've been wondering too. I'm no Denzel, but I'm not a bad looking guy."

Lightly moving her fingers along my knuckles, Mya said, "You're far from being a bad looking guy, Ahmad."

"Thank you," I said, enjoying the feel of her subtle yet not so subtle caress. I continued. "I don't have the most muscular physique, but I can pull off a tank top."

"Yes . . . you can."

"Then why can't I get any damn sex?"

Just as I'd said that, the waitress brought our meals. I knew she'd heard what I said because her eyes were wide and her face an even deeper shade of red. Mya pulled her hand away again. When the waitress left and again hustled to gossip to her co-worker, Mya said, "I don't know what to say, Ahmad. I really don't understand Shay not appreciating what she has."

"Yeah well, I'm getting tired of feeling unappreciated. Shit, I'm a man. A damn good one."

"I know," Mya said.

"Then what's the problem?" I asked, too frustrated to even touch my food.

Mya looked down at her plate of food. "I really wish I had an answer for you, Ahmad. I just hope Shay wises up before someone else comes along hoping to get your attention."

Nothing but silence passed in between us after Mya's comment. Mya kept her head bowed and ate some of her food.

I picked up my fork and before sliding the food into my mouth, said, "You already have."

Mya lifted her head to look at me, and as if on cue, my cell phone rang. I sighed when I looked at the caller ID and saw Mike's name. I answered the phone. "Hello."

"Yo, is Mya close to you?"

I looked over at Mya and said, "Nah, Mya's not around. She's in the bathroom."

"She doesn't suspect anything, does she?"

"Nah. She has no idea."

"Alright, cool. Listen, man, you're gonna have to keep her out a little longer. The DJ's having some problems with his equipment and he's gonna need more time to set things up. I need you to keep Mya out until at least seven o'clock."

I looked at my watch. "Okay, but that's another three and a half hours."

"I know, man, but he has to drive all the way back to Alexandria, grab some things and then come back. That'll be about an hour and a half right there. Then I gotta run to the store to buy the liquor and party favors."

"I thought Max was getting that stuff."

"Man, I don't know where that nigga is. I've been calling him all damn day on his cell and I haven't gotten him, and he hasn't called me back."

"Damn, that's weird."

"Yeah well, his ass better have a good excuse for leaving me hanging. Anyway, besides all that, Mya's mom needs more time with the food."

"Alright. So what should I do?"

"Take Mya to the movies or something. She wants to see that Nicole Kidman flick."

"You mean *The Stepford Wives*?"

"Yeah, that's the one. Take her to see that."

"Alright."

"Cool. Yo, I really appreciate this, bruh. It's nice to be able to count on my boy."

I frowned and looked away from Mya, who had been watching me intently. "No problem," I said. "Hey listen, Mya's on her way back. Let me jet."

"Alright. Thanks again, man."

I hung up the phone and massaged my temples. I could feel Mya's eyes on me. Damn, why did Mike have to go and talk about relying on me? "We're going to have to stay out a little longer than originally planned," I said.

"I kind of gathered that. I guess he needs more time to finish screwing whoever's over there, huh?"

"He's not doing anything like that," I said.

Mya sighed. "I don't even care anymore. Until what time?"

"At least seven."

"Okay."

We finished our food in almost complete silence. My guilt was beating the hell out of me. The waitress came by to ask if we needed anything else. I was about to ask for the check when Mya asked for the dessert menu. The waitress brought the menu and when she walked away, Mya looked at me and said, "I don't really want dessert."

"You don't?"

"No. I just wanted more time here where we have no choice but to face each other."

"Face each other?"

"Yes. We both know that we need to talk."

I sighed and massaged my temples. "I know."

"Ahmad, what's happening between us?"

I clenched my jaws. I regretted ever opening my mouth and saying what I'd said. Damn it, this was wrong. "I don't know, Mya."

"Ahmad, what happened last Friday . . ." Mya paused and took a breath. "What happened wasn't right."

"I know."

She took my hand. "But it was real, wasn't it?"

I looked at her hand in mine and then at her. I was about to answer her when she spoke again.

"Ahmad, I want to say that it wasn't, that you and I were both emotionally vulnerable, but I can't. Dammit, what happened was wrong on so many levels. Mike is my husband and one of your best friends. You have Shay and Nicole. There's so much for both of us to lose."

I sighed. "I know, Mya. Believe me, I do."

"Then why do we want it to happen again? Why do we want to be in each other's arms again?"

I pulled my hand away from hers and gritted my teeth. As wrong as it was, I knew that it was time to lay all of my cards out on the table. "Mya, I'm going to be honest with you. I can't stop thinking about you. And believe me, I want to—every time I look at Shay and my little girl, every time I talk to Mike. I want to stop thinking about your smile, your eyes, your kiss, your touch. I don't want to think about how much I want you. But as hard as I try, I can't stop thinking about those things and more."

"Ahmad, we can't do this."

"I know. But we are. Mya, I think I'm falling in love with you. I've tried to deny it but I can't."

"Ahmad . . ."

"Please let me just get this off my chest. I know that I'm crossing a line that should never be crossed. Mike is my boy, one of my best friends. Shay is my wife. I'm betraying them both by saying these things to you. It's wrong, I know, but I can't deny what I'm feeling for you."

Mya shook her head. "Ahmad, you're just unhappy right now. Things with you and Shay—"

"What's happening with me and Shay has nothing to do with what I feel for you, Mya. You are a beautiful woman. I've always felt that. For years I've watched Mike disrespect you and I've hated it. You don't deserve to be treated the way he treats you. I wanted to say something so many times, but because of my friendship with him and because you seemed so in love with him, I held my tongue. Eventually I met Shay and I moved on, but I never stopped caring about you and wondering how it would be if you were my woman."

"Ahmad, stop," Mya said. "Don't say anymore. Please. This is wrong. All wrong. We're married and we have to respect that no matter how we feel. Believe me, if our situations were different, I wouldn't hesitate to be with you. You are everything a woman could want.

You're handsome, intelligent, caring. Shay doesn't realize what she has in you. If she did, she wouldn't do what she's doing. Or not doing. But as much as I don't like how she's treating you, I have to respect the fact that she is wearing your wedding ring. And you should too. Besides, we're friends, Ahmad. I would hate to do anything to cause us to lose our friendship."

"I would too," I admitted.

"So then you agree that what happened last Friday night can never happen again?"

I exhaled slowly. "Look, Mya, everything you're saying is right. We should respect the lives we have. And last Friday shouldn't have happened."

"Thank you."

"But it did. And as right as you are about everything you've said, you and I both know it's going to be impossible for things to go back to being the same between us. We have feelings for each other—strong feelings—and we can't deny that."

Mya lowered her head and covered her eyes. I could hear her sniffling. I reached out and took her hand in mine. "Mya, I don't mean to make you cry. I just know that I can't get you out of my head, and I know you're in the same boat. We need to do something. Maybe not today, or tomorrow, but eventually we need to do something."

"What, Ahmad?" Mya asked, pulling her hand away. She looked up and stared at me with hard, intense eyes. "What should we do? What are you willing to do? Leave your marriage? Are you willing to give up Shay and Nicole to be with me? Are you willing to lose one of your closest friends? Are you willing to lose all of those things?"

I looked away from her gaze, her questions in my mind. What was I willing to lose? My wife? My family? My life-long friendship? Damn it, why did I have to feel so strongly for her?

"Ahmad, you are a beautiful man and I care about you. Deeply. That's why even if you were willing to give up all of those things for me, I couldn't let you. Please let go of your feelings for me. Please." She reached across and lightly touched my cheek, making me warm. I took her hand and kissed her knuckles. Mya pulled her hand away slowly. "Let's keep our friendship, Ahmad. Let's do that because it's the right thing and it's the best thing to do."

I stared at her but didn't respond. She was such an incredible woman. How was I ever going to be able to let go of Friday night and how it felt? How was I going to be able to ignore my feelings for her? "You are a beautiful woman, Mya," I said. "Mike doesn't deserve you."

"Ahmad . . ."

"Don't worry. I won't say anymore."

Just then the waitress came back to our table. I had a feeling she'd been listening because her timing was just too damn perfect.

"Have you picked a dessert?" she asked Mya.

Mya shook her head. "I've changed my mind about dessert. I think we're ready for the check."

After I paid the bill, we left and walked around the mall section of Arundel Mills, not really speaking. Eventually we went to see the movie, which helped to lighten our moods temporarily. After the movie I called Mike. "What's up, man? Are you ready for me to bring Mya home?"

"Yeah, bruh, everything's ready. The people are here, the food's done, and the music is right."

"Alright, cool." I hung up the phone and turned to Mya. "Are you a good actress?"

Mya smiled. "I'm no Nicole Kidman, but I think I can give an Oscar-worthy performance."

We laughed and then slipped on our coats. Before stepping out into the cold, Mya took my hand. "Ahmad, before we go, I just want to make sure that you're alright with what we talked about. Like I said, if our situations were different . . ."

I put up my hand for her to stop talking. "It's cool, Mya. I'm cool with what we have."

"Good. So am I."

"Alright then. Let's get you home."

Mya squeezed my hand. "Okay." She smiled and stepped out into the cold ahead of me. I watched her for a few seconds before moving to catch up to her. Although she'd said one thing, her eyes were telling a whole different story.

Shay

"Surprise!"

I wasn't yelling as loud as everyone else when Mya walked through the door. I was busy staring at Ahmad. I hadn't seen or spoken to him since our argument the night before. I'd hoped to talk to him this morning. I wanted to apologize for leading him on the way I had, but he was gone before I woke up. I didn't know where he went until Mike called and told me that he'd needed Ahmad to take Mya out since I couldn't. I tried to call Ahmad once. When he didn't answer his cell, I knew it was because he was still pissed, and I couldn't blame him. I wanted to have sex with him. I really did. He had me so damned turned on with the intensity of his kiss, I was practically dripping in my panties. I wanted him inside of me. But as things started to get hot and heavy and he tried to put his hand underneath my shirt, I just shut down. I didn't want him to feel my rolls. I couldn't bear the thought of him feeling my stretch marks and being disgusted by them. As excited as I was, I just had to have him off of me.

I lay in bed alone, crying all night. I was hurting my marriage; I knew it. After going without a good man for years, the last thing I wanted to do was lose Ahmad. I cried until I had no more tears then I got out of bed and went into the bathroom to take a long, hard look at myself in the mirror. I looked at my eyes, searching for the woman my husband had been attracted to. I took off my clothes and looked at my body, only this time I looked for the good in it as opposed to the bad that I always saw. It took a while before I finally realized something: I may have gained some extra weight after Nicole's birth, and I had a little extra cushion by my stomach, but overall, I wasn't looking half as bad as I'd thought. My hips were wider but I still had a figure. My breasts were sagging but were still desirable. For the first time in months I didn't see a cow, but a fine sistah who was now a mother but could still turn heads. I wanted to share my revelation with Ahmad, but when I walked into the living room and saw him snoring on the couch, I decided to wait until the morning. Of course, he was gone before I ever had the chance.

I watched my husband step through the door behind Mya. He was smiling and seemed to be in a good mood. I loved him so much. He was everything to me. I hated that I'd let my insecurities cause tension between us. I hated that he ever spent a night on the couch away from me. Last night lying alone, I'd made up my mind to do everything in my power to make sure Ahmad never strayed into the arms of another woman, because I knew that if I didn't make things right between us, that's what was going to happen. I just hoped it hadn't already.

I walked up to my husband with purpose in my step. After taking my mother to see her friend in the hospital, I went to the salon and had my hair done, while my mother watched Nicole. It had been a couple of months since I'd had my hair done and I was due. After the salon, we went to the mall so that I could buy an outfit to wear. The salon and mall weren't part of my original plan, but like I said, I was trying to keep my husband's attention. I figured the sleek black dress with spaghetti-straps would do the trick. I was just glad it was warm in the house.

"Hey, baby," I said above the hip-hop that was now being played. Ahmad looked at me and his smile abruptly disappeared. I frowned. "You don't have to be that excited to see me."

"What's going on, Shay?" he said, his voice void of any emotion.

I reached up and gave him a kiss on the lips, trying to ignore the fact that he never returned the favor. "I missed you today." I took his hand.

Ahmad looked down at my hand and then up at me. Then he looked in Mya's direction. "Yeah well, I was busy today."

I looked over at Mya, who was receiving birthday wishes from her friends. She took a quick glance over at us and when my eyes locked with hers, she quickly looked away. I put my focus back on Ahmad and stepped in front of him. "So, do you notice anything different about me?" I was dying to know what he thought of the light blond streaks I'd put in my hair. He didn't respond right away because he was too busy looking over at Mya, who was wrapped in Mike's arms.

Finally, after a curious sigh, Ahmad looked down at me. "Yeah, you have that ridiculous dress on," he said. The callousness in his voice shocked the hell out of me.

"Ridiculous?"

"Yeah, Shay. It's forty-something degrees outside."

"I just wanted to look nice for the evening, Ahmad."

"Yeah well, it'd be nice if it were spring or summer." He looked past me again. Without checking, I had no doubt where he was looking, and that bothered the hell out of me.

"Ahmad." I tugged on his hand. "Ahmad, what did you and Mya do today?"

I watched him closely and noticed a subtle twitching of his jaws before he said, "Nothing much. We went to Jillian's and played some games and had a bite to eat."

"That's it?"

"Yeah, pretty much. We also went to see a movie."

"Really?"

"Yeah."

"What movie did you see?"

"That one with Nicole Kidman."

I opened my eyes wide. "*The Stepford Wives*? I asked you to take me to see that a couple of weeks ago."

"Yeah well, we had the baby."

"My mother was going to watch her."

Ahmad shrugged his shoulders. "That wasn't a good night to go, anyway. I had work to do, remember?"

"No. I remember you saying that you didn't want to go because you didn't want to see the movie. Then you found work to do." I couldn't believe he went.

"Look, Shay, it's Mya's birthday and she wanted to see it, so I took her. Stop making a big deal out of it."

"Stop making a big deal?" I looked at him with dark eyes. I knew he was still angry about me turning him down, but he was being unusually nasty. I was about to rip into him for taking Mya and not me, his wife, when Mya walked up to us.

"Shay," she said with a smile. "I'm so glad you're here."

I put on a fake smile. "Hey, happy birthday, girl."

We kissed each other on the cheek and hugged. When we let go, Mya looked at Ahmad then back to me. I didn't know why, but there was a tense feeling in the air around us.

"So," Mya said, still smiling, although her smile seemed to mirror my own insincerity. "Where's Nicole? I'm surprised you didn't bring her."

"She's at home with my mother. It was too cold to bring her out tonight. Besides, this is a grown-up party."

"Yes it is," Mya said. "By the way, your dress is slamming, girl."

"Thank you," I said. "So, I heard you were at Jillian's today."

"Yeah. Ahmad took me there. I had such a good time. It was the perfect distraction. Thank you again, Ahmad."

I struggled to keep a smile on my face as she looked at Ahmad, who smiled at her.

"I also heard you went to see *The Stepford Wives*," I said.

"Oh yeah. Girl, that movie is good. You should go see that."

"I would," I said looking at my husband, "but someone didn't want to take me because they didn't want to see it."

The sounds of the music overtook the conversation as an uneasy silence fell among us. I had a bad feeling in the pit of my stomach. I looked Mya up and down casually. The snug jeans she wore left little to the imagination, and despite her sweater, her breasts still demanded attention. I couldn't help but wonder just how much attention Ahmad had given them.

Mya cleared her throat. "Well, I guess I better go and mingle. It was so nice of Mike to do this."

I agreed. "Yes, it was nice of your husband." I turned to Ahmad. "You've got one hell of a friend, baby."

Ahmad nodded. "Yeah, I sure do. Speaking of friends, where's Max? I haven't seen him yet."

"I'm sure you didn't see him," I said under my breath.

"What was that?" Ahmad asked.

"I said I'm sure you haven't seen him . . . with this crowd in here."

Ahmad and I looked at each other for a short, but very intense second. "Is he here?" Ahmad asked Mya, looking away from me. "I need to talk to him."

"No, neither Max or Trina are here."

"Really? I didn't expect Trina to come, but I'm surprised Max isn't here yet. He's usually never late. I'm gonna go and find Mike and ask about Max."

Ahmad walked away, leaving Mya and me alone. We stood side by side, soaking in the atmosphere in silence. The queasy feeling in my stomach seemed to be getting worse. Mya cleared her throat again.

"Something wrong with your throat?" I asked.

Mya shook her head. "Not really. It just keeps drying up on me."

"Mine usually does that when I'm nervous. Are you nervous?"

Mya looked at me. I made sure not to blink. "No," she finally said. "I guess it must have been all the screaming I did today. I had a lot of fun. Ahmad really showed me a good time."

"Did he?" I asked. We continued to stare each other down while the tension around us grew thicker.

"Yes, he did," Mya said. "You have one hell of a husband Shay. A definite keeper."

"Yes . . . he is."

"Well, I'm gonna go and mingle. We'll talk more later."

"Yes, we will," I said.

I watched her as she sashayed past Ahmad and Mike, then I watched Ahmad's eyes trail behind her. I don't know what was going on, but that feeling in my stomach was telling me to watch my back.

For the rest of the party, Ahmad did his best to make sure that we were never alone; he also did his best to ignore my attempts to get close to him. Eventually, I got tired of being ignored and sat on the sofa with a drink that I didn't really want, and kept my eyes on my husband, who just couldn't seem to keep his eyes from wandering to wherever Mya was. She, in turn, couldn't seem to avoid looking over at him, or giving me a look from time to time that could almost have been called a stare-down. As a matter of fact, that's just what I was calling it. I finally got tired of being alone and walked over to Ahmad, who was standing talking to Mike and a few other guys. "I'm ready to go," I said bluntly.

Ahmad looked at me. "What?"

"I'm ready to go," I said again.

"Just relax, Shay. It's still early."

"Yeah, Shay, chill out," Mike slurred.

I cut my eyes at him. "Because your ass is drunk, I'm gonna let that go, but don't put yourself in my business again, because drunk or not, I'm not having it." A few of Mike's boys oooh'd. I turned back to Ahmad. "Let's go, Ahmad."

"Shay, can't you just relax and have a good time? It's not like we have to rush home to Nicole."

"No, I can't relax, Ahmad, and I can't have a good time. Not with you eyeing Mya every damn minute."

The DJ had just cut the music to make an announcement, so everyone had heard what I'd said. Ahmad was glaring back at me while Mike was looking at him. From the corner of my eye, I could see Mya turn and walk out of the living room. Ahmad's whole body tensed. "Shay, don't start any bullshit, okay?"

"I haven't started anything, Ahmad," I said angrily, "but I will if you don't take me home." I walked off to get my coat. I didn't care about the stares coming from everyone.

I grabbed my coat from the closet and before I left I heard Mike say, "Yo, what's she talking about, man?" He was drunk, but obviously not so drunk that he'd missed that. I slammed the door shut as I stepped outside. Ahmad came out seconds later.

"Shay, what the fuck was all that about?"

"Like you don't know," I said, sucking my teeth. "The whole night, Ahmad. The whole fucking night you couldn't keep your eyes off of Mya."

"Shay, stop talking shit."

"Stop talking shit? Ahmad, don't you even try to deny that you were practically drooling over Mya because I watched you the whole damn night."

"Come on, Shay."

"Come on, Shay nothing. You ignored me all fucking night."

"Damn, Shay, it's a party. I didn't know I had to be your babysitter."

"My babysitter? You know what? Fuck you, and take me home. I'm your fucking wife. Spending time with me shouldn't be considered babysitting."

"My wife? That's a joke."

"What the hell does that mean?"

"It means, Shay, that you sure have a weird way of showing it."

"Look, Ahmad, if this is about sex—"

"Sex is only part of the problem, Shay. For six fucking months you've been a mother to Nicole and a stranger to me. I don't understand the distance you've wedged in between us. You don't talk to me, Shay. You're dealing with something and for whatever reason you won't open up to me. I don't know what the hell's happened, but you used to be able to communicate with me."

"Ahmad, I've told you what I'm dealing with has nothing to do with you."

"I don't give a shit if it does or doesn't, Shay! I'm your husband. You're supposed to be able to talk to me. I've never made you feel like you couldn't confide in me. It's always been an I-lean-on-you, you-lean-on-me type of relationship. That's why we exchanged vows."

"I know that—"

"No, you don't, Shay. If you did, we wouldn't be here arguing, and you damn sure wouldn't be accusing me of bullshit. If you want to know the real truth Shay, I should be the one spitting out all of the accusations. I mean, let's face it—all of the shit you've been pulling is pretty suspicious. The distance, your inability to talk to me, your unwillingness to have sex—that's what happens when someone else is in the picture."

"Don't you even try to go there, Ahmad."

"Why not? Are you afraid to tell the truth? Is that what's going on, Shay? Are you fucking around with another man? Was your own guilty conscience making you accuse me?"

Ahmad stood with a smug look on his face and waited for me to entertain his bullshit with an answer. I couldn't believe he'd tried to turn the tables on me. This was a side of him I'd never seen before. "You know what, Ahmad? I'm not even going to waste my time with what you just asked me."

"Because I'm right."

"Go to hell, Ahmad!"

"Answer the question, Shay. Are you or are you not fucking around on me?"

I twisted my lips into a snarl. I was so angry I didn't even feel the wind that cut through my coat. "Give me the fucking car keys," I said, putting my hand out. "I'm leaving. You and your BS can stay here and stare at Mya all you want."

Ahmad pulled the keys from his pocket and dropped them in my palm. "There you go with that Mya crap again."

"Oh, please! You want to try and turn the tables on me, you go right ahead. But you and I both know that what I saw was real."

"It's about as real as the chance of you having sex with me."

"For your information, asshole, I was going to try and give you some tonight, but now you can forget it. As a matter of fact, don't even bring your ass home."

"Maybe I won't," Ahmad said defiantly. "Maybe I'll find someone else to satisfy me. Shit, maybe I already have."

No longer able to contain the anger that was boiling inside of me, I stepped forward and spat in his face. "Fuck you!" Without saying another word, I turned and walked away. When I got to the car parked across the street, I looked at Ahmad as he wiped his face. "Bastard," I whispered. I unlocked the car door. Before I got inside, I caught a glimpse of a figure standing in the bedroom window upstairs. I could tell by the shape of the figure that it was Mya. I could also tell that the bedroom window had been open. "Bitch."

I got in the car and drove off, angry, hurt and filled with regret. I was losing the one man I truly loved, and it was all my fault.

Mike

"Nigga, I'm gonna kill your ass!"

"Wait, Mike, don't shoot, man. Please!"

"Don't shoot? Nigga, you're supposed to be my fucking boy and you're fucking my wife, and you expect me not to kill your ass?"

"Mike, please, man. Please don't do this. You've already done enough. Man, you killed your wife. You killed Mya."

"Hell yeah, I killed that bitch. You think I'd let her live after what she did?"

"Come on, man. Put the gun down. You don't want to do this."

"Fuck you Ahmad. You crossed a line you should have never fucking crossed. You're dead."

"But you'll go to jail!"

"Nigga, I'm a cop. The only place I'm going is to your funeral to spit on your grave. Say hello to Mya."

"Noooooo!"

Bang!

I jumped up, breathing heavily, and looked around frantically to get my bearings. I was enveloped in darkness in my bedroom. I'd been there since getting home from work. I looked to my right side; Mya was there, sleeping quietly. I eased out of the bed and went downstairs to the kitchen to get something to drink. I was covered with sweat, but welcomed the chill from the air because it was helping to cool me down.

This was the second night I'd had a nightmare starring Mya and Ahmad. It started when Shay made her comment to Ahmad during Mya's surprise party.

The first night, I dreamed that Mya and Ahmad were naked and fucking on my bed while I sat bound to a chair, forced to watch. I could hear every moan, every gasp. A few times, Mya looked at me and smiled. I didn't think I could have a worse dream until tonight.

I shook my head to get rid of the unwanted picture that danced in my mind, and tried to steady my hand as I poured some orange juice. I looked at the clock; it was two-thirty in the morning. I knew that it would be a couple of hours before I'd fall back to sleep.

No, I can't relax, Ahmad, and I can't have a good time. Not with you eyeing Mya every damn minute.

I knew that I was drunk as hell that night, but I wasn't so drunk that I missed the seriousness and hurt in Shay's voice. After Ahmad and Shay went outside, I looked around for Mya, but she'd disappeared and I was just too out of it to go looking for her. When Ahmad came back inside, I asked him about Shay's comment.

"Yo, what was all that about?"

Ahmad shook his head. "Man, don't worry about that shit. Shay and I are just having some problems."

"So, what's up with her comment about you eyeing Mya?" I looked at my boy as hard as my vision-impaired eyes would let me.

"Come on, Mike. Are you really gonna pay attention to that?"

"It's just an off the wall comment, bruh."

"Exactly. Like I said, we've been having problems. She just said that because she's pissed off I wasn't paying her any attention."

"Yeah, why not?"

"I just got into it with her about it outside, man. I don't feel like talking about it now."

"Understandable. So, where's Shay?"

"She went home."

"Really?"

"Yeah. And get this; she told me not to come home tonight."

I looked at Ahmad. "Damn, man, what kind of problems are y'all having?"

Ahmad sighed. "Big ones. I'll tell you about it later, man. I just want to get a drink and have a good time."

I stared at him for another long second then shrugged. "Alright, man, but we're definitely talking later."

"No problem. Hey, have you heard from Max? I thought he'd be here by now."

"Yo, I don't know where that punk is, but he better have a good-ass explanation for dissing me today."

"It's not like him to not show up. Maybe he finally got Trina to talk to him."

"Yeah, maybe. He still left me hanging, though."

"Yeah, but you know he wouldn't do that unless he had a good reason."

"Whatever. Anyway, man, I'm gonna go and check on Mya." I turned to walk away but didn't get too far before Ahmad asked me one more question.

"Hey, where is she, anyway?"

I turned around and I didn't know why, but Shay's comments came to my mind. "She's upstairs. Why?"

"I just want to apologize for what Shay said."

I nodded. "Man, I doubt that Mya even heard what she said."

"Yeah well, maybe I'll run up and apologize just in case she did."

"Nah, don't sweat it. Besides, I think she's sleeping."

"She is?"

"Yeah," I said, locking my eyes on his. We silently watched each other for what seemed like minutes, but in reality had only been seconds.

"Alright," Ahmad finally said. "Well, like you said, maybe she didn't hear."

"Exactly. Anyway, you said yourself that Shay was tripping, so there's really no need to talk to Mya about it."

Ahmad looked at me. "Right."

I swallowed the orange juice down along with the recollection of my exchange with Ahmad. I wished I had something harder, but I was bone dry after the party. I poured another glass, went into the living room, and turned on the TV. I needed something to distract me. I flipped through the channels but got frustrated when I couldn't find a decent show. I shut it off to sit in darkness. "Ahmad's my boy and Mya's my wife," I whispered to myself. "There's no fucking way."

Still, Shay's comment beat at my brain. Ahmad said she was just pissed off and that's why she said what she did. But of all things to say, why say that? If they were having problems, why bring Mya's name into the drama?

Her comment had ruined the rest of the night for me. I didn't have another drink and I couldn't relax. I went upstairs to find Mya. When I went up, she was standing at the window.

"Hey, there's a party for you going on downstairs," I said, standing next to her.

Mya looked at me and smiled. "Yeah, I know."

"So, what's going on? How come you're up here?"

Mya shrugged her shoulders. "I'm just a little partied out. It was a long day."

"So, I guess you and Ahmad had a good day."

"Yeah. We had a lot of fun."

"That's cool. I'm glad my boy could be there for me like that."

She turned away from me without responding. I looked out the window, which was open slightly, even though it was cold outside. "Shay left the party," I said. I turned to look at her; I wanted to see her reaction.

"She did?" Mya said softly.

"Yeah. Ahmad's still here, though."

"He is? What happened?"

"He and Shay had an argument."

"What about?"

I looked to the opened window and then back at Mya. "I don't know. Ahmad didn't want to talk about it. He just said they're having some big problems. You don't know about any problems they're having, do you?"

Mya shook her head. "No, I don't. Excuse me, honey. I need to go to the bathroom." She walked into our bathroom and locked the door behind her.

"Mya, you okay?"

"Yeah. I'm fine." I could hear a strain in her voice. I leaned my ear against the door, but only heard her turn on the faucet.

"Hey, open the door, baby. I need to go too."

"I'm going to be a while, Mike. Use the one in the hallway, okay?"

I knitted my brow. "You sure you're okay?"

"Yes."

"You gonna come back down?"

"I don't think so. Tell everyone I'm sorry. I'm just really tired."

I looked at the closed door and listened to the running water, then shook my head. I went back downstairs and played the upbeat host while I watched my boy out of the corner of my eye. Every now and then I would catch him looking toward the staircase. Eventually he caught a ride home. I had my first nightmare that night. I called Ahmad the next day to talk to him about what was going on with him and Shay, but I never got him.

I didn't like the thoughts running through my head, and I damn sure didn't like the sleepless nights. I swallowed down the rest of my second glass of juice then went back upstairs. Mya was still sleeping. Ever since the party, she'd been distant, and that bothered me. I looked down at her and thought about what I'd done to her in my dream. It all seemed so real. The hatred and rage I felt were so intense. I'd shot Mya and enjoyed it. I could smell her blood as it oozed from her dead body. I relished in the fear in Ahmad's eyes. I climbed back into bed, hoping that it was just my guilty conscience fucking with me.

Trina

I had just finished washing my mouth out after another bout of vomiting when my phone rang. Being pregnant was a real pain in the ass. The fatigue, the bloated feeling, the vomiting—and I was only at the tail end of my first trimester! God knew what he was doing when he made it so that only women could give birth. If men had to go through this, the world would cease to exist. I wiped off my mouth with a towel and went to grab the phone. I looked at the caller ID; my sister's number registered on the screen. I sighed. It had been a few days since Max had last called me, begging for another chance. Although there was no chance in hell that I was going to give him one, for God knows what reason, I missed the calls. "What's up, Nikita?" I asked, trying to sound as normal as I could. I still hadn't told anyone about the pregnancy.

"Trina!" Nikita yelled into the receiver, hurting my ear.

"Damn, Nikita, why you tryin' to blow out my eardrum with your loud ass? What's going on sister dear?"

"Trina, please tell me you had nothing to do with it," Nikita said, her voice filled with anxiety.

"Nothing to do with what? Nikita, why do you sound all flustered?"

"You don't know anything about Max?"

"Max? Why would I know anything about him? I don't even speak to his friends anymore. What's wrong?" I had a feeling she was about to give me some very bad news. "What should I know?"

"Trina, Max is in the hospital. He was beaten up and shot."

My knees buckled slightly. "What? Nikita, what did you just say?"

"Trina, I found out from a friend who works at Johns Hopkins that Max is in the hospital, barely holding on. He was listed as a John Doe because he didn't have ID on him."

"What? Oh my God!"

"My friend recognized him from when you Max and I had gone to visit Uncle Earl after his heart attack."

Tears started to fall from my eyes. I had to sit down. "Oh my God. I can't believe this!"

"Are you sure you don't have anything to do with this? Maybe you had someone do it for what he did. I would understand if you did."

"No, Nikita. I'm mad at him for what he did, but I wouldn't have someone try to kill him."

"Well if you didn't, who would?"

I wiped tears away. I didn't even have to think. "Sharon," I said, balling my hand into a tight fist.

"Her? But why?"

"Because Max slapped her, that's why. And even though her trifling ass deserved it, she would never let something like that go. You know how ghetto she is. She probably ran her mouth off to Jamal."

"How can you be so sure, Trina?"

"Trust me. I'm not wrong. Oh God, I can't believe this is happening. Nikita, I have to see him. Max can't die." The tears were falling down my cheeks faster than I could wipe them away, dripping onto my naked leg. "Come and pick me up, Nikita. I love him. He can't die. I'm carrying his baby."

"You're what?" Nikita asked, raising her voice to a high-pitched shrill.

"I'm pregnant with Max's baby. He doesn't know. That's why he can't die. Oh my God. Come and get me, please."

"What do you mean you're pregnant?"

"Just come and get me, Nikita, please. I'll explain everything later. Just come now. I need to get to Max. He needs to know that I still love him and that he's going to be a father."

"But Trina—"

I hung up the phone and buried my face in my hands. I loved Max. As much as I hated him, I loved him even more. That's why I'd never deleted any of the messages he'd left for me. That's why I never went to see the divorce lawyer Nikita had used and recommended. I loved Max. As I admitted this to myself, the torrent from my eyes fell harder and faster. Somehow I managed to stand up to get dressed. I had to see Max. He couldn't die. I needed him.

Ahmad

"Shay, it's been four days. Don't you think we should talk about what happened now?"

We were sitting at the table, eating in complete silence. I think we might have spoken three times since our argument at Mike's house, and that was only because it had to do with Nicole. Other than that, there was nothing but silence and tension. After catching a ride home that night, I sat on the couch for a long time with the television on but barely audible. I felt horrible about the blowup we'd had. Shay didn't deserve to be the bad guy, but she was so right about my eyes being on Mya the whole night that I had no choice but to turn the tables on her.

I still couldn't believe she called me out in front of Mike like that. I did my best to assure Mike that she was talking shit, but I had a feeling that he didn't believe me completely. He'd called my cell the next day, but I never answered. I just didn't want to have to lie to him again.

I put down my fork and looked at Shay. She hadn't answered me and hadn't looked up from her plate. "Shay," I said, "are you willing to talk?"

She sighed loudly and looked up at me with a whole lot of attitude. "I said all I needed to say on Saturday."

"So, you still think there's something going on between me and Mya?"

"I never accused you of that, Ahmad. I just said that you were staring at her the whole damn night."

"Yeah well, you were wrong," I said, defiantly standing on my shaky ground.

"You know, I wish I was wrong, Ahmad. It's just too damned bad that I can see in your eyes that you're lying."

I wanted to say something, but I didn't know what, because no one knew me better than she did. "Shay—"

"Ahmad, listen. I know I'm not wrong about what I saw Saturday night. Nothing you can say will make me believe I was. As far as there being something going on between you and Mya, all I can say is I hope not. For the sake of our marriage and your friendship with Mike, I really hope not."

"Shay, there's nothing going on," I said quietly. "I promise."

"Don't promise, Ahmad. Promises are made to be broken."

"Shay, nothing's going on," I said again.

"I'll give you the benefit of the doubt, Ahmad, because you are my husband. But you know, I'll be honest with you. If there was something going on, I couldn't put all of the blame on you. I've been a terrible wife these past five months. I know it. I also know that if I don't find a way to deal with my issues, you're going to fall into the arms of another woman."

I gritted my teeth at the sadness in her voice. "Baby . . . that's not going to happen."

"Don't lie to me and don't lie to yourself," Shay said. "You can only go for so long having a stranger for a spouse. Eventually someone will come and catch your eye and maybe even your heart. It may or not be Mya, but it will be someone."

"Well, if you're so sure of that, why won't you talk to me? I'm here dying for you to open up and tell me what it is you've been dealing with."

"I know you have."

"So then why won't you talk to me?"

"Because it's not easy, Ahmad."

"Who said it had to be, Shay? We're supposed to help each other get through rough periods in our lives. That's what being a married couple is all about."

"I know that."

"Then talk to me," I said sternly. "For the sake of our marriage, talk to me, because the only piece of thread that's holding us together right now is our little girl."

"I love you, Ahmad," Shay said softly as teardrops fell from her eyes. I reached across the table and took her hand in mine.

"I love you too, Shay."

"I . . . I feel like I'm losing you."

I shook my head. "You're not losing me, baby. Just talk to me."

Tears dripped from her chin while I held onto her hand reassuringly. Neither one of us said a word. I sat and waited patiently, hoping the next time she opened her mouth it would be to tell me what she'd been dealing with. I meant it when I said that I loved her. I really did. I wanted to mean it when I said that she wasn't losing me, but deep down I wasn't sure if I believed my own words, because even as we sat there, Mya came to my mind again. I gently squeezed Shay's had. I had to make this work between us. More importantly, I had to let thoughts of Mya go. "Talk to me, baby."

Shay smiled at me weakly and wiped tears away with her hand. "Ahmad, I don't know how to start."

"Just start from the beginning."

She wiped away another teardrop and sighed. I gave her a reassuring and warm smile. "I'm here," I said.

Shay nodded and opened her mouth to speak. That's when the phone rang.

"Damn," I said, jumping up to grab it. I didn't want the ringing to wake Nicole. I hit the talk button and looked at Shay. I was hoping it would be a telemarketer so I could hang up on them and get back to saving my marriage. I should have looked at the caller ID. "Hello?"

"Ahmad."

The sound of Mya's voice made my heart beat faster. My eyes were still locked on Shay's. "Mya?"

It didn't even take a second for Shay to suck her teeth and get up from the table and walk away. I frowned as she walked out of the kitchen. "What's going on, Mya?"

"Ahmad, have you spoken to Mike today?" Mya asked, her voice filled with distress.

"No, I haven't. What's wrong?"

"Ahmad, Trina just called here. Max is in the hospital."

"What?"

"Max is in the hospital," she repeated. "He's been there for the past couple of days."

"Jesus," I whispered. "Is he alright?"

"Trina says he'll be okay. He was in a coma for a while."

"Damn. How did this happen? When did it happen?"

"I don't know the particulars."

"Alright. What hospital is he in?"

"He's at Johns Hopkins."

"Okay."

"Ahmad, I've been calling Mike, but I haven't been able to reach him. He's not at work and he's not answering his cell."

"Okay, let me try to reach him."

"Ahmad, can you come by and get me?"

"Yeah, I'll come."

"Is Shay coming too?"

"I don't know. Nicole's sleeping."

"I think she should."

"Okay, I'll make sure she comes. I'll be by you in twenty minutes."

"I'll be ready. Oh, and if you reach Mike, tell him that his wife is looking for him."

"Okay." I hung up the phone and bowed my head. Max had been shot. Damn. I said a prayer for him then dialed Mike's cell phone, hoping that he'd answer. I cursed out loud when his voice mail picked up. "Mike, it's Ahmad. Max was shot he's in the hospital. He's at Johns Hopkins. I'm going there now, and I'm gonna pick Mya up on the way. Yo, where the fuck are you, man? Call me back or meet us there." I hung up and raced upstairs to get dressed. Shay was sitting on the bed with Nicole.

"Have a nice conversation?" she asked with an attitude that I didn't need.

I looked at her. "Max was shot."

"What?"

"He's at Johns Hopkins. We have to leave now. Get Nicole ready."

"Who shot him?" Shay asked. "When did it happen?"

"Shay, I don't have any answers. That's all Mya told me. Now get ready, please. We have to stop and pick her up on the way." I slipped into a pair of jeans, ignoring Shay's displeasure as she sucked her teeth. Before we left the house, I tried to reach Mike again, but still got his voice mail. I left another message.

Mike

"You know, Cynthia, if I keep fucking with you, I could end up in a world of trouble."

"No, if you keep fucking like that, you could end up with a promotion."

"So, I take it you were satisfied?"

Cynthia smiled. "Let's just say that your use of the handcuffs and stick are exemplary. But you know what?" Cynthia slid her hand up my thigh.

"What?"

"Before I start giving out a passing grade for the day, I think another test is needed." She grabbed hold of my manhood, making me instantly erect.

"No problem," I said. "Just let me hit the bathroom."

Cynthia let go of me and rolled over onto her stomach, giving me a nice view of her firm ass. "Handle your business so that you can handle your business."

I smiled then got up from the bed and went into the bathroom, smiling in the mirror at myself and my good fortune. Cynthia was my captain's wife, a sophisticated, sexy woman, rich with old money. Her great-great grandfather was a paranoid carpenter who was one of the first people to discover gold in California back in the 1800's. I don't know how much gold he collected, but I knew that Cynthia's family never had to want for anything.

I met her at my captain's end of the summer barbecue the year before. They were engaged then. As soon as I laid eyes on her, I knew she was a freak who loved brothers, because she was watching me like I was a prime piece of steak. She wasn't shy about her interest in me, either. With the way she was eyeing me every chance she got, there was no doubt in my mind that I could have met her upstairs and tapped her ass without anyone knowing. But I was on chill mode that day because Mya and I had a big argument the night before about me not paying enough attention to her, and I promised her I'd do better. I figured a brief hiatus from some pussy on the side wouldn't hurt. Besides, she was my captain's wife.

A few minutes before I left the barbecue, Cynthia approached me as I was coming out of the bathroom upstairs and handed me slip of paper with her cell phone number on it. She said, "Bud loves me, but he loves my money more. I can get him to do anything I want."

It was on after that.

We started fucking two weeks later.

I smiled at myself in the mirror again. I was just too damned smooth. I washed my hands and then stepped back into the room. Cynthia was just getting off her cell phone. "Everything alright?" I asked.

Cynthia smiled. "Everything's just fine. Bud just asked me to pick up some beer from the store."

"Alright." I looked over at my phone on the dresser against the far wall. I had it off because I knew Mya would be calling for me. I was about to go and check it when Cynthia cleared her throat.

"Are you ready to handle your business?" she asked, laying on her back and spreading her legs.

"Mm-mmm," I said. Forgetting about the phone, I sauntered over to the bed. I looked down at her. Cynthia was one of those thick, older women who was always in the gym making sure her ass and tits were firm. She reminded me of Stifler's mom in the movie *American Pie.* "MILF," I said out loud. *Mom, I'd like to fuck.*

"What?" Cynthia asked.

I smiled while staring at her shaved pussy. "Nothing, baby." Without warning, I dove headfirst in between her legs. Cynthia moaned, gasped, trembled and eventually came as I licked her up and down until she said stop. When she was done getting hers, she laid me back on the bed and snarled.

"How does a fifteen thousand dollar increase feel?" she asked, mounting me.

"Feels damn good," I said.

For the next twenty minutes, Cynthia rode me like a wild tiger until I exploded. When I was finished, she slumped down and kissed me on my chest. "Honey, I'd give you a letter grade higher than an A, but there is none."

"A pay increase will do just fine," I said.

Cynthia kissed me again then rose off of me. "Don't worry about that. It's yours. All yours." She winked. "I better take a shower. I can't go home to my husband smelling like satisfaction." She walked into the bathroom and closed the door. I was glad she didn't ask me to join her because I was worn out. I just wanted to lay down for a few and recuperate.

As Cynthia was showering, her cell phone rang. That reminded me of my own phone. I got up and grabbed it from the dresser and turned it on. As I expected, I had messages waiting for me. I checked the call history and saw that Mya had called me four times and surprisingly, Ahmad had called me twice. I guess he'd finally returned my call. I decided to call him back before Mya. I'd deal with her later. I lay back on the bed and dialed his number. When he answered I said, "Yo, what's up, man?"

"Mike, man, where the fuck have you been?"

"Yo, what the fuck is bugging you? What's up with coming at me like that?"

"Man, Max is in the hospital."

I bolted upright. "What?"

"He was shot, man. We're just now getting to Johns Hopkins."

"Is he alright?"

"Trina says he's gonna be okay."

"Shit. Alright, I'm on my way." I hung up the phone and grabbed my clothes from the floor. I was getting dressed when Cynthia came out of the bathroom.

"Where are you going?"

"I gotta go. An emergency came up."

"You sure you have to go?" Cynthia asked, stepping toward me, her naked body dripping.

"Yeah, I'm sure. I'll talk to you later. I'll drop the room key off." I raced out of the room before she could say anything else. Hopefully, she wouldn't take my quick departure as a dis. I got in my cruiser and without hesitation, turned on the siren

Trina

I touched Max's forehead lightly as he slept. For two days he'd been in a coma with no one by his side. The doctor who treated him told me all about finding him outside the emergency room on the ground, unconscious. Whoever dropped him there never bothered to stick around to see that he'd made it inside. He was registered as a John Doe because he had no ID or personal belongings of any kind on him. He'd been shot in the chest and they had to operate on him immediately. He was given a blood transfusion to replace all the blood he'd lost. In addition to the gunshot wound, he'd also suffered a slight skull fracture, two broken ribs, a fractured cheekbone and a swollen eye. Whoever did this to him had only one intention, but thankfully, someone was watching out for him, because had the bullet been an inch over to the right, he'd be in the morgue instead of a hospital bed.

When I first laid eyes on him I nearly fainted. The person in the bed was not the man I'd married. His face was swollen and covered with bruises, and the bandages around his head were stained with blood. I stayed by his side, talking to him, until he awoke from the coma a day later. I'd like to think my voice brought him back.

"I'm sorry I wasn't there for you," I said, whispering again the apology I'd given him when he'd first become conscious the day before.

Tears fell from my eyes, and I broke down for a few minutes. I wanted to ask him so many questions about who'd done that to him and how he'd gotten to the hospital, but he was still too weak to talk much. I did try once, but the only thing he'd say was that he didn't remember anything. Of course, I didn't believe him.

Whether he told me or not, I had no doubt in my mind that Sharon was behind this.

Bitch.

If it was the last thing I did, I'd make sure there was no way in hell she got away with this shit. If I wasn't pregnant, I'd beat her ass. Lucky for her I had to think of another way to hurt her.

"You're gonna be a daddy, Max," I said quietly as he slept. "Sharon won't get away with this. I promise."

"Mrs. Winters," a voice said from behind.

I turned around and looked at the nurse who'd just come into the room. "Yes?"

"Your husband's friends are here."

"Okay. I'll go get them."

"If you don't mind, can you have them wait before you bring them back? We'd like to check his blood pressure and apply fresh bandages."

"No problem." I turned back to Max. "Baby, I'm going to be back soon. I love you." I kissed him softly then walked out of the room and went back to the waiting area where Ahmad, Shay and Mya were waiting.

Mya greeted me first with a hug. "Trina, I'm so sorry this happened."

Shay came next, with Nicole in her arms. "Do you need anything?"

"No, I'm okay."

Ahmad wrapped his arms around me. "Are you sure you're alright?"

I nodded. "Yeah, I'll be fine."

"You know I'm mad you didn't call us sooner, right?"

"I know, and I'm sorry. I was just stressed and didn't want to leave his side."

"No apologies needed, Trina," Ahmad said. "I understand. Can we go and see him now?"

"Not yet. The nurse is checking his pressure and reapplying his bandages. Along with being shot, he was beaten up pretty badly. He has a slight skull fracture, some broken ribs, and a swollen eye."

"Damn," Ahmad whispered.

"The nurse will come and let us know when he can have visitors."

"Alright. I'm glad he's okay."

"Yeah. The doctor said that if the bullet had been an inch to the right he would have died."

"Damn. Who did this to him?"

"I don't know. I tried asking him, but he won't tell me anything." Ahmad gave me a look that said he suspected the same person. "Ahmad, I was so afraid of losing him, especially now that I'm pregnant."

"What?" Ahmad asked, looking down at me.

"Trina, did you say you were pregnant?" Mya asked.

I nodded. "Yeah."

"Congratulations, Trina!" Shay said, giving me a kiss. "Welcome to the club. How far along are you?"

"Two months."

"That's great, Trina," Ahmad said with a smile. "I can't believe Max didn't tell me."

"He doesn't know yet," I said.

"Really?"

"I hadn't spoken to him since everything happened with Sharon, and I didn't want to break the news so soon after he came out of the coma. I didn't want to get him worked up."

"Wow. He's going to be happy," Ahmad said.

"Yeah, I think so. Hey, where's Mike?"

At the mention of his name, Mya's lips formed a thin, angry line.

"He's on his way," Ahmad said, glancing at Mya.

I nodded. It was obvious that Mike was out somewhere doing what he always did. "I'm gonna go back now. This is the longest I've been away from him.

I'll send the nurse to come and get you guys when it's clear."

"We'll be here," Ahmad said.

I smiled then went to see my husband.

Shay

I was trying as hard as I could to focus on Trina and Max. I thanked God for bringing them through their ordeal, for delivering Max from the evil that had happened to him. I said a prayer for the health of the child that Trina was carrying, then I wondered if I'd end up going to hell because my attention wasn't focused solely on prayer. As I prayed and thanked God, my eyes remained open and fixed on Mya.

We'd barely spoken a word to each other since Ahmad and I picked her up. I know Ahmad swore there was nothing going on between them, but you wouldn't know it by his body language and Mya's fake-ass smile to me. Mya and I exchanged another glance when Trina went back to be with Max. We'd been doing a lot of that the whole time we were in the hospital. She'd been challenging me with her gaze, and I'd been cursing her with mine.

I was just about to open up to Ahmad when she called. Our marriage depended on my talking about my personal issues. It was vital that I leaned on him for support and comfort. That moment was the fork in the road and I'd finally chosen to take the path to Ahmad, but then the phone rang, and of all people, it had to be her. Even though the call had nothing to do with her, it was still her calling. Now we were exchanging glares while Ahmad sat uncomfortably and did his best to avoid looking up from the magazine he'd picked up. With Mya's call, I'd backpedaled to the beginning of the fork again. Only this time, I didn't know what path I wanted to take.

I exhaled hard. I was angry at Mya and, whether he did or didn't do anything, I was angry at Ahmad. I was also pissed at myself for allowing an opportunity for someone to capture my husband's attention.

Anger. Deep anger. That's what I felt when Mya and I looked at each other. That's what was bubbling inside of me as I thought about the distance that Ahmad had placed in between us since Mya stepped into our car.

Nicole stirred, taking me out of my seething trance. My negative energy must have disturbed her. I kissed her forehead and caressed the back of her tiny head. I rocked her slowly until she eventually settled back into deep slumber.

"She's precious," Mya said with a smile.

I looked at her, but didn't say a word. We stared hard at each other again until she looked away. I tightened my lips and looked at Ahmad, who'd been watching me. I gave him a hard, burning glare until he frowned and looked away. I kissed Nicole again and wondered which path in the fork I was going to take.

Ahmad

I watched Shay shoot daggers from her eyes at Mya and cringed. We were so close, so damn close to taking a step toward rebuilding our marriage. After months of non-communication, Shay was finally going to open up and let me know why she couldn't talk to me and why she didn't want to be intimate. Then the bottom fell out from underneath us. I sighed again as Shay gave Mya another hard glare. If anyone else had called and given me the news about Max there would be nothing for me to stress over. But because it was Mya on the phone, I had a bad feeling that the door that had finally been cracked open had now been slammed shut and dead bolted. Only time would tell, of course, but judging from the fact that Shay had chosen to sit across from rather than beside me, I didn't know if time would matter.

Damn.

I looked away from Shay, who'd taken a moment to bore a hole into me, and switched my thoughts away from the drama of my life. I thought about Max. I couldn't help but wonder if this all had to do with his affair with his mother-in-law. For a brief moment, I'd wondered if Trina had gotten someone to teach Max a lesson for what he did, only they'd taken things too far. But that thought quickly went away when I saw her. It was obvious that despite what he'd done to her, Trina loved the hell out of him, and no matter how pissed off and hurt she was, she wouldn't go there. Letting go of that thought, there were only two other options: Either he was just randomly attacked, or he'd gone looking for Sharon to get a little payback and his plan backfired. Knowing Max like I did, it was safe to assume it had been the second option.

Damn.

I know Trina said he'd be fine, but I still said a prayer asking God to allow him to pull through for Trina, for their unborn child, and for his boys.

Speaking of boys, where the hell was Mike? I took a look over at Mya and couldn't help but frown. She was such a beautiful and special woman. Mike didn't deserve her. Or better yet, she didn't deserve Mike. She deserved to be with a man who would show her day in and day out that she was a queen. She was a treasure to be cherished and adored. Maybe in another life, another time, I would have been that man.

These past couple of months, my friendship with Mike had really been strained. It just became harder and harder for me to ignore his behavior or accept it as just 'Mike being Mike'. Not only that, but the sadness and hurt in Mya's eyes really began to show. When he threw the surprise party, I thought that maybe he was going to make an attempt to change. Obviously that wasn't the case. I took another quick look at Mya, who was chatting with Trina's sister, Nikita, who'd just arrived.

Another lifetime—maybe.

"Ahem."

I looked away from Mya to see Shay beating me down with an accusatory glare. I sighed, dropped the book in the empty chair beside me and stood up. "I'll be back," I said. I didn't wait for Shay to say before I walked outside. Mike was just arriving when I did. He was dressed in his uniform, his shirt hanging outside of the pants. It was obvious that he'd gotten dressed in a hurry.

"Yo, how's Max doing?" he asked.

I looked at him hard for a long second. Mike looked back at me. Finally, I said, "He was in a coma for a few days, but he's ok now."

"Damn," Mike whispered. "Who the fuck would do this to him?"

"I don't know, man. I've been wondering the same thing."

"Shit. Trina okay?"

"Yeah, she's fine. She's also pregnant."

"What? Are you for real?"

I nodded. "Yeah. She just told us."

"Damn. And it's Max's?"

I looked at Mike and shook my head. "What kind of question is that?"

"Man, I'm just saying. I mean, they were apart for a few weeks."

"Mike, shut up, man. Just because they were apart doesn't mean Trina was out there sleeping around."

"Yeah well, it could have happened."

"Whatever, man," I said.

We were silent for a few seconds until Mike said, "Damn, a coma. Have you seen him?"

"Not yet. The nurses are redressing his wounds. Along with the gunshot, he was beaten up pretty badly. Suffered a slight skull fracture, couple of broken ribs, and swollen eye. Whoever did this was clearly trying to take him out. An inch over to the right and Max would have been gone."

"Damn." Mike clenched his fists. "I wonder if this has to do with Sharon."

I shrugged. "I don't know, but I've been wondering the same thing."

"Yo, whoever did this better hope I don't find out. I have a gun and a badge. They'd have no fucking chance. Fucking cowards. Shit. Come on, man. Let's go inside."

"Yo, before you go in, I think I should warn you that Mya is pretty pissed off right now."

Mike groaned and rolled his eyes. "Yeah, I'm sure she is. She called me about fifty times."

"You should have answered your phone at least once, Mike."

"Couldn't man. I was handling some business." He gave me a smirk and then said, "Besides, man, I figured she was calling to hassle me. I didn't think she was calling for this."

"Yeah well, she wasn't. Man, if you keep fucking around like that, you're gonna lose your woman."

"Ahmad, bruh, do me a favor and spare me the lectures. I've heard them before."

"I'm just saying, man."

"Yeah well, how about you don't say? I'm a big man, Ahmad. I know how to handle my business. I've told you before, whether she knows about the pussy on the side or not, Mya's not going anywhere."

"What if you're wrong, man?" I asked, biting my tongue to keep from saying anything about his attitude.

"Trust me, I'm not. Now, let's go see our boy."

Without waiting, Mike walked past me to go inside.

"Mya," I heard him say suddenly.

I turned around to see Mya standing by the entrance to the emergency room with her arms folded across her chest and her eyes ominously fixed on Mike.

"How long have you been there?" Mike asked, his voice tight with worry.

"Long enough, asshole," Mya answered bitterly.

I stood silent and watched as Mike approached her and tried to take her hand, only to have her pull it away.

"Baby, let me—"

Before he could finish his sentence, Mya did something that shocked the hell out of me at the same time. She kneed Mike in his balls, sending him to the ground instantly.

"Go to hell, Mike!" she yelled as he squirmed in pain. "And take your balls with you. I'm tired of putting up with your shit!"

Mya walked away from him and approached me. My hands instinctively went to my own balls. She looked at me without saying a word. Pain and sadness was all I could see in her eyes, then they welled up with tears. I wanted to reach out to her, but I couldn't. I stood and waited for her to speak.

"You can go see Max now. I came out to tell you. Please tell Trina I'm sorry I couldn't stay." She turned and looked back at Mike, who was still down for the count.

"Mya, you can't go," I said. She turned and fixed her eyes on me. I didn't look away until Mike moaned. I cleared my throat. "I brought you here, remember?"

Mya nodded. "I'll call a cab."

"Come on, Mya, you don't want to do that. Why don't you just wait a little while and then I'll take you home?"

She gave me a sad smile. "No, that's okay. I want to take a cab. I want to be alone right now. Thank you though for offering."

"Are you sure?"

"I'm sure. I think it's best if you stay here."

I sighed. "Okay."

Mya gave me another half smile. "Thank you, Ahmad for the things you said. It didn't mean shit to him, but I appreciated it."

I squeezed her hand. "No problem."

She looked back to Mike, who was rising slowly. She left as tears began to run down her cheeks.

I sighed then looked over at Mike. I felt for him. Hell, I felt for any man who took a knee to the groin, but he'd had it coming. I approached him. "You alright, man?" I asked, trying not to crack a smile or laugh at the pained look on his face.

Mike moaned and looked at me. "Do I look like I'm alright? I can't believe she did that shit. Goddamn, I feel like throwing up." Mike bent over and I took a step away from him. If he was about to vomit, it wasn't going to be on me. He cursed out loud again and squeezed his eyes. "Goddamn," he whispered painfully.

I watched him deal with his pain and resisted the urge to say, "I told you so." Mya's blow must have made him telepathic though. "Don't say shit to me, man," he snapped. "Don't say one fucking word. Goddamn!" He bent over again and this time I couldn't stifle my smile. I patted his shoulder.

"Max is awake," I said.

Mike moaned again and when he looked back at me, he was near tears. "Yo, I don't think I can walk."

I couldn't hold it back any longer. I exploded with laughter.

"This shit ain't funny, man," Mike yelled. "I think she fucked my shit up. I may not be able to have kids, man."

His comments made me laugh even harder. "Come on, man," I said, helping him stand erect. "Let's go see Max."

As slowly and gently as I could, I led him towards the emergency room. Without warning, Mike stopped our movement. "Yo, you think I lost her?"

I shrugged. "I don't know, man," I answered honestly.

"Damn, Ahmad. I think I lost her."

I looked at him; it actually looked like there was regret in his eyes. But then again it could have also been pain and discomfort. "Only time will tell," I said.

"I don't want to lose her. I love her."

"Don't tell me," I said.

Mike nodded then eased himself away from me. "Let's go."

As we walked inside, I wondered if Mya was okay.

Max

I was alive. My head and body ached and I felt like I had taken a thirty round beating from the 90's Mike Tyson, but I was alive.

"Hey, baby."

"Hey," Trina said, smiling. "Ahmad and Mike are here."

I smiled. "Let them come in."

"I sent the nurse to get them already."

I tried to sit up but the pain in my body wouldn't let me.

"Relax, baby," Trina said, touching my cheek.

"Have you gone home yet?" I asked.

"No. But Nikita's been bringing me a change of clothes."

I frowned. "I'm sorry to have put you through this, baby."

Trina gave me a slight smile. "At least you pulled through," she said.

I nodded. "Yeah. At least."

"Max, I know you've answered this already, but are you sure you don't remember what happened? Who did this to you? Why did they do this?"

I looked at Trina as she waited for an answer and thought back to before I'd woken up. The last thing I remembered doing was sitting in a bar drowning my sorrows in beer and shots of Hennessey. I was pissed off at myself because once again I'd tried to get Trina to talk to me and she wasn't having it. She'd cursed me out and told me to go to hell. She wasn't trying to forgive me for what I'd done. After failing to get her to hear me out, I did what she recommended and went straight to hell. I stopped at the first bar I came across and went in to drink until I couldn't drink anymore. I'd been miserable without Trina. I downed one beer after another and threw in who knows how many shots of Henny. The more I drank, the angrier I became at Sharon and myself.

Bitch.

"Max, please tell me if you do," Trina said, breaking me from my thoughts.

I stared at her but still didn't say anything. I was back at the bar drunk, sad and heated. My recollection began to get sketchy now. I remembered staggering off the barstool with my car keys in hand. I remembered stumbling to my car. I didn't remember driving, though. I just knew that all of a sudden I was standing outside Sharon's apartment, yelling for the bitch to come out. I wanted payback for what she did. Like I said before, I didn't normally hit women, but I wanted to slap her again.

"What the fuck do you want?" I remembered her screaming as she came outside.

"Bitch, I'm gonna kick your ass for opening your mouth."

"You better leave now, nigga, or else your ass is the one that's gonna get kicked."

"Bitch," I spat out again. "What the fuck did you open your mouth to Trina for? You fucked up my marriage!"

"Good. You should be glad I did. You can do better than her stuck up ass anyway."

"Bitch, I'm gonna kill you!"

I think I started to rush toward her, then Jamal and three of his friends appeared. I didn't remember anything after that, although there really was no need to.

"Max?"

I blinked and focused back on Trina. "I don't remember what happened," I said.

"Are you sure?"

I nodded. "Yeah, I'm sure." I knew that if I told her what had happened she'd make it her mission to get Sharon back. As good as that seemed, I didn't want her to. I deserved everything I'd gotten.

"Okay," she said.

"Well, look who finally decided to wake up," came a voice from the doorway. I turned my head. Ahmad and Max were coming in with Shay and Nikita following behind.

"Fellas," I said smiling, although it hurt. I raised the head of the bed so that I was sitting up.

"Good to see you made it through," Ahmad said, patting my shoulder.

"Yeah, man," Mike said, his voice sounding funny. I looked at him. He seemed to be in pain.

"You alright, man?"

Mike winced. "Yeah, I'm cool."

I looked at Ahmad, who was doing a terrible job of stifling a smile. He gave me an I'll-tell-you-later look. I looked at Shay, who had Nicole in her arms. She smiled. "I'm glad you're okay, Max," she said.

"Thanks, Shay." I looked at my sister-in-law. From the venomous look in her eyes, it was obvious that she knew what I'd done. She'd obviously been there for Trina's benefit. We watched each other for a few short seconds before she leaned down to Trina.

"I'm gonna get going, sis."

Trina stood and hugged her sister. "Thank you for everything, Nikita."

When they parted, Nikita looked at me. "My sister's a better woman than I am. Trina, call me if you need anything." She turned and left.

I cleared my throat and looked at Mike. "Mike, where's Mya?"

Mike frowned and then winced in pain again.

"She had to leave," Ahmad said.

"Yes, she certainly did," Shay said. There was a lot of attitude in her tone. I looked at my boys then at Trina.

"Baby, would you and Shay mind leaving the room for a few? I want to talk to my boys."

Trina nodded and stood up. She bent over and kissed me gently on my lips. "Don't make it too long. You still need to rest up, and we also have a lot of things we need to talk about." She looked at me seriously and kissed me again, then she and Shay walked out.

When the door closed behind them I asked, "What happened, fellas? Mike, why you keep wincing like you need to be laid up in a hospital bed?"

Mike groaned, but didn't say anything. I looked at Ahmad.

"Mya kneed him in the balls," he said.

"Are you for real?" I turned to Mike. "Is he for real, man?"

Mike frowned again. "Yeah, he's for real."

It hurt like hell, but I had to laugh. Ahmad joined me. Mike shook his head. "Fuck both of you. Let me kick your nuts and then we'll see how fucking funny this shit is. Goddamn. I think I'm gonna piss blood."

With pain racking my insides I laughed even harder. Ahmad was doubled over with laughter. "Yo, stop man, you're gonna kill me," I said, trying to stop laughing.

"Yeah, whatever," Mike said. "This shit ain't funny to me."

Ahmad and I laughed for a few more seconds. Finally, the pain just too intense, I had to stop laughing and catch my breath. After a few seconds, I looked at Ahmad. "What about you, man? What's up with Shay's attitude?"

Ahmad sighed. "We've been having a lot of problems."

"Well, I hope you two work them out."

"So do I," Ahmad said with another long sigh.

"Who did this to you?" Mike asked me. "Did this have to do with that trick Sharon?"

I looked at Mike for a few seconds. I could see in his eyes that he already knew the answer. I just had to confirm it for him, but I wouldn't. Instead of answering the question I asked him a simple one. "Mike, do you love Mya?"

Mike looked at me curiously. "What kind of question is that? Of course I love her."

"Are you in love with her?" I pressed, grimacing a bit. "Do you feel like you wouldn't be able to breathe without her? That nothing would be right without her by your side? Because that's how I felt the day Trina found out about me and Sharon and kicked me out of the house." I paused to catch another breath.

"You okay, man?" Mike asked, watching me.

I nodded. "I'm cool," I said. "Just hurts a bit."

"You want us to leave?" Ahmad asked.

"Nah. It's cool. Besides, what I'm saying you guys need to hear anyway. Especially you, Mike."

Mike looked at me and opened his mouth to say something, but changed his mind and remained quiet.

"Remember when you drove me away from my house with my shit thrown all over the front yard?"

"Yeah. Why?"

"Well, I realized in that instant how much I loved and needed Trina. She was my better half and without her, I couldn't function."

I paused momentarily as Mike watched me, I'm sure wondering where I was going and why I hadn't answered his question yet.

I continued. "Mike, if you're in love with Mya, then you felt the same thing when her knee got you in the groin. If you're in love with her, man, then I'm willing to bet that the pain of possibly losing her is hurting you much more than your nuts are." I paused again to

breathe as Mike leaned against the wall with his arms folded across his chest and his head bowed. He still hadn't said anything. Maybe I was getting through to him.

"Ahmad was right, man," I said, taking a quick look in Ahmad's direction. "Every lecture he gave, every time he got on our case about losing the good women that we had, every time he said that our actions would come back to bite us in the ass—or in your case, knee you in the balls—he was right. Our boy wasn't trying to be a nuisance, man. He was just trying to keep us from going through what we are now.

"I learned a hard lesson, man, one that I won't forget. I don't know what's gonna happen with me and Trina. There's not much I can say explanation-wise. I mean, shit, I was fucking her mother. I just know I have a lot of groveling to do. Mike, my brother, if Mya means the world to you and you don't wanna lose her, I suggest you get rid of your old philosophy, buy some knee pads and do the same thing."

I turned and looked at Ahmad. "Ahmad, I don't know what's going on with you and Shay, but work it out."

Ahmad nodded. "I plan on it."

"Since when did you become so damn philosophical?" Mike asked.

I looked at the bandages around my chest and winced a bit. Very honestly, I said, "Getting shot will do that."

"So, you're not gonna tell us who did this to you, are you? Because I know you know, and I'm sure we know, too."

"Nah, man," I said, shaking my head. "I'm just gonna chalk this one up to experience. I'm alive and that's what matters. Now I just gotta try to fix my marriage. You do the same."

"Yeah, I got you," Mike said. I hoped he did.

"Just make sure your ass wears a cup the next time you speak to her," I said.

Ahmad burst out laughing again. I tried not to join in, because the laughing was painful, but couldn't help it.

"Fuck both of you," Mike said, laughing with us.

Just then the door opened and Trina stepped inside. "Sorry to break up your party but Ahmad, Shay wanted me to come and get you. She wants to take Nicole home."

"Okay," Ahmad said. He came over to me and gave me a pound. "You take it easy, man. I'll come and check on you tomorrow."

"Alright. Thanks for being there," I said.

He looked at me and understood my double meaning. "Hey, we're boys. Take care of him," he said, giving Trina a hug goodbye.

"Alright." Mike grunted as he pushed himself away from the wall. "I'm gonna make my exit too."

"Remember what I said, man." I touched his knuckles to my own.

"Yeah, yeah, Plato. I got you. Take it easy, man. Trina, congrats."

Trina smiled. "Thanks."

Mike left and closed the door behind him. I looked at Trina. "Congrats?"

She sat down on the bed. "How are you feeling?"

"Sore as hell, but better now that you're here. So, what did Mike mean by congrats?"

Trina's face became serious. "We need to talk, Max."

I sighed. "I know."

"Max—"

"Before you say anything, Trina, let me speak. Please?" I took her hand. "Baby, I know you hate me for what I did, and I'm sure a small part of you is glad for what happened to me."

"I didn't want you to die."

"Maybe not," I said, "but I'm sure you imagined me beaten and bloodied a thousand times since everything went down."

"More," Trina said, giving me a no-joke glare.

"I don't blame you. Baby, I wish there was something more that I could say than I'm sorry for what I did. But unfortunately, sorry is all I can say. I regret everything that happened. I hate that I betrayed you the way I did."

"Max, the fact that you betrayed my trust isn't what hurt me the most."

"I know," I said, feeling shameful.

"Sharon, Max. Of all the women in the world to screw, you screwed her. Why, Max? What did I do to you that would make you do something so fucking hateful?"

"You didn't do anything."

"Then why fuck her? Wasn't I doing it for you? Was I neglectful? Was I not supportive enough for you?"

"No, baby, you were—are the best thing that's ever happened to me."

With tears falling slowly from her eyes, Trina asked. "Then how could you do that to me?" She let go of my hand to wipe the tears away.

I frowned as I thought about what to say. "I was an ass, baby. I was immature and insensitive."

"What was it about her, Max? What made that bitch so special that you had to fuck her in our home, our bed?"

"There was nothing special about her. There is nothing special. I was a jerk. She came on to me and the bastard I was saw it as an exciting conquest."

Trina squeezed her eyes tightly at my brutal honesty. I shook my head and let out a long sigh again. This was the worst.

"I hate you, Max," Trina said softly.

"I know you do. I hate myself."

"I'm pregnant."

"What did you say?"

"I'm pregnant. You're gonna be a daddy."

I watched her to see if she was playing around. When she didn't crack a smile, I asked, "Are you serious?"

"Yes."

"You're pregnant?"

"That's what the doctor says."

"When did you find out?"

"Before I kicked you out."

"Oh shit! I'm gonna be a dad. We're gonna be a family." Despite the aching in my body, I wrapped my arms around Trina and kissed her. I let her go and put my hand on her stomach. "Somewhere in there is my little boy," I said proudly.

"Or girl," Trina reminded me.

"Right, right. Or girl. A little you. Damn. We're having a baby! That's what Mike meant by congrats. How long has he known?"

"I just told everyone tonight."

I touched her belly again. "A father," I said happily. This was truly one of the best feelings I'd ever had. Having grown up without the supervision and guidance of a father, I always swore that when my time came, I would be the best father a man could be. I didn't want my son or daughter to have the same type of void inside of them that I'd had my whole life. I didn't want them to grow up constantly searching and looking to the wrong type of man for a male role model. Having kids was no picnic and was one hell of a commitment, but I know I would have turned out differently had my father been present in my life. I wasn't doing that to my kids.

I wanted to get up and dance around, but there was no way my body would have allowed that. "We have to start working on names," I said, smiling. "Shit, I gotta start working on changing the spare bedroom into a nursery." I was amped. I was going to be a dad.

"Hold on a second, Max," Trina said.

I smiled and nodded. "I know, I know. One step at a time. First the name and then the room. I'm just excited."

"No, that's not what I meant." Trina stood up and walked to the window then turned around.

"Well, what did you mean?" There was a change in her posture, a look in her eyes that I didn't like.

"Max, we're having a baby. A baby that I considered not having."

"What?"

"Yes, Max. I thought about it. I was going to have an abortion and not say a word to anyone, but I couldn't do it, because I love this child more than anything in this world."

"So, what's the problem?" I asked. The look in her eyes hadn't changed.

"Max, I love you."

"I love you too, Trina. More than you could possibly imagine."

"I know. I believe you. But—"

"But what?" I hated buts; there was never a good but.

"Max, I don't know if I can go on with us."

"What? What do you mean? We're having a baby."

"Yes, we are, Max, but that still doesn't erase what you did. My anger, my pain is still there. I love you, Max, but I just don't know if I can stay married to you."

"But Trina—"

"I need time, Max."

"Time?" I couldn't believe this was happening. I mean, I knew that the road to us getting back to normal was going to be bumpy as hell, but with a baby coming, I couldn't believe she was saying that she might not be able to stay married to me.

"Yes, time. I need to think about what I want. What I need. I need time to let this anger that's burning inside of me die out."

I clenched my jaws. "How much time, Trina?"

"I don't know, Max. I don't have a time limit. Just do me a favor."

"What's that?"

"Don't call me and don't come to my job or the house."

"What? What do you mean don't call you? That's my baby you're carrying."

"Max, if you want to be with me like you say, then you'll abide by my wishes. I need time and space. I can't see your face, I can't hear you. If I do, this rage won't go away, and that's the only way we can work. This rage has to die out on its own."

"But . . . but that's my kid," I said, defeated.

"I know, Max, and I promise, no matter what decision I make, I will never prevent you from having a relationship with your child."

"But I love you, Trina."

Backing away slowly to the door, Trina said, "I believe you, Max. I just don't know if I believe in us anymore. I'll call you."

"But—"

Before I could say another word, she walked out of the room. I sat immobile with disbelief. I was going to be a father. Was I going to lose Trina in the process? I lay back and stared up at the white ceiling, wishing that I could have still been asleep.

Mike

Mya wasn't home. I don't know why I was surprised, but I was. Even though she'd heard my conversation with Ahmad and kneed me in the balls, I guess the arrogant bastard in me expected her to be home waiting. Pissed, but waiting nonetheless. I stepped inside, closed the door and sighed. At least my shit hadn't been thrown out on the lawn like Max's. I went to the kitchen and grabbed an ice pack from the freezer and a beer from the fridge. I went back into the living room, sat down gingerly on the sofa and tossed my cell phone on top of a stack of magazines on the coffee table.

I was hurting. I'd received glancing blows here and there while playing sports, but I'd never received a blow to the groin as fierce as what Mya had done. Initially, I almost passed out, it hurt so fucking bad. Had Ahmad not been there, I would have been shedding tears. I Very gently laid the ice pack on my crotch. I didn't know if it would do me any good, but I had to try something. "Jesus Christ," I whispered. This was definitely the worst pain I'd ever felt.

I leaned my head back and closed my eyes as my balls throbbed viciously. How the hell was I going to sleep with pain like this?

Ring.

"Shit." I looked at my cell phone. Why the hell couldn't I have tossed it beside me?

Ring.

"Fuck it," I said. I'd let it go to voice mail and check it later.

After a few seconds the ringing stopped, but the cell never beeped to let me know there was a message.

"Must not have been important." I closed my eyes again and enjoyed the numbing cold from the ice pack.

Ring.

I opened my eyes and looked at my cell again. *Mya?* I smiled. "I knew she couldn't do without me." I didn't want to, but I had no choice. I moved the ice pack away and slid forward on the couch to reach for my cell.

Ring.

"I'm coming, I'm coming," I said, grimacing with each slow movement. "I'm injured, goddammit," I said, annoyed by the ringing.

I finally reached the phone and looked at the caller ID. I didn't recognize the number displayed on the screen, but who knows where Mya could have been calling from. I hit the talk button as I painfully sat back. "Hello."

"Mike." It was a female voice I didn't recognize.

"Who's this?"

"You don't remember me?"

"No."

"It's Raquel."

"Raquel? Do I know you?"

She sucked her teeth. "You better know me. I sucked your dick and rode you in the backseat of your car."

"Huh?" I still had no clue who she was. She was just one of many females who'd done that to me in my backseat.

Obviously not pleased by my selective memory, Raquel breathed heavily into the phone. "It's Raquel from Giant."

Raquel, Raquel? I was racking my brain, and then it hit me. "Ohh," I said, putting a name with the face. It was the Tyra Banks lookalike I'd hooked up with. I forgot I'd given her my number. She'd been so good with her ride that I wanted to hit it again. "What's going on?" I asked, trying to put some mack in my voice.

"How come I ain't seen you in Giant?" she asked, cracking gum in my ears. There was a lot of attitude in her voice.

"I've been busy," I said, putting the ice pack back on.

"Yeah well, you need to come by tonight. I need to talk to you."

"You know I can't do that. I'm married, remember?"

"Yeah, I remember."

"Alright then. Maybe I can try to swing by in a couple of days." If I was going to hit it again, I needed at least a couple of days to recuperate.

"Unh-uh," Raquel said. "You need to come tonight. I got to talk to you, and what I got to say can't wait."

"What do you want to talk about, Raquel?" I was getting aggravated.

"Not over the phone. I want to see your face."

"You need to see my face for what?"

"I need to tell you something."

"Tell me now, then."

"I told you I don't wanna do it over the phone."

She was really beginning to piss me off, which was only making my balls hurt more. "Look, Raquel, I've had a pretty fucked up day and I'm not in the mood for any games. Now, you know I'm married, so you know I can't just up and come and see you because you want me to. Whatever it is that you need to say, just say it."

"No you didn't just come at me with all that attitude," Raquel snapped.

I gritted my teeth. I was two seconds away from hanging up on her. "Look, Raquel—"

"No, you look, Mike. You wanna talk all about your day being fucked up, where's here's something else for you—I'm pregnant."

"And you're telling me because?"

"I'm telling you because you the baby's daddy."

I sat upright. "What are you talking about?"

"I'm pregnant with your baby."

"Get the fuck out of here with that bullshit," I said. I couldn't believe she was trying to play me like that. "Your ass isn't pregnant with my child. Did you forget I wore a fucking condom? Try your fucking games on some other fool."

"You're the only fool I need to deal with, and this ain't no fucking game. I ain't fucked nobody since I was with you that night."

"Whatever, Raquel. I'm not falling for your shit. I didn't get your ass pregnant. Like I said, I had on a condom."

"Well, your condom musta broke or else it had a hole or somethin'. All I know is I ain't fucked no other nigga since you and I'm two months pregnant now. And just to show you I ain't playing, we can do a paternity test."

I shook my head. I couldn't believe this was happening. There was no way she was pregnant. There was no way that condom broke or had a hole. I was about to snap at Raquel when a voice interrupted my conversation.

"You asshole!"

I didn't want to turn around. I closed my eyes and held my breath.

"You fucking asshole!"

Shit. I turned slowly as my heart tried to beat through my chest. I'd been so caught up with Raquel that I never heard Mya come inside. Damn.

"You fucking asshole!" Mya screamed again as tears poured from her eyes.

"Mya…" I said then stopped, not knowing what to say.

"Mya?" Raquel said. I forgot I was still on the phone with her.

I hung up without saying anything to her. "Mya."

"You got some bitch pregnant? I gave you all of me and you get some bitch pregnant?" She was crying so heavily that her chest was heaving up and down.

I dropped the phone and stood up slowly. "Mya, just hear me out, please," I begged.

"I don't want to hear shit, Mike! You cheating motherfucker! I can't believe I was coming back here to try to be with you still. I hate you, Mike. You are a filthy dog!"

"Mya, please. That bitch was just trying to play games. She can't be pregnant by me. I wore a condom."

"Is that supposed to make me feel better? I don't care if she's pregnant or not. You fucked her and who knows how many other women."

Ring.

Shit. Both Mya and I looked down at my phone.

"Your baby momma is calling you back, Mike."

"Mya, I don't give a shit about her. Baby, it's all about you." I took a slow, painful step toward her.

Ring.

"Fuck you and go to hell, Mike! It's all about me? You're so full of shit. God, why have I stayed with you so long? And if you come any closer, I swear I will send your balls up into your throat."

I stopped moving immediately.

Ring.

I looked down at my phone. I wanted to stomp the hell out of it. "Mya, she . . . she's not pregnant by me."

"I don't give a shit, Mike. It's over. Fucking over. Here's your fucking ring!" She pulled the two-carat diamond off her finger and threw it at me. To add insult to injury, it hit me in the groin.

"Mya, please! Don't do this."

Ring.

Mya looked down at the phone again then back up at me. "Talk to your bitch, Mike. I'm finished." Mya turned and walked out of the house, slamming the door behind her so hard that a couple of pictures fell from the wall. I sighed and sat down, no longer feeling the pain in between my legs. I looked at my phone and shook my head; the ringing had stopped. I cursed and kicked the phone across the carpet. There was no way Raquel was pregnant by me. No fucking way. Condoms had never failed me in the past and they damn sure hadn't now. I cursed out loud again as a what if question popped into my head. What if I was the baby's father?

"No fucking way!" I said. I got up and walked to the door. I don't know why I was checking, but I wanted to see if maybe Mya was out there. She wasn't.

I closed the door and went back inside remembering Max's comment about the pain of losing Mya being worse than the pain from the knee. I was listening to him when he was speaking, but I wasn't listening at the same time. Buying kneepads and groveling wasn't an option because I just knew that Mya was going to come back. She'd never had much of a backbone and even though she'd kneed me, I didn't think she'd leave me for good. Even though she was pissed off after the conversation between Ahmad and me, I still had a feeling she would come back to me. And she did, only to hear me on the phone with Raquel.

I squeezed my temples. The venom in Mya's eyes and the hurt in her voice made my head hurt. Damn. Max was right. The pain of possibly losing her was a beast. I leaned my head back on the sofa as another question popped into my head. What if Raquel wasn't trying to play me? Damn. Now I had sore balls, a hurting heart, and a mind full of questions. I really wasn't getting any sleep tonight.

Ahmad

Not again. I couldn't believe this was happening. For the past day and a half Shay and I had been strangers again. I was hoping that we were going to be able to get back to talking things over and working on our marriage after seeing Max, but Shay wasn't having it. As I feared, she'd climbed right back into her shell and wouldn't talk to me. I let it go the first day. Although the call was a necessary one, I knew that she was still bothered by the fact that Mya had called. Was it a little immature on Shay's part to be upset? Sure. But whatever. I could deal with her cold shoulder during day one. Halfway through day two, though, I was tired of being patient and understanding. I was fed up with the cold shoulder and accusatory stares. I was tired of the silent treatment. And I was fed up with Nicole being the only thing we talked about.

"Shay, let's talk."

I could tell that she was going to protest, so I gave her a look to let her know that I wasn't taking no for an answer. She sat down across from me. We were in the kitchen again. Nicole was asleep.

"Shay, before everything happened with Max, you were going to say something."

"Was I?" Shay asked.

"Come on, Shay. Don't make this harder than it has to be. Just open up to me. I told you I want our marriage back the way it used to be, and I know you do too." I looked at her with imploring eyes. After everything Max had said, I really wanted to work on our problems. For a few seconds, Shay watched me watching her. Then she sighed.

"Okay."

I couldn't help but smile. We were finally on our way.

And that's when the phone rang.

Goddamn, I thought, looking at the number displayed on the caller ID. I looked at Shay. She didn't even bother to ask who it was. She got up and walked out. I shook my head and exhaled a long, frustrated breath. In a flat voice I said, "Hey, Mya."

"Ah-Ahmad," Mya said on the other end, sniffling. "I need you."

I clenched my jaws. She was still upset about overhearing my conversation with Mike, and as bad as I wanted to be there for her, I couldn't. "Mya . . . uh, listen, right now's not a good time for me. Shay and I were just talking, and—"

"She's pregnant, Ahmad," Mya said, cutting me off.

"Who? Trina? I know. I was there when she told everyone."

"No, not Trina. Raquel."

"Raquel? Mya, who are you talking about?" I was confused and worried by the anxiety in her voice.

"Raquel. She's some bitch Mike fucked. She's pregnant."

"Huh?"

"That asshole got her pregnant, Ahmad." Mya broke down over the phone. I could only listen. "Ahmad, please . . . I need you. I need a friend. Please?"

I took a slow, deep breath and thought about Shay. Goddamn. "Mya, where are you?"

"I'm at the Sheraton by the Harbor. That asshole's paying for me to shed my tears in a suite." Mya laughed momentarily, though it was hardly out of happiness. "I hate him, Ahmad. I hate him so much. Please, Ahmad. Please come."

I sighed. This was the last thing my marriage needed right now, but I couldn't leave Mya hanging when she was hurting like this. A friend—a real friend—wouldn't do that. "What room are you in?"

"Six-ten."

"I'll be there in a half hour." I hung up the phone and massaged the building tension in my neck. How the hell was I going to explain this to Shay? I wanted to say no to Mya, but she sounded so broken up that I couldn't bring myself to do it. I was going to have to have a talk with Mike later about this situation with Raquel. I took a deep breath and released it slowly, hoping to relieve some tension. It didn't work, though. I was about to put my marriage through a huge test.

I walked out of the kitchen and into the living room where Shay was sitting, waiting for me. There was no need for me to beat around the bush. "Shay, I have to go out for a few," I said evenly.

Shay looked up at me. "Was that Mya?"

I nodded. "Yeah."

"And where are you going?"

I hesitated before I answered. This was the moment of truth. "Mya needs someone to talk to."

"I don't give a fuck what she needs!" Shay yelled out suddenly, shocking the hell out of me.

"Shay, it'll only be for a short while. She's going through something really difficult right now."

"Fuck her and what she's going through," Shay yelled vehemently. "I'm going through something difficult. Are you going to stay and be here for me?"

"Come on, Shay. Don't be like that. Don't put me in a predicament like that."

"No, Ahmad, you don't put me in a predicament. Don't make me choose divorce over this marriage."

"Damn it Shay, she's a friend."

"I don't give a fuck, Ahmad. I'm your fucking wife!"

"I realize that."

"Then sit your ass down and let's work on us like *you* wanted to."

"You know, it's really funny to hear you talking about me sitting my ass down to deal with our problems when I've been trying to get you to do that for the past six months."

"Don't try to turn this around, Ahmad."

"Why not?" I asked defiantly. "I've begged you for six months to talk to me. I've had my ass sitting in a chair hoping that you'd open up to me. And what the hell did you do? Nothing. Not a fucking thing! Well, you know what, Shay? I'm tired of sitting my ass down. I shouldn't have to beg you to communicate with me."

"Sit down, Ahmad."

I clenched my jaws and hesitated for a brief second before I said, "I can't do that."

"You can't or you won't?" Shay asked coldly.

"Shay—"

"I'm telling you, Ahmad, don't leave your wife and child to go and be with her ass."

"I'm not going to be with her!" I yelled. "She just needs a friend to talk to. Why can't you just understand that?"

"Oh, I do understand her needing someone to talk to. What I don't understand is how come all of a sudden she doesn't consider me a friend anymore. I think Mya needs to learn a few things about being a good friend and not trying to take her friend's man. I need my husband here, Ahmad. I'm your concern, not Mya. She's a grown fucking woman. Let her deal with her own problems. We have enough of our own."

"Shay, what the fuck do you want from me?" I was boiling inside.

Shay pointed to the couch. "I want my husband to sit his ass down so we can work on our issues. And I want my husband to remind himself that Mya is Mike's concern."

"I know that Mya is Mike's concern, but unfortunately, he's the cause of the pain she's dealing with right now. And you know what? As many times as I've tried to get you to sit your ass down, not once did you ever give in. Yet I'm supposed to now? To hell with that! If working out our problems was so damned important to you we would have been sitting down a long time ago. The only reason you want me to now is because of your feelings about Mya. You don't want to talk to fix our marriage. You just want to talk because you're insecure. Whatever. Mya's a friend who *wants* to talk, Shay, and I'm not turning my back on her."

Silence took over after my last comment, giving us a chance to hear Nicole, who'd been crying from her crib. With all of the yelling we'd been doing, who knows how long she'd been crying. Shay turned her head toward the bedroom then back to me. "Don't go, Ahmad."

"Shay . . ."

"Ahmad, this is our marriage. Don't go."

I lowered my head and closed my eyes. I listened to Nicole cry and that made me think of Mya. "I have to," I said, looking at her apologetically.

"The only thing you have to do, Ahmad, is stay black and die."

"Shay, please."

"If you leave, Ahmad, don't come back."

"This is my house too," I said.

"Fine. Then don't expect to find me or Nicole here when you get back."

"Don't do this, Shay."

"No, *you* don't do this."

I closed my fists tightly at my sides. I wanted to say something, but nothing I could say was going to make things any better. Instead of talking, I turned around, grabbed my keys from the key ring and walked out the door. As I walked to the car, I heard Shay yell out the word *bitch,* then I heard something shatter. I stood with my hand on the hood of my car, knowing that I should turn around and walk back inside. I drummed my fingers, too pissed to listen to my voice of reason. I damned myself as I got in the car and drove off.

* * * * * *

"Thanks for coming."

I looked at Mya but didn't say anything right away. I was still having a hard time with the fact that I was there. I'd come so close to turning the car around on my way to the hotel. I knew I needed to be back at home with Shay, but every time I came close to making the U-turn I'd think about the strain in Mya's voice and that would keep the car going forward. Besides, Shay really pissed me off when she started demanding that I sit down to talk about our problems. Like I told her, she never gave in when I begged. Why the hell should I now?

"No problem," I said, stepping into the room.

Mya let the door close then stepped past me. "Would you like something to drink? I have wine. I ordered it from room service."

I took off my jacket and looked at the half-consumed bottle of red wine sitting in a bucket of ice then looked at Mya. She looked as bad as she'd sounded. Her eyes were swollen from crying. Her nose was red, no doubt from constant nose blowing. Her hair was wild and unkempt. "I'm good," I said, shaking my head.

Mya nodded. "Okay." Tears spilled from her eyes.

I dropped my jacket and wrapped my arms around her. She laid her head against my shoulder.

"I hate him so much, Ahmad," she whispered.

I tightened my hold around her. "I know," I said.

"Why the hell did I stay with him so long? He's never changed. I knew he never would. Why did I let myself be his fool?" Mya cried harder into my shoulder.

"Because you love him," I said softly.

Mya pushed herself away from me. "Yeah well, now I hate him," she snapped angrily. She reached for the wine bottle and a glass. From the unsteadiness in her step it was obvious that another drink was the last thing she needed. I wrapped my hand around hers. Mya looked up at me. With my eyes I told her to stop drowning her sorrows.

"No more drinks," I said.

She collapsed into my arms again. "I was always so good to him, Ahmad. With everything he's done, I've always been so good to him. I feel so used. How could he hurt me like this?"

"I don't know," I said with an exasperated sigh. "I wish I had an answer for you. I wish I could tell you why he does the things he does."

"Why wasn't I ever good enough for him?" Mya whimpered. "What is it about me? What is it that I don't do for him?"

I shook my head, upset at what Mike was putting her through. "Mya, listen." I put my finger underneath her chin and lifted her head so that she was looking up at me. "Don't start beating yourself up, okay? There was nothing, absolutely nothing that you didn't do."

"That's not true," Mya said, her tears running down her cheeks and wetting my hand. "If it were, Mike would never treat me this way."

"Mya, it's not about you. That's just the way Mike is. I've told you before you're an extremely beautiful and special woman." I paused and stared intensely at her. "Any man would kill to have you at his side. You're the woman that every man wants." My voice trailed off as Mya stared back at me.

"Mike doesn't," she said softly.

"Mike's a fool," I said, my fingers caressing her back gently.

Mya exhaled. "I feel so much better now that you're here, Ahmad. It means so much to me that you came."

My body temperature rising, I said, "We're friends, Mya. I couldn't not be here for you."

Mya's hands crept slowly from my waistline to my back. My hands slid down from her back to the top of her behind. Even if we wanted to, the rising passion couldn't be denied. We looked at each other in silence. I inhaled the scent of the wine on her breath and felt myself becoming intoxicated. My manhood throbbed as my blood flow increased and my imagination worked. I could see in Mya's eyes that she felt it. I can't say that I minded that she did. Mya licked her lips slowly, making me catch my breath. Deliberately, her lips moved toward mine, mine toward hers.

"I would never be going through this if I were with you," Mya said.

"No, you wouldn't."

"I would never let you be unhappy either," she said, her lips near mine.

"I know you wouldn't," I said.

Right or wrong, our lips were about to meet until my cell phone suddenly vibrated against my leg. Mya cleared her throat and moved away from me. I frowned and grabbed my cell. My home number was displayed on the screen. I didn't want to answer, it but I knew I had to. I hit the talk button. "Hello?"

There was a brief of silence then Shay spoke. "Tell me that you're at the bar drinking. Tell me that you're sitting in your car cursing me. Tell me you're out robbing a fucking bank, Ahmad. Tell me you're anywhere but with her."

I took a deep breath. "Shay—" She cut me off.

"Tell me that you didn't go to her, Ahmad."

"Shay," I said again as Mya sat on the bed with her back toward me. Again I was interrupted.

"Ahmad, I'm begging you to tell me that you didn't go to her. Our fucking marriage is begging you."

I sighed. There was so much pain and anger in her voice. I closed my eyes. "I'm here, Shay." Silence was my answer after I spoke. Damn. "Shay?" I said after a few seconds passed. I looked at the LED screen to make sure I hadn't lost the signal; I hadn't. "Shay?" I said again. "I know you're there. Say something."

Another couple of seconds went by before I heard Shay speak. "Ahmad, I changed my mind."

"Changed your mind about what?"

"I'm not leaving."

"You're not?"

"No."

I smiled. Maybe we would survive this after all. "I'm glad you're not, Shay."

"So am I. I mean, this is my house too. Besides, if anyone should leave, it should be your ass."

"What?" My smile quickly disappeared as Shay's voice became jagged ice.

"That's right, you son of a bitch. Your ass should be the one to leave. And you know what? You already did!"

"Shay—"

"Don't come home Ahmad."

"Shay—",

"Stay with that bitch you piece of shit! Stay wherever the fuck you want, but don't bring your ass home."

"Shay," I said again.

The line went dead. I hung my head low.

"Is this my fault?" Mya asked.

I sighed and shook my head. "No. It's mine."

"Maybe you should leave and go home to her."

I dragged my hand down over my face. "I don't think that would be the best thing right now."

Neither one of us spoke. Suddenly my stomach growled.

"Are you hungry?" Mya asked.

I put my hand on my stomach. I hadn't eaten since lunch. "A little."

"I tell you what." Mya stood up. "I'm going to take a shower and wash away some of this frustration. Why don't you call room service and have some food brought up here while I do that?"

I was going to decline but my stomach growled again.

"I think your stomach likes my suggestion," Mya said with a smile.

"Okay."

"Good. The menu's by the phone. Order me some lobster and order more wine. You order anything you want. This is Mike's treat. I'll be out in a few."

"How long do you plan on being here?"

Mya shrugged. "Until I figure out where I'm going. Back to Mike is not one of those places." She turned around and disappeared into the bathroom.

I sighed and reached for the menu.

Shay

All he had to do was say that he wasn't with her. That's all his ass had to do. Why the hell couldn't he? Hell, I would have even accepted a fucking lie. He could have at least done that. Bastard. If he would have only said something other than that he was with that bitch, then I wouldn't have had to pick up the phone and call Trina to get the number of the locksmith that she used. If he didn't tell the truth, I wouldn't have had to decide that I was through with his ass. I couldn't even cry right away after his ass left. I was too angry and too shocked at the choice he'd made. To hell with him. He was going to be in for a rude awakening when he brought his sorry ass home. I wasn't playing. Choose that bitch over this marriage? Oh, hell no! It doesn't work like that. Remember when Angela Bassett burned all of her husband's shit up in *Waiting To Exhale*? Well, I was gonna do one better.

After I got Nicole back to sleep I went about making the changes Ahmad had forced me to make in my life. First step was to call Trina and get the locksmith's number. I didn't want to have to go into detail about why I needed it, so I told her that some of our keys came up missing and we were changing the locks as a precaution. I was able to have the locksmith come the same night by using a damsel in distress routine and offering to pay extra for the prompt service. After that, I went around the house grabbing all of Ahmad's clothes, shoes and whatever else I could, stuffing it all into Hefty trash bags. In two days' time, he'd realize how serious I was about him making the choice to leave.

I would have done more, but Nicole woke up again, which was surprising because she normally slept through the night. It was almost as though she knew something wasn't right at home. I picked her up and took her in the bed with me. Lying alone with my little girl only made me angrier at Ahmad. I really expected him to change his mind about going to Mya when I said I would take Nicole and leave. I didn't think there was any chance of him sacrificing his family for Mya's ass. Piece of shit. He chose her over us. Acknowledging that opened the floodgates in my eyes and allowed the tears to fall. Because of Mya, my marriage was falling apart.

Mya

I pushed my rear end into Ahmad's crotch and felt his manhood poke against me. We were spooning on the bed. We'd been there for the past few hours since finishing our meals. His arms were wrapped around me; my hands were on his. I smiled when his penis poked at me again, and thought this was the way it was supposed to be. Ahmad and I together, we were perfect for one another. The connection, the spark, the fit—it was all too real, too obvious. I realized how much we were meant to be together when Ahmad was holding me, letting me cry on his shoulder.

I knew Ahmad felt the same thing because I saw it in his eyes when we were about to kiss. Damn Shay for calling when she did. I knew I said that it was wrong for Ahmad and I to take things further than we already had, but the more things happened around us, the more I started to wonder why it was wrong. Mike was never going to change. As much as I wanted him to, I knew it wasn't going to happen. And it just seemed like Shay was going to continue to make Ahmad's life miserable. Both of us deserved better. We deserved to be happy. If that meant that we should be together, then so be it.

I actually decided to try to make Ahmad mine before I overheard his conversation with Mike at the hospital, and before I walked in on Mike's phone conversation with Raquel. I'd made my decision at my surprise party. It just pissed me off the way Shay opened her mouth in front of Mike and everyone else, and then gave Ahmad grief when they were arguing outside. I heard the whole argument from upstairs. I heard it all; the anger and frustration in Ahmad's voice, the ignorance in Shay's. God, she didn't deserve him. I was dead serious when I told him he'd never be unhappy with me. I would never put him through what Shay was putting him through. I'd make sure that he always had a smile on his handsome face. He would never have to worry about not getting enough love and attention from me. And he damn sure wouldn't have to worry about not being pleased sexually. I'd make him feel like the man Shay obviously didn't realize he was.

When I went into the bathroom to shower, I did so with a plan in mind. Ahmad was going to be mine. After Shay called I really expected him to leave, but when he didn't, I knew that my chance had come.

I soaped my body down with some tropical scented body wash I'd bought from the gift shop in the lobby, then rubbed my entire body with lotion. I'd bought the scented soap and lotion hoping that if Ahmad had indeed agreed to come and comfort me, he could be enticed enough to take things further than we'd gone on his couch. I left my hair wet for that sultry look, and—remaining naked—wrapped myself up in the plush cotton robe the Sheraton provided. When I stepped out of the bathroom, Ahmad's jaw dropped a notch. Obviously, I had caught his attention.

We sat across from one another, not really speaking much, just eating our meals. Every now and then I would smile at Ahmad and he'd smile back.

"Feeling better?" I asked after he'd finished the steak he ordered.

He nodded. "Yeah. But the real question is do *you* feel better?"

When he asked me that I could have very easily said I was feeling much better. Instead, I let my smile drop and lay my hands out on the table. "A little," I said with a melancholy sigh. "I'm still so hurt. He's scarred me, Ahmad. Emotionally, he's scarred me."

As I'd hoped he would, Ahmad reached across the table and took my hands in his. "I know this is hard,

Mya, but just give it some time. Things will get easier. I promise. You just have to give it some time. Maybe you and Mike—"

"Me and Mike nothing," I said sharply. "I'm done with him. He got another bitch pregnant. There is no more me and Mike."

"Have you spoken to him about the situation?"

"What is there to speak about?"

"Maybe this baby's not his. Or maybe the girl is lying about the whole thing."

I pulled my hands away from his. This was not the conversation I wanted to be having. I could feel myself growing angrier by the second. "I don't care about any of those possibilities, Ahmad. He fucked her and who knows how many other bitches. That's all that matters."

"I understand that, Mya, but maybe you should just talk to him. I know it may not seem like it, but I know Mike loves you."

I moved away from the table with tears welling in my eyes. It was just too much for me. "Mike doesn't love shit but his damn self," I snapped, walking over to the window. "He's a no-good, lying-ass, piece of shit. A womanizer. He always has been and will always be nothing more than a womanizer."

"Maybe he can change, Mya. Maybe this will be the wake up call he needs."

"I don't care about maybes, Ahmad."

"But, Mya—"

"No buts, Ahmad. I don't want to hear any buts. Now, can we please change the damn subject?" I slapped my palm against the glass, wishing that I could lash out at Mike instead. "I'm tired of being his fool, Ahmad. I've been his fool for so long. I'm not willing to be that anymore." I rested my forehead against the cold glass and watched my tears run down my cheeks in the reflection. Behind me I heard Ahmad rise from the table.

"Look, I didn't mean to upset you, Mya. Maybe I should get going."

I turned around quickly; that was the last thing I wanted. "Ahmad, don't leave, please. I'm sorry I lashed out like that. I'm just so angry and so damn frustrated. I've been hurting for a long time, but walking in and hearing him on that phone, hearing him talk about a possible child that he didn't have with me was the straw that broke my back. I have no more rope to hold onto, Ahmad. Don't leave, please. You're the last lifeline I have left. You're the only positive light in my dark world." I let tears cascade down my cheeks for him to see. I couldn't let him go.

Ahmad sighed and walked over to me. Placing a hand on my shoulder he said, "You have every right to feel the way you do, Mya. Mike fucked up time and time again."

"Then why try to get me to talk to him?"

Ahmad shrugged. "I guess I was just suggesting that because you guys have been together so long, and I care about both of you, I just want to see you both happy."

"You're a good friend, Ahmad. Mike's lucky."

"Yeah, Mike's lucky. Lucky to have you."

"His luck has run out. Now it's someone else's turn to be lucky."

Ahmad watched me and then cleared his throat. "Maybe I should leave," he said, although I could tell he didn't fully mean it.

"Don't go, please," I said, taking his hand. "Just stay with me for a little while. Lay down with me."

"Mya," Ahmad started.

I put up my hand. "I'm tired, Ahmad, and I just don't want to fall asleep alone. Just lay down with me for a little while. That's all I'm asking." I stared at him as he tried to make up his mind. "Please?" I asked softly.

Ahmad looked at me for a few more seconds and then his shoulders dropped. "Okay."

I smiled. "Thank you."

I pressed my behind into him again, only this time when his manhood reacted, I moved my hands from on top of his to in between his legs, feeling his hardened member. Ahmad didn't react as I did so, although his body did become rigid. I slowly stroked him above his pants as thoughts about our moment of passion on his couch went through my mind. Then I reached for his zipper.

"Mya," Ahmad said as I pulled the zipper down.

"Shh," I said. I reached beneath his pants and found my way past his boxers to his erection. I stroked slowly as he began to moan.

"Mya," he said again, though there was little fight in his voice.

"Shh." I turned around and faced him, watching him as I stroked. Ahmad moaned and slid my robe off my shoulders. He took my breasts into his hands. "Ahmad," I whispered, as he ran his tongue around my nipple. I began to stroke him faster as my body heat increased. Ahmad moaned and squirmed from the magic I was working. I used my free hand to gently caress his strong face while he sucked on my breasts. I exhaled from the pleasure and warmth of his mouth. I gently pulled my breast away and lifted his face toward mine, planting my lips on his. We kissed deeply, our tongues merging to become one. As we kissed, I took his hand and guided it to the pool in between my legs. I wanted him to feel what he'd done to me. He gently fingered my clitoris, making bumps rise from my skin. Then he guided his fingers inside of me, making me gasp, bringing me to the brink of explosion. My caress on his manhood became faster, my grip tighter.

I wanted to feel him inside of me.

I unbuttoned his jeans and slid them, along with his boxers, down past his ankles. I removed my robe while he peeled off his shirt. We lay naked, exploring the inside and outside of one another. "Take it, Ahmad," I said breathlessly. "Take it. It's yours."

He lifted himself above me as I readied myself for his penetration. I'd been imagining what it would be like to feel him deep inside of me and now I was about to find out. I closed my eyes as he brought his body down closer to me and opened my walls. But before sliding inside, he paused.

I opened my eyes and looked up at him. "What's wrong?" I asked, not liking the distressed look on his face. Ahmad stared at me, but didn't answer. "What's wrong, Ahmad?" I asked again.

He shook his head. "I can't do this." He moved from above me.

"Can't do what? Ahmad, we've already done it."

"No, we haven't," he said, sliding into his boxers.

"But we were so close. I know you wanted to. Why are you fighting what's natural?"

Ahmad stood up and grabbed his jeans from the floor. "I love Shay, Mya."

"Why?" I covered myself with the bedspread. "She doesn't love you."

"Yes, she does."

"Not like I could."

"Mya, this is wrong. We can't do this. You're my boy's wife."

"So? Do you think Mike stops to think about me before he sticks his dick into another woman's pussy?"

Ahmad shook his head and grabbed his shirt. "I'm sorry, Mya, but this can't happen."

My eyes welled with tears, but I refused to let them fall. "Don't go, Ahmad. You said you were falling in love with me, remember?"

"Yeah, I remember."

"Was that a lie?"

"Mya . . ."

"Just answer that, Ahmad," I demanded.

Ahmad breathed out slowly. "No, I wasn't lying."

"Then come back in the bed and take me."

"Mya, I can't."

"Why? Why can't you? This is right. You and I both know it. The feeling is real. You have to admit that."

"Mya . . ."

"Admit it," I pressed as the tears won the battle and started to fall.

"I'm sorry, Mya, but I love Shay. I'm in love with her. Honestly, I should have never come here."

"But . . . but I needed you."

"I know." He sighed. "But so did my wife. I have to go."

"Ahmad, don't go." He ignored me and picked up his coat. "Ahmad," I called out again as he opened the door. "Ahmad!" I said when the door closed behind him. I screamed out and flung the pillows from the bed. It wasn't fair. "Ahmad!" I yelled again. "Come back! I need you."

I lay back and brought my knees to my chest and cried hard tears. "I need you," I said softly. "I need somebody." I cried until I eventually fell asleep.

Trina

I sat down for the first time all day, sighing along with the sofa cushion as I sunk into it. I looked over at the clock to see the time. It was four in the afternoon. I'd been cleaning the house since the crack of dawn. I started first in my bedroom, wiping away every speck of dust I could find, changing sheets and organizing the closet. From there I moved to the bathroom and scrubbed the sink, toilet, tub, tiles, and anywhere else that could be scrubbed. I even got down on my hands and knees and scrubbed the floor. After the bathroom I went from room to room, dusting, straightening, vacuuming, rearranging, and didn't stop until now. Although I'd read about it happening, I didn't think I'd ever have an overwhelming need to clean like that, especially feeling as uncomfortable as I was with my belly which was growing bigger and getting heavier by the second. Or at least that's how it seemed.

I sighed and looked around my now spotless home. I couldn't remember the last time it was this clean. I'd always wanted to do a thorough cleaning like this, but I just never had the time or energy to devote. Work took so much out of me during the week that on the weekends, the last thing I felt like doing was cleaning. I did what I had to do to keep a clean house, but other than that, I never over-extended myself. Now, with all of the drama going on in my life, that had all changed.

I closed my eyes and tried to let my body relax, but the phone rang. I thought about getting up to answer it, but changed my mind. It was probably Max again. He'd been calling me steadily since I left him at the hospital, begging me to give him another chance. I didn't know how he expected me to give him that chance when he wasn't giving me the time that I needed. Didn't he understand how badly he'd hurt me? Wasn't he listening when I said that I needed the time and space to let my anger burn out?

I shook my head with disdain. He was making this harder on himself, because every time he called, all it did was make me think about him and Sharon. Goddammit; my neck was starting to stiffen up again. "Stop calling me, Max," I said softly. I took a few deep breaths and released the air slowly, trying to calm down. I didn't need my blood pressure to rise. The phone rang a few more times and the answering machine clicked on. I sighed and listened to another one of Max's messages.

Uh, baby . . . It's me again. Listen, if you're there, pick up the phone. Please. I just want to talk to you for a few. I know you said not to call because you need the time, but all I'm asking for is a couple of minutes. That's all. So, can you pick up? Okay, I guess you're not there. Either that or you're sitting there listening to me right now. Well, whichever it is, I guess I'll just say what I have to say like I did all of the other times. Baby, I'm sorry for everything that's happened. I'm sorry for fucking up the way I did. I know I keep saying that, but until you give me a chance to show you how much I regret what I did, saying sorry's all I can—.
Beep.

The machine clicked off. I did a slow backward count from ten; by four, the phone was ringing again. *Damn you, Max.* I waited until the machine clicked on again.

Uh, yeah, it's me. I ran out of time. Anyway, I'm begging you to give me another chance. I don't want to be without you. Please. Just let me show you that I'll do right by you. You're having our baby, Trina. A little you or a little me. I know you said I could be a part of the baby's life even if we weren't together, but that's not good enough for me. I want—

Beep.

I did my count and waited again.

You should reset the machine for a longer record time. Anyway, like I was saying, being a part of our baby's life without us being together isn't good enough for me. I want us to be a family. A whole family, living under one roof. Baby, let me make it up to you. Give me a chance to be a real man. An honest and faithful man. I miss you. I love you. I need you. I need you and the baby—

Beep.

I sighed and did my count again, only this time the phone never rang. "Damn you, Max," I said out loud this time. "I hate your ass so much. How could you do this to me? How could you fuck that bitch? That trashy, disrespectful bitch." I slammed my hand down on the cushion of the sofa. *Stay calm*, I reminded myself, but the more I tried, the harder it was to quell my rage. I screamed out loud and threw a pillow from the couch to the floor. "Low life bastard!" I would have thrown another pillow but the nearest one was out of my reach. I cursed Max again for putting me in this predicament. A baby. I was carrying his baby, and he'd fucked my mother.

The phone rang again.

"No! No more fucking calls!" I got up as quickly as my stomach would allow me to and went to the phone. "Max, will you stop fucking calling me?" I yelled into the receiver. "I told you I need some damn time. Can't you understand that?"

"I would if I were Max."

"Nikita? I'm sorry, sis. I wasn't expecting it to be you."

"Yeah, I can see that. So, he keeps calling?"

"Every damn minute. Leaving message after message. He just won't stop."

"What's he saying?"

I sucked my teeth. "He keeps apologizing for what he did and begging me to give him a second chance."

It was Nikita's turn to suck her teeth. "Give him another chance? Fuck that asshole. What you need to do is call up my damn lawyer and have divorce papers drawn up. Trifling nigga."

"It's not that simple a decision, Nikita."

"Not that simple? Why the hell not? He fucked our mother in your fucking bed, and you're telling me that divorcing his ass isn't a simple decision? Please. His ass is lucky he's not my husband. I would have had papers served to him right when he woke up from that damn coma."

"I hear what you're saying, Nikita, but have you forgotten I'm carrying his child?"

"So?"

"So leaving him isn't as easy as one, two, three. This child is going to need a father."

"Max can still be the baby's father, Trina. That don't mean you have to stay married to his ass."

"I know, but it's more complicated than that. There are things to consider."

"Like what?" I could hear my sister scowling over the phone.

I hesitated and then said, "Like my feelings for him."

"Your feelings? Please. After everything he's done, don't tell me you still care about his ass."

I thought about it for a second. "Yeah, I do."

"Come on, Trina!"

"Nikita, I know what he did is trifling and damn near unforgivable—"

"Damn near?"

"But as much as I hate him, I'm not gonna lie and say that I don't still love him."

"Please Trina, that Negro doesn't deserve your love."

"You're probably right, but I still do love him. I'm angry, but my feelings are still there and they're still strong. I'm having his baby. He's my husband."

"Trina, please spare me the dramatic speech. So, he'd be your baby daddy. So what? You don't need him. Kick him to the curb and find a real man. It's not like you can't. Besides, Max wasn't pulling in any kind of money anyway."

"He was working on his dream," I said, defending him.

"How many artists has he gotten deals, Trina? Please. He wasn't about shit. Dream my ass. He was living off of your paycheck."

"He's gotten some independent deals, Nikita. It's a tough industry, and it was a give and take relationship. I supported him."

"While he was fucking our mother! Drop his ass like a hot potato, girl. Forget love. He did when he slept with that bitch. Speaking of which, you won't believe what I heard."

"What?"

"I don't know how, but she found out you were pregnant."

"Oh, really?" I asked, my blood starting to boil.

"Yeah. But that's not the real news. Apparently she's been walking around her neighborhood bragging about how she's gonna be a grandmother."

"What?"

"Believe me, I know exactly what you're thinking."

"Who the fuck does she think she is?" I snapped. "If that bitch thinks she's going to have any kind of association with my child she's got another thing coming. A grandmother? Fuck that bitch. I hope she doesn't think I'm going to let her get away with what she did to me. Bitch. Ghetto-ass, trifling, hoochified bitch!"

"Calm down before you go into labor, Trina," my sister warned me. "Damn, if I would have known you'd blow up like that, I wouldn't have said anything."

"Nikita, I hate that bitch. I swear."

"I know, girl. I do too."

"If it were up to her ass, you and I would still be living in the dumps with her."

"Don't I know it."

"All our life she's treated us like shit just because we were determined to rise. You'd think she'd be proud that we made something of ourselves. You'd think she'd try to do the same. But instead all she can do is call us stuck-up bitches. What sense does that make? You know what? Fuck her and her ghetto mentality. A grandmother?"

I paused. My heart was racing from the venting. I couldn't believe she had the nerve to be happy about my pregnancy. A grandmother. That's the last thing she would ever be. I took a deep breath and let it out nice and slow. I had to calm down, but between Max and Sharon, that was a damn hard thing to do. I rubbed my belly. "Nikita, I need to get going. I need to relax."

"No problem. Are we still on for movies tonight?"

I managed a smile. Ever since all of this shit happened, Nikita and I had become even closer than we already were. She had really been my rock through this ordeal. "Yeah, we're on."

"Alright. I'm coming over around seven."

"Bring popcorn," I said.

"You sure you can eat that?"

"Yeah, I'm sure."

"Okay. You know I gotta make sure you feed my niece or nephew right."

"Don't worry. I'm taking good care of the little one."

"Alright. Don't make me have to call grandma," Nikita said, laughing.

"Whatever," I said, laughing with her. "Go ahead and call her. She's liable to get slapped."

"I know that's right. Anyway, are you sure you don't want to know whether you're having a boy or girl ahead of time?"

"I'm sure. I want to be surprised."

"Haven't you had enough surprises? Besides, it'll make gift buying a lot easier."

"Just buy neutral colors."

"Well personally, I hope it's a girl."

"Why?"

"Because the men in our lives ain't shit."

"I know that's right," I said.

"You sure you love Max, Trina?"

I sighed. "I'm sure."

"Don't take him back, sis."

"I gotta go, Nikita," I said, not wanting to get into it again.

"Okay. I'll see you at seven."

"With popcorn," I reminded her.

"With popcorn. Bye."

"Bye.

I hung up the phone and smiled again. I loved my sister. She'd always been there for me. I knew she was only looking out for my best interest when she said not to take Max back, but making that decision just wasn't as easy for me as it was for her. Whether I liked it or not, Max still had a hold on my heart, and I needed time to figure out what I wanted to do, what I could and couldn't live without. At this point, I was sure of only a few things. One, I loved this child I was carrying and wanted to be nothing but the best mother I could be.

Two, the last thing Sharon's bitch ass would ever be was a grandmother. And three, if Max didn't stop calling and give me what I demanded, he was going to make my decision easier.

Ahmad

I was driving. My music was loud, Jaheim blasting from the speakers, singing about how he forgot to be his girl's lover. I was singing along with him, only I changed the words. If it wasn't for being an ass and messing with my boy's wife, I could remember. If it wasn't for neglecting my vows and not being there when I was needed, I could remember; and if it wasn't for putting others before my family and forgetting what was truly important, I could remember. "I know in my heart that you need love too. I'll spend my life making up to you. Oh, oh, oh, Shay, I forgot to be your husband." My voice was scratchy and I couldn't sing to save my life, but verse after verse, I belted out the song, which I had on repeat.

I sighed as the song ended, and strangled the hell out of my steering wheel as I thought about the over-abundance of drama and stress I endured the night before, all starting when I walked out of my house to go see Mya. Damn, I should have never done that. I knew I was asking for trouble, but I was so pissed off and caught up in my 'fuck it' attitude that I let all logic fly out the window.

Jesus, I thought. *Mya and I almost had sex.*

My thoughts went back to us lying on the bed. The whole time we were there I kept thinking to myself it was wrong. I'm no fool. I knew what Mya was doing when she pressed her behind into my crotch, making me harder than a lead pipe. I could have stopped things right then and there and left. Hell, I should have, but damn it if the arousal didn't feel so good. With every push from Mya's behind my blood flowed more and more and my will became weaker and weaker. I went from thinking about how doing anything would be an act of betrayal to my wife and best friend to thinking how good it would feel to be inside of Mya.

I really lost all sense of right and wrong when Mya started to massage me. Once she did that, the animal instinct in me took over and I wanted nothing more than to enjoy the pleasure of her body. Truthfully, with her lying naked, eagerly waiting and wanting for me to slide inside of her, it's amazing that I didn't do just that. God knows I wanted to. I hadn't had sex in six months, and I was harder than a steel pole left out in the cold—I was ready, willing, able and needing to erupt. But as I was just inches away from the ecstasy between Mya's legs, I looked at her as she lay with her eyes closed and saw not her but Shay. At that moment, I realized that I did indeed want sex, but not with Mya. I wanted my wife. Immediately, Shay's words came to my mind again. *Don't come home.* I wasn't trying to hurt Mya's feelings by leaving the way I did, but I wanted to get home as quickly as possible to save my marriage.

I cruised down I-95 not even giving a second thought to the state troopers hidden in the shadows. I was focused. For better or worse I loved my wife. And I loved my little girl. It was time for me to put my women first. No more idle fantasies about Mya. Shay was all the woman I needed.

As I got to my neighborhood I nearly collided with a locksmith's van. Lucky for me I had quick reflexes and veered over to the right, narrowly avoiding an accident. On any other night I think the van and I would have crashed into each other, but not that night. It was my night. When I finally got to my house, I shut off the engine and jumped out of the car so fast I forgot to take my keys out of the ignition. It was a good thing I'd been too excited to remember to lock my doors. I grabbed the keys and raced to the front door.

I paused at the door to prepare myself. I had no doubt that Shay was gonna give me some serious hell, but I was more than up for the challenge. I was on cloud nine, ready for battle.

And then the cloud number changed.

I stood at my front door confused when my key wouldn't fit into the keyhole.

What the—?

I tried it again. I was excited, after all. Maybe I was holding the key upside down.

What the—?

I tried the key one last time.

"What the fuck?"

I thought about the van I'd almost run into. "No way," I said, shaking my head. "She did not change these locks." I tried the key again and when, like the other times, it didn't work, I rang the bell. I waited for a few minutes and when Shay didn't answer, I pressed the bell again—five times.

"I told you not to bring your ass home," Shay said from behind the door.

Here we go, I thought. "Shay, open the door."

"You should have never walked out of this house, Ahmad."

"Shay, I'm sorry. You're right, I shouldn't have left. Now please open the door, baby, so we can talk."

"We have nothing to talk about," Shay said.

I sighed. "Look, Shay, you have every right to be upset. I know I've been an insensitive jerk to you. I admit it. But was changing the locks really necessary?"

"Only the people who live in this house can have keys, Ahmad," she said bitterly.

"Come on, Shay, stop playing games and let me into my damn house." I knew I was in the wrong but I was losing my patience and cool very quickly.

"I'm not playing games with your ass, Ahmad. And this is not your damn house. You gave it up when you left to be with Mya."

I banged on the door. "Open the damn door, Shay!"

"Go to hell, Ahmad!"

I banged on the door again, harder this time. "Let me in, damn it!"

"Go back to Mya, you son of a bitch!"

I pounded on the door and kicked it. "Stop the bullshit, Shay, and open the fucking door!"

"Fuck you, Ahmad! And if you kick my door one more time, I'm calling the police!"

"The police? Call them for what, trying to get into my own home?"

"I told you, you don't live here anymore!"

I couldn't believe this was happening. "Shay," I said, trying my hardest to calm the anger in my voice. "Open the door, please. Let's talk about this calmly. I told you you have every right to be pissed off. I shouldn't have left. But Shay, I'm back now."   There was a long moment of silence after I spoke. So long, in fact, that I called out her name again. "Shay? Are you there?" A few more seconds of silence passed and then I heard her voice.

"Yes, that's right. His name is Ahmad Jefferson. I'm at 1394 Steel Mill Court. Yes, he's out there right now. He's upset and threatening to break the door down. He's already tried to kick it in. Hurry. It's just me and my baby girl."

What? There's no way I just heard what I think I heard. "Shay, who are you talking to?"

A couple of seconds went by before Shay said, "Ahmad, you have about fifteen minutes before the police get here."

"What? Shay, you did not just call the fucking police."

"Didn't I?"

"You better not have called them!"

"I told your ass to leave!"

I pounded on the door and kicked at the base. "Open this goddamned door, Shay! I'm tired of these fucking games!" I hit the door again.

"Go ahead, asshole! Keep banging!"

I hit the door again. "Goddammit! I'm your fucking husband and this is my home! Now let me the hell in!"

"Go to hell, Ahmad! I told you this is not your home anymore."

"Goddammit, Shay, open the door!"

"No!"

The exchange went on for several minutes. I hit the door again just as I heard a police siren wailing in the distance, getting louder by the second. I turned and looked down the dark street and saw the flashing blue and red lights coming closer. I couldn't believe it; she'd really called them. I turned back to the door. "This is some real bullshit," I said, pounding on it again.

"This is your fault, Ahmad."

"Goddamn," I whispered as a police cruiser came to a stop in front of the house. I turned around and watched as two officers stepped out. One of them I recognized as Mike's boy, Kenny.

"Ahmad, is that you?" Kenny asked, walking up to me, his partner trailing behind.

I sighed and met him halfway. "Yeah, it's me."

"Man, we got a call for a domestic disturbance. What's going on?"

"Nothing, man. Me and my wife are just having an argument. She just called you guys to give me hell."

Kenny looked past me to the house. "I see. Well why don't you go inside and settle this?"

"Man, I'm trying, but she won't let me in the fucking house."

"Don't you have a key?"

"A key?" I dug in my pocket and turned to face my house. "Yeah, I have a damn key," I yelled loudly. "Too bad it won't work on the new fucking locks!" I threw my keys at the front door.

"Why don't you calm down, man?" Kenny suggested, putting his hand on my shoulder.

"Calm down? How the fuck am I supposed to do that? That's my fucking house. My daughter is in there."

"Why don't you let me go and talk to your wife and see what I can do?"

"Fine. Let's go."

"Do me a favor and wait here, alright?"

I gritted my teeth. "Whatever." I stood with my arms folded across my chest as Kenny walked to the door. To think I left Mya, naked and wanting me, to come home to this. She changed the damn locks. That's some real bullshit.

"Mrs. Jefferson, can you open the door?" Kenny said, after he knocked.

"Don't call me Mrs. Jefferson. My name is Shay Reynolds."

"Okay, Shay, can you open the door?"

I shook my head; she used her damn maiden name. "The marriage certificate says Shay Jefferson!" I yelled out.

"That's gonna change, asshole!"

Kenny looked at me. "Relax, man," he said.

I frowned as Kenny turned back around. "Can you open the door Shay?"

"I'm not letting his ass in this house."

"I promise I won't let him inside."

I shook my head and looked over to Kenny's partner, a short dark-skinned brother, who looked like he was fighting a losing battle to keep from smiling. I frowned and looked back to the front door as it swung open. Shay stood defiantly with her hands on her hips.

"Asshole!" she screamed at me.

"Relax, Shay," Kenny said. "Let's try to resolve this as peacefully and quietly as we can."

"The only resolution I need is for his ass to be gone."

"I'm not going anywhere but in my damn house," I said.

"Both of you relax!" Kenny said sternly. "Ahmad, back up a bit and let me talk to your wife."

"Don't call me that!" Shay protested.

I groaned and backpedaled a few steps.

"What's the problem, Shay? Why won't you let Ahmad inside?"

Shay sucked her teeth loudly. "The problem is that that nigga over there decided to run to his best friend's wife's side instead of staying here where his ass belonged. Isn't that something? I mean, did he really think I'd let him disrespect me by being with her ass? What does he take me for? What, he thinks I'm some weak-ass woman who would accept his bullshit about her being a friend in need? Well, I have news for him. You hear that, Ahmad? I have news for your ass! I'm not some silly bitch who'd let you do your thing while I sit and wait for your ass to come home. Go back to her, nigga. Go anywhere you want, but one thing's for sure— you ain't bringing your ass into this house!"

Before Kenny or I could respond, Shay stepped back into the house and slammed the door shut. I sighed while Kenny's partner chuckled. "I don't think this shit is funny," I said, looking at him. He gave me a hard stare that said, *Watch it buddy. I'm wearing the badge and carrying the gun.* I dragged my hand down over my face in frustration and looked away.

"Yo, I think you're gonna have to find another place to crash tonight," Kenny told me.

"Come on. That's my home. My daughter's in there."

"Just let your wife calm down for tonight, Ahmad."

"This is bullshit, Kenny. I pay the damn bills in there."

"Yeah, I know, man, but you know women have right on their side when it comes to us cheating."

"Man, I didn't cheat on her!"

"You didn't?" he asked, looking at me skeptically.

"No. I just went to make sure a friend was okay."

"A friend?"

"A friend."

"Right," Kenny said, obviously thinking I wasn't serious.

"Man, I'm telling the truth! I didn't cheat on my wife!"

"Alright, Ahmad, whatever you say. Just do us both a favor and give up on trying to be here tonight."

"Man . . ."

"I know it's your home too, but I've seen arguments like this escalate into something worse. So let's just keep that from happening and take my advice. Give her time to calm down. Maybe she'll be more willing to talk tomorrow. Alright?"

I looked toward my house and watched as the living room lights went off. *Damn.*

"Alright, Ahmad?" Kenny asked again.

"Yeah, whatever," I said.

"Good. Well, now that my job is done, we're gonna head out of here. Oh, before we go, I gotta ask, this best friend's wife . . . that's Mike's wife, isn't it?

I looked at Kenny as he waited for his answer. I nodded. "Yeah, but believe me, Kenny, it's not what you think."

Kenny put up his hand. "Hey, you don't have to explain anything to me, man."

"I'm for real, Kenny. Nothing's going on between me and his wife."

"Like I said, man, I don't need any explanations. Hell, you wanna fuck her, you go right ahead. I won't say shit."

I gave Kenny a confused stare.

"Look, man, you can bang her all you want. Just between you and me, I don't like Mike's cocky ass. So like I said, I don't have shit to say. Anyway, we need to leave, but I'm gonna need you to leave first."

"Me? Why?"

"Because I need to make sure you take my advice."

I gnawed on my bottom lip and looked back to the house, now completely dark. This was not how I envisioned things going down. "Alright," I said.

"Know where you're gonna stay?"

"Doesn't really matter, does it? Just as long as I'm not here." I walked to my car, got in and drove off. I drove around for an hour after that, unsure about where I wanted to go. I knew I didn't want to go to a family member's house because I didn't want them in my business. I couldn't go by Max's since he was still in the hospital, and going back to Mya was not an option at all. I drove, music on loud, trying to drown out my frustration. I thought about going back to the house, but I was sure the police would have someone there in a hurry if I did. Stressed, I eventually drove to the one place I didn't want to, especially after what happened at the hotel.

"You look like shit, man," I said as Mike opened his front door.

Mike frowned. "Yeah well, I feel like it, too." He stepped to the side and I walked in. He closed the door after me. "What are you doing here at this time?"

It was my turn to frown. "Man, Shay's tripping right now."

"Damn. For real?"

"Yeah. Like I said, we've been having problems." We walked into the living room and sat on the sofa. "So, what's up with you? Why do you look so down in the dumps? And where's Mya?" I hated to put on an act for my boy, but I had no choice.

"Man, I fucked up."

"How?"

"Man, Mya's been gone for the past two days."

"Why? What happened?"

"Some girl I fucked a while back is trying to say she's pregnant by me."

"You for real?"

"Yeah. This girl, Raquel. She called me on my cell after I got home from seeing Max at the hospital, and told me that she was pregnant."

"Damn, man, don't you use a condom with these women?"

"Man, what you think? Of course I do."

"Then how could she say the baby's yours?"

"She's trying to say the condom must have broken."

"That's pretty weak."

"Yeah, I know. She even said that she hasn't been with anyone since we were together."

"I know you don't believe that."

"Of course not, but it doesn't matter because Mya heard my whole damn conversation with her."

"She did?"

"Yeah. Man, I never heard her come in the house. She left right after she cursed me out."

"Damn, man," I said, trying to sound as sympathetic as I could. "And you haven't seen or heard from her since then?"

"Not a peep. Man, this shit is really depressing the hell out of me." Mike hung his head low. He looked so distraught and miserable. I felt for him, but my feelings of sympathy only went so far because I couldn't help but think about how badly Mya was hurting too.

"You try calling her family?"

"Yeah, and they haven't seen or heard from her either. I tried her friends—nothing. Her job—she took a couple of personal days. She's gone, man. Fucking disappeared."

"Geez, man."

"Damn, Ahmad," Mike said, looking as though he were going to cry. "Max was right. This shit hurts far worse than my balls ever did." He sighed heavily. "So anyway, man, enough of my drama. What happened with you and Shay? You never told me what kind of problems y'all were having."

I looked away from Mike and looked down at the carpet. I didn't want to look him in the eye. I stood up. "You have any beer in the fridge?"

"Yeah. Grab me one while you're at it."

I went to the kitchen, grabbed two beers from the refrigerator and went back into the living room. I handed Mike his beer but didn't sit down. I took a long swallow.

"So, what's up, man?" Mike asked. "I spilled my drama."

I exhaled. "Shay and I haven't had sex in more than six months."

Mike's eyes got wide. "What? You're kidding, right?"

"I wish I was."

"Damn! Six months! Bruh, that's half a damn year. You went without ass for half a year. Shit, that makes you a born-again virgin." Mike laughed out loud.

"This shit isn't funny," I snapped.

"My bad, my bad. You're right, that shit ain't funny at all. So, why aren't y'all having sex? You having problems with your tool?"

"Hell no, I'm not having problems. Shit, I wish I was. At least then I'd know why I can't get laid."

"What do you mean?"

"For whatever reason, Shay won't have sex with me and she won't tell me why."

"What do you mean she won't tell you why?"

"Every time I try to have sex with her and she turns me down, I ask her for a reason and she won't give me one. I figured it must have had something to do with me, but she swears it doesn't."

"So, what's her problem then?"

"Fuck if I know. She says it's all about her and has nothing to do with me, but that's all she tells me."

"Damn, Ahmad, that's some horrific shit. Six months? And you haven't stepped out on her?"

"Hell no," I said quickly.

"Why the hell not? Bruh, she hasn't given you any ass for six months. You should have been found some ass on the side."

"Look, man, I'm not like your unfaithful ass, alright?" I said sharply.

"I'm just putting things in perspective and keeping it real for you," Mike said.

I swallowed the rest of my beer angrily and put it down. "Do me a favor and don't. I mean, look at your situation. You had a wife willing to give it up to you and what did you do? You fucked anything that walked. Now your wife is gone and you may have some chick pregnant. I told you, man. I told your ass all that fucking around would come back to haunt you."

Mike set his beer down and stood up. "Look, man, we've been down this road before. Let's not do it again, alright? And as far as that bitch goes, she's not pregnant by me. I'll prove that shit."

"So what if you prove it, man? You already screwed things up and hurt Mya."

"Nigga, Mya may be gone, but I'll get her back."

"You sure about that?" I asked, staring at him hard.

Mike stared back. "I'm sure," he said, although I could see in his eyes that he wasn't. "All I have to do is find her."

"Yeah, right," I said. "That's all it takes because you're the fucking man, right?"

Mike took a step toward me. "You know what, nigga? I'm tired of you and your righteous bullshit. Always talking shit about being a faithful motherfucker. Man, I may do a lot of things, but at least I haven't been living my life like a fucking monk for the past six months."

"Yeah, but you're fucking everybody but your wife."

"Nigga, I've already told you that's just ass. Those other tricks don't mean shit to me."

"And Mya does?"

Mike and I stared at each other for a few seconds as the tension between us grew.

"Mya is everything to me, motherfucker."

"How the hell can you say that but not be faithful to her? And don't give me any bullshit about ratios. Mike, Mya loves your ass, but I'm gonna be straight with you. She's been hurting for a long time. She's cried on my shoulder over the way you run around on her. You're always talking bullshit about how she wouldn't leave you because you're all she knows, but man, you're so far off from the truth. Mya loves you. That's why she's stayed with you. Not because you're her be-all-end-all. Did you ever once consider that?" I stopped talking to take a breath while Mike watched me with burning, unblinking eyes. There was so much more that I wanted to say, but I held my tongue. I'd already taken things too far.

"So Mya's cried on your shoulders, huh?" Mike asked.

"Yeah, she has," I answered.

"So what other intimate moments have passed between you two?"

I closed my eyes a fraction as the tension became charged. "What are you getting at, Mike?"

"You know, it's all starting to make sense," Mike said, his eyes getting darker.

"What do you mean?" I asked again, hoping he wasn't going where I thought he was going.

"I mean I've been racking my brain since Shay made her little comment at the party. I know you said that she was talking shit, but that just never made sense to me. I mean, of all people, why would she call out Mya's name the way she did?"

"What are you getting at?" I asked again, my muscles tightening.

"You know exactly what I'm getting at, nigga. The way you get pissed off when I talk about fucking other chicks, Shay's comment, the way Mya disappeared right afterwards." Mike took another step close to me. "You want to fuck Mya, don't you?" he asked, his voice tight.

"Come on, man," I said, my heartbeat quickening.

"Come on, man nothing. I can see it in your eyes, bitch. You want my wife. Shit, what's to say you haven't already had her? Talking about her crying on your shoulder. what other tender moments have you two shared?" Mike took another step closer. We were inches away from one another. Mike's eyes had gone from brown to black. I clenched fists.

"Mya loves you, Mike."

"You didn't answer my question."

"Mya loves you."

"You betraying-ass nigga!"

Before I had a chance to react, Mike hit me with a blow to my mouth, sending me reeling backwards. "You fucked her, didn't you?" he yelled, rushing me before I could recover. He hit me with another blow, this one connecting with my eye, and then in my midsection, knocking the wind out of me and sending me down to one knee. "I'm gonna kill your ass, nigga!" Mike grabbed me by my collar and brought my face centimeters away from his. I wanted to throw a punch, but I was in too much pain from his heavy body blows. I coughed and grunted as he shook me. "Answer my question, Ahmad. Did you fuck Mya?"

I coughed again and licked at the blood trickling from my mouth. "No," I said, staring at him through clouded vision.

"You're lying, motherfucker. I can see it in your eyes." Mike hit me again in my stomach then pushed me back, causing me to tumble over the coffee table and fall to the ground. I coughed and spit blood as Mike stood, his nostrils flared, his hands clenching and unclenching. He closed his eyes tightly and shook his head. "You're supposed to be my fucking boy," he said.

"Mike, listen to me, man. I didn't sleep with Mya. I swear to you."

"Then what the fuck happened between you two? And don't fucking lie to me."

I took a labored breath. The pain from seeing what my betrayal to my lifelong friend had done almost hurt worse than the physical pain I was feeling. "We shared a kiss," I said softly. "That's all, man. I swear." Mike didn't respond right away, but from the look in his eyes, I could tell that my admission hurt him far worse than any retaliatory blow I could have given. "It wasn't a planned thing, man. It just happened."

"You know where she is, don't you?" Mike asked evenly.

I nodded slowly.

"Where?"

"She's hurting, man."

"Where, motherfucker?"

"She's at the Sheraton at the harbor."

"What room?"

"She's hurting, man."

"What fucking room, nigga?"

"Six-ten."

Mike swung out at a lamp sitting on an end table. "Get the fuck out of my house, Ahmad," he said in a vehement whisper.

I coughed. "Mike, listen to me."

"Nigga, I'm going upstairs to change and to get my gun. If your ass ain't gone by the time I get back down, I promise I will shoot you."

He walked away without saying anything else. As much as I was hurting, I got up as quickly as I could. Onc thing Mike never did was make empty threats. I left the house, got in my car and drove to the nearest motel.

* * * * * *

The night's events faded away as Jaheim's song finished again. I switched from Jaheim's CD to the radio. Ironically enough, "What Kind of Man Would I Be" by Mint Condition was playing. I shook my head and took a quick glance at myself in the rearview mirror. My right eye was swollen, black and blue all around it. My bottom lip was busted and my ribs hurt like hell. I frowned and looked back at the road. My friendship with Mike was undoubtedly over, and my marriage to Shay was questionable.

I drove until I ended up back at my house. I parked the car, got out and walked painfully to the front door. I was about to ring the bell when my neighbor, Ms. Rosario, opened her door.

"Shay's not home."

"She's not?"

"No." Ms. Rosario gave me a disapproving stare.

I sighed. "Do you know where she went or when she's coming back?"

"No."

"Damn."

"And don't think about breaking in. I'll call the police and have them come back if you do."

I looked at Ms. Rosario then walked to my car. I got in and sat behind the wheel. "Damn," I whispered. I turned the key in the ignition, pulled away from the house and drove to the mall to wait for it to open. I had to buy some clothes to wear.

Mike

I was at the bar swallowing down some Hennessey. My hands were unsteady and everything around me seemed to be moving in erratic, slow motion. This was my fifth drink, but the funny thing was, I couldn't tell if it was the alcohol or the emotional pain I was feeling that had me fucked up. I threw down the rest of my drink, enjoying the burn at the back of my throat, and immediately ordered another one. I'd been sitting alone at the bar for the past three or four hours, drinking and reflecting at the same time. In a span of a few days, my life had flipped upside down and was rocking back and forth, teetering on the edge of chaos.

I dropped my head and squeezed my eyes tightly as images of the fight between me and Ahmad flashed in my mind. He'd kissed Mya. I'd had nothing but the image of them kissing and doing more in my head ever since he told me that. He kissed my wife. He betrayed me and our friendship. He was lucky that I didn't have my gun with me downstairs, or else I would have been in jail right now for manslaughter. I had every intention of killing his ass. At the very least, I was going to put him in the hospital with Max.

After I got dressed, I drove to the hotel where Mya was staying. I didn't really know what I was going to say to her, but I had to see her. I stood outside her room for a few minutes doing nothing but breathing, trying to calm myself. It was damn hard because of the thoughts running through my mind.

Ahmad knew where Mya was.

He said all they did was kiss.

He betrayed me.

Mya was in a suite at the Sheraton.

Ahmad knew where she was.

What if they'd done more?

I knocked on the door, my head pounding, my heart beating, my anger rising. A couple of minutes went by without an answer. *I know that nigga better not be up in here.* I knocked again, harder this time. Another couple of seconds crept by before I heard the locks turning.

"You came back," Mya said, opening the door. And then her eyes grew wide. "Mike!"

"Expecting someone else?" I asked, my voice tight, my hands clenched at my sides.

"What are you doing here?"

I didn't answer right away. Another image of her and Ahmad ran through my head, making the anger inside of me burn even hotter. "We need to talk," I said finally.

Mya watched me watching her. She was worried; I could see it in her eyes. "There's nothing to talk about." She tried to close the door, but I wouldn't let her. I pushed against it.

"I just got done kicking Ahmad's ass," I said evenly. Tense seconds went by and then the pressure on the door eased as Mya opened it wide again. She looked at me but didn't speak. I looked at the robe she was wearing; she was naked underneath, and she'd answered the door expecting it to be someone else. I clenched my fists tighter. "We need to talk," I said again, not even trying to hide my anger. Mya looked at me for another second then stepped away from the door. I stepped inside, closed the door behind me and walked into the room, my eyes focusing immediately on a room service cart littered with remnants from a meal for two. I stared at the empty plates and empty wineglasses and breathed slowly. Not wanting to, but needing to know, I looked over to the bed. The sheets were tussled, the covers pulled back and in disarray; the pillows were on the floor. An unwanted image of Ahmad and Mya having sex in the middle of the mattress invaded my thoughts. She was straddled on top of him, chest against chest, moaning softly.

So good . . . So good, Ahmad.

He doesn't make you feel as good as I do, does he?

No. Oh God, no!

I looked away from the bed quickly and looked at Mya. "How the fuck could you do this to me?" I yelled out. "How could you?" I paused, unable to believe she'd done this to me. "How could you fuck Ahmad? You're my wife. You're not supposed to fuck my best friend!" No longer able to hold myself together, I walked to the cart and overturned it, sending the plates, glasses, and wine bottle crashing to the floor and against the wall. "How could you betray me like that?"

"How could I betray you?" Mya snapped. "How dare *you* ask me a question like that. All you've ever done is betray me."

"Ahmad is—was my boy. You don't fuck my best friend!" I looked toward the bed, seeing the image again. "I've given you everything you ever wanted, everything you needed."

"Are you saying that I wanted or needed you to be an unfaithful dog?"

"Those other women don't mean shit to me. I come home to you. It's you I provide for."

"So, because all those other bitches are just fucks I should forgive you? I should be happy that I'm your number one ho?"

"I never called you that!"

"You didn't have to, asshole! That's how you treat me. They don't mean shit. They're just ass. But I take care of you, so I'm the one you take care of. A ho, Mike. That's all I am to you."

"You fucked my best friend! Do you know how much that hurts?"

"How much it hurts?" Mya asked.

Suddenly there was a knock on the door. "Is everything okay in there?"

"Everything's fine!" I yelled.

"You'll have to quiet down or else we will call the police."

I groaned, went to the door and opened it. "I am the fucking police," I said, flashing my badge to a scrawny concierge. I slammed the door in his face and turned back to Mya.

"What bothers you the most, Mike? That it was Ahmad that I slept with, or that I finally decided to play your fucking game?"

I clenched my jaws, but didn't say anything.

"You are a piece of shit, Mike. I let you disrespect me day after day, hoping you'd change, but knowing you wouldn't. I gave you all of me. Everything. My blood, my sweat, my tears. And you want to stand there and talk about how much you've given me? What about heartache? Why didn't you mention all of the goddamned heartache you've given me? You got another bitch pregnant. Do you know how much *that* hurts?"

"I told you that baby's not mine!"

"I don't give a shit! Some other woman is calling you her baby's father. In all of our years together, I've never gotten to say that to you. Never. You want to scream about me fucking Ahmad, which, by the way, didn't happen. You want to scream about how painful it is. I have a question for you. How do you think it feels being a wife and never getting the chance to tell my husband that I'm pregnant by him, while a woman who doesn't mean squat to him gets to say those words? Huh, asshole? How much do you think that shit hurts?"

I stood unmoving as tears erupted from her eyes. I wanted to respond to her but I didn't know what to say. The pain and anger in her voice rocked me; left me speechless. Mya sniffled and wiped away some of her tears.

"I wanted to fuck Ahmad," she said, staring up at me with cold eyes. "I wanted to know what it was like to have a good man inside of me." She paused, giving her brutal words time to sink in. "If Ahmad's love for Shay weren't as strong as it was, he could have had me."

I didn't say anything right away. I stood confused and wondering how I should feel—relieved because the images I'd seen weren't real, or hurt because had he not turned her down, Mya would have allowed another man to enter her. I erupted. "Bitch!" Although it was an unfair double standard, her willingness to cheat was a blow that I couldn't bear. "You may not have fucked him, but you would have. Now you truly are a fucking whore!"

"Fuck you!" Mya screamed back at me.

I lashed out and knocked over the lamp sitting on the night table, causing it to break against the wall.

"What's going on in there?" It was the same concierge. "I don't care if you are the police, I'm calling them anyway!"

I looked at Mya, who stood defiantly with tears trickling from her eyes. "I hate you," she whispered. "I hate you."

A knot rose in my throat. She wanted to fuck Ahmad. That shit hurt me more than anything's ever hurt me before. I turned away from her and went to open the door. Several other people had joined the concierge now. They all stood quietly, watching me, waiting to see what I would do, and wanting to see what I had done. I dug in my pocket, removed my wallet and pulled out a card. I looked at the bony concierge, whose name badge read *TONY*. He seemed to shrink back as though he thought I was about to hit him.

"Here," I said, holding the card out for him. "My office and cell numbers are listed. Call me when you get the bill." I gave him the card then turned around to take one last look in the room. Mya was sitting on the bed, her back facing me. She wanted to fuck Ahmad, but he'd turned her down. I walked through the small crowd and left to drown my sorrows away.

I gulped the rest of my Henny and signaled the waiter for another glass. He gave me a concerned look. I flashed my badge at him. He nodded and poured the drink. When he handed it to me, I snatched it out of his hand and told him to get another one ready. "No, scratch that," I said. "Bring me a whole bottle and a pen and paper."

The bartender walked away and got what I wanted. He put the bottle down in front of me. "Anything else?"

I nodded. "Yeah." I grabbed the pen and paper and started scribbling. "Here," I said, pushing it to him. "In ten minutes call a cab. The paper has my address." I reached into my wallet. "This will cover the fare and his tip."

The bartender looked at me, took the fifty-dollar bill and the paper, and walked away. I lifted the bottle. "Here's to my life." I tipped my head back and swallowed the Henny. That was the last thing I really remembered.

Ahmad

How much more drama would I have to endure? That's what I was wondering while the kids in my fourth period class sat, some doing homework, others drawing pictures, passing notes and talking. I'd given them a free study hall session because I was just too stressed to teach. Hell, all of my classes that day were getting free periods.

How much more drama would I have to endure?

I sighed and stared blankly at the numerous papers I had out on my desk. Like my students, I was pretending to do work. My head ached with a dull pain from the stressful weekend I'd had. Even after getting all of Saturday to calm down, Shay still wouldn't let me in the damn house. That really pissed me off. I'd gone two days without seeing my little girl. I tried to plead my case to Shay, hoping to reach her compassionate side.

"Come on, Shay. I won't even stay. Just let me see Nicole." Once again I was standing outside begging.

"I'm not letting you in here, Ahmad!"

"Damn, Shay. At least bring Nicole out here. I'm her damn father!"

"You should have told yourself that before you walked out of here Friday night."

"Bring my daughter outside, damn it!"

"No!"

"You're being unfair, Shay!"

"Damn right I am! I've earned the right to be as unfair as I want to be."

That was the basic gist of our argument. No matter what I said, Shay wasn't bending. After she threatened to call the police again, I left, homeless and frustrated.

Once again, I had to make a shopping trip to the mall and spend another night at the hotel.

"Ahmad." I snapped out of my trance and looked over to the door. Irene was standing at the threshold. Things had gone back to normal after the tape recorder incident. Actually, they were better than normal. Because she was terrified of the tape ever being heard, Irene went out of her way to make sure that I was satisfied. She smiled whenever she passed me in the hallway. When we were in the teacher's lounge, she'd make small talk and ask me how Shay and Nicole were. These were both things she never did before. Irene was kissing my ass so much, I was sure her lips were imprinted there.

"Yes?" I asked.

"There's a UPS driver in the office. He has some packages for you."

"Packages? For me?" I didn't remember ordering anything. "Are you sure?"

"Well, you're the only Ahmad Jefferson in this school, and that's who he said they were for."

I stood up. Packages? I don't know why, but I didn't have a good feeling about this. "You said packages. How many are you talking?"

"From what I saw, about five boxes."

"Boxes?" I was really not getting a good feeling. "Can you watch the class for me?"

"Only for a few minutes. I have a meeting in fifteen minutes that I need to prepare for."

"Okay. Well, this shouldn't take too long." I hoped.

I headed down to the office, taking short, slow, reluctant steps, the bad feeling getting worse the closer I got. I finally made it there and stepped inside. The UPS driver, a short, pudgy white guy, was standing by the counter holding a clipboard and talking to our secretary, Mrs. Westworth. I didn't say anything right away because I was busy staring at the five boxes stacked beside him.

"There you are," Mrs. Westworth said with a smile.

I forced a smile of my own. "Here I am."

The UPS driver turned away from our secretary and lifted his clipboard and a pen toward me. "I just need you to sign for these and I'll be on my way."

I looked from the boxes to the clipboard, then at the driver. "Are you sure those are for me?"

The driver nodded. "You're Ahmad Jefferson, right?"

"Depends on what's in those boxes. Who sent them?"

"I don't know. There's no return address."

"You weren't given a name?"

The driver shook his head.

"Nothing?"

"No."

"So they were just sent by anonymous?"

The UPS driver looked at me for a short second then pushed the clipboard to me. "Sign by the X," he said, the pleasantry in his voice gone.

I looked from him to the boxes. "Do I have to accept them?"

The driver had had enough. "Look, man. Just sign by the X so that I can get back out on the road. I don't care what you do with the stuff afterwards."

I sighed and took the clipboard, feeling like I was signing away my last rights.

"Thank you," the driver said. He took back his board, waved goodbye to Mrs. Westworth and left. I didn't move. Five boxes. Five U-Haul big-enough-to-hold-sweaters-pants-shirts-shoes-and-a-whole-bunch-of-other-things boxes.

"Well, aren't you going to open them?"

I gave Mrs. Westworth a hard look, causing her to turn away. I went back to staring at the boxes. All five of them. The dull pain at the back of my head had moved to the front and wasn't so dull anymore. I took a hesitant step to the first box and placed my hand on it lightly as if it were a bomb set to go off at the slightest touch. I pulled on the duct tape holding it closed. I paused after tearing off the last piece, took a slow, deep breath, then opened the box. "Shit," I said with a long sigh.

It was stuffed with clothing—my clothing from the house that I couldn't get into. "Shit," I said again softly. "I don't believe this." I ignored Mrs. Westworth as she peeked at me from behind the counter, and opened another box. Again I found my things inside—underwear, socks, T-shirts. "Shit."

Except for Mrs. Westworth, the office was mercifully empty. I sat down on the bench usually reserved for students who were in trouble, and dropped my chin to my chest. How much more drama would I have to endure? That was my 'to be or not to be' question. Now I knew my answer.

I dragged my hand down my face. I couldn't believe Shay had taken things this far. Being upset was one thing, but this was too much. I stood up and looked at Mrs. Westworth. "Is there room in the back for these?"

Mrs. Westworth nodded. "Mr. Dunbaldt isn't in today. His office is open."

"Okay." I moved to pick up the first box and then stopped. I turned back to our secretary. "Do we have duct tape?

After resealing the boxes, I moved them into our assistant principal's office and rushed back to the classroom. I'd reached the end of my rope. I was tired of playing Shay's game. I walked in the room and grabbed my coat.

"Mr. Jefferson," Irene said, standing. "I told you I had a meeting."

"I'm leaving," I said bluntly.

"What? You can't leave."

"I have a family emergency. I'm leaving."

"What about your classes?" Irene asked.

"I'm sure you'll think of something." I turned and left, not caring if she had anything else to say. I got in my car and raced home. I didn't care if Shay called the cops. There was no way I wasn't getting into my damn home this time. Twenty minutes later I pulled to a stop in front of my home and jumped out of the car. I was a soldier, walking to battle.

I walked straight up to the door and pounded. "Shay, open up this goddamned door right now!" I waited for a few seconds then pounded again when she didn't answer. "I know you're home, Shay. Open up this fucking door or I swear I'll break it down. And I don't give a shit if you call the police or not. This is my fucking home too!" I beat on the door again. "Open it up, Shay. Now!" Another couple of seconds passed without a response. I thought about the boxes filled with my things back at the school. "Alright. You want to play like that? Fine. Don't say I didn't warn you." I backed up a few steps to get a nice start to throw my elbow into the door. Would I be able to break it down? I had no idea, but I was damn sure gonna try.

I was about to charge forward when I heard the locks turning. When I heard her feet shuffling away, I walked to the door, placed my hand on the knob and breathed a sigh of relief when it turned. I pushed the door open and walked inside. I couldn't keep the smile from forming on my face; in spite of everything, it felt good being back home. I closed the door, walked toward the living room and let my smile drop when I saw Shay on the sofa.

I opened my mouth to speak, but before I could get a word out, she put up a finger, signaling for me to wait. She got up, went to the bedroom and closed the door.

When she came back, I didn't wait for any cues. "I got your packages," I said.

With a satisfied look on her face, Shay said, "There's a couple more in the other bedroom."

"That was real dirty of you, Shay."

"No dirtier than you leaving your family for another woman."

I bit my bottom lip in an effort to keep from snapping. Now that I was back in the house, no matter how pissed off I was about the boxes, I had to remain as calm, cool and collected as I could. Besides, I really missed being at home with Shay and Nicole and I just didn't want to argue anymore. "Look, Shay," I said, keeping my voice as even as I possibly could. "I'm not trying to go down this road with you again. Whether you believe it or not, I didn't leave to be with Mya like you're thinking. I was just trying to be a good friend because I know she needed one."

"Then you should have told her to call someone else. You had a family."

"I *have* a family, Shay," I said.

"Do you?"

I clenched my jaws. I was trying to be calm and civil, but she was making it damn hard. "Yes, I do, so stop acting like our marriage is over."

"I'm acting? If anyone was acting like our marriage was over, it was you! You left, asshole. You walked out and left my ass alone with *our* child."

"I was trying to be a good friend!"

"You should have tried being a good husband first!"

"A good husband? That's all I've ever fucking been to you! I've always been there for you! Anything you needed, no matter what the hell it was, any goddamned time, all you had to do was ask and I made sure you had it. A good husband? What about you being a good wife? How about pleasing your husband once in a while? God knows I deserve it for all the shit I've put up with these past six months. No communication, no affection, no sex . . . What kind of shit is that? Any man in my position would have fooled around on your ass, but I didn't. Why? Because I love you. But you know what? That didn't get me shit but the humiliation of sitting in a classroom and having all of my things boxed and delivered to me for everyone to see."

"You know what, Ahmad? You are a selfish son of a bitch! I can't believe you're coming out of your mouth talking about me being a good wife. So you haven't gotten some ass. Is that the end of the world? Is that all you care about? I mean, did you ever once try to think past satisfying that dick of yours? There's a reason why I didn't want to have sex, Ahmad, and it had nothing to do with you! Nothing. I was going through some things. Things that I wasn't ready to talk about. All I asked was for you to give me some time to sort through my issues. That's all."

"I did that, Shay. Month after goddamned month, that's all I did. How much more damn time am I supposed to give you?"

"As much as I need, jerk!"

"As much as you need? What about me? What about my needs?"

"To hell with your needs!"

"To hell with my needs? What kind of shit is that to say? How about to hell with your imaginary needs?"

"Fuck you, Ahmad!"

"I wish you would fuck me, Shay," I snapped.

"Asshole! Get out!"

"Get out? You must be out of your damn mind if you think I'm leaving."

"You did it before, so you can do it again. Get out!"

"I'm not leaving," I said adamantly.

"Fine. Then Nicole and I will." Shay made a move to head toward the bedroom, but I blocked her before she could go too far. "Get out of my way, Ahmad."

"You're not going anywhere with my daughter, Shay," I said sternly as we stood just inside the hallway to the bedroom.

"Get out of my way, Ahmad," she demanded again. She tried to push her way past me, but I wasn't budging.

I put my hands on her shoulders and pushed her back a step. "I said you're not taking Nicole anywhere. If you want to leave, fine, then you can leave. But my daughter is staying here with me."

"Get your hands off of me, Ahmad." She pushed my arms and tried again to move past me.

I stuck out my arms and pushed her back again. "Nicole is staying with me, Shay."

"Get off of me, asshole! Nicole is not staying with your unfaithful ass!" Once again she shoved my hands away and tried to force her way by, but to no avail. I was dead serious—Nicole wasn't going anywhere. I raised my hands to push her back again, but instead of getting her shoulders, I missed and pushed her face instead, causing her to fall and bang the back of her head against the wall.

"Asshole!" she screamed. "You abusive piece of shit! I can't believe you just did that."

"Come on, Shay. You know that was an accident."

"Accident, my ass!" She stood up and rubbed the back of her head. "I can't believe you put your hands on me."

"You put your hands on me first, damn it. Anyway, stop exaggerating. I didn't push you that hard."

"Tell that to my lawyer, ass!"

"What?"

"You heard me."

"What do you mean by that?"

"I want a fucking divorce, Ahmad."

It took me a second to respond. "A divorce? You're kidding, right?"

With eyes that could kill, Shay said, "Do I look like I'm kidding?"

"That's not funny, Shay."

"I said I wasn't kidding, Ahmad. I want a damn divorce."

I stared at my wife for a long, intense couple of seconds. She'd just said that she wanted a divorce. I shook my head. "You don't mean that," I said quietly.

Shay tightened her lips and cocked her neck back a bit. "Don't I?"

"No . . . you don't."

"Fuck you, Ahmad. I want a divorce and I mean that with my whole being. I want a divorce."

"Come on, Shay. Mailing my shit was one thing, but you're taking things way too far now."

"Go to hell, Ahmad. You took things too far when you walked out of this house."

"But nothing happened!"

"I don't give a damn, Ahmad. You still left Nicole and me for her."

"It wasn't like that, Shay, and you damn well know it!"

"Oh, yes it was!" Shay screamed back at me. "You left me home alone with your daughter to take care of Mya. I don't give a shit if anything happened or not. You still left. You still chose her over your family. I want a divorce, Ahmad. I'm tired of your shit. I've had enough."

"Shay—"

"Don't say another word, Ahmad, and get the fuck out of my way before I scream."

I stared down at her, but didn't move. She wanted a divorce. Demanded it. I didn't want to believe it. Shay glared at me with hard eyes. I wanted to say something, anything to change the direction of our conversation, but I could tell by her stare that it would have been an impossible task. Her mind was made up. As painful as it was, I had to accept that. I lowered my head and let out a long sigh. "It doesn't have to be this way," I said.

Shay looked up at me. "You made it like this," she said bitterly. She forced her way past me and headed to the bedroom.

I called out her name. I didn't know what I was going to say. "Shay," I called out again. Just like the first time, she refused to stop. "Shay, wait. Please?" Her response was to slam the bedroom door.

I sighed and leaned against the wall. Thirty minutes later, Shay came out of the room with Nicole in her arms and a bag around her shoulder. I started to say something, but she put up her hand. "Don't say a word, Ahmad, and don't you dare try to stop me."

"Shay—"

"Goodbye, Ahmad." She walked past me, slowly, daring me to touch her. I thought about it, but decided against it. Shay walked out the door, and I was fearful that she had walked out of my life too.

Max

I hung up the phone when Trina's answering machine came on. I'd been doing this for the past day now, hoping that by some miracle she'd answer. I'd given up on leaving any more messages after the last million that I left. I knew she said not to call her, but it was hard not to. She was having my baby.

I sighed and groaned as I got up slowly from my cousin's couch. I'd been staying with him since getting out of the hospital. My body still hurt, but this was the best I'd been feeling since everything happened. My wounds were healing, the bruises were disappearing; soon I'd be back to my old self. Well, not exactly. After everything I'd been through, my old self was the one thing I wouldn't be going back to. Mercifully, God had seen fit to spare my sad life and give me a chance to turn things around. And believe me, I wasn't gonna let this second chance go to waste.

Since I couldn't get Trina back right away, I decided to put my focus on making the groups that I was managing as large as I could. I wanted my female singers to be divas, and my rappers to be the next 50 Cent. With all of the ideas that had been running through my head, I was determined to make them all a success. Like I said, I was gonna make my second chance count. I didn't know what was gonna happen between me and Trina, but I at least wanted to try everything in my power to make sure that my baby's future would be a comfortable one. I wanted to be a good father like mine wasn't. Hell, I wanted to be a good husband too.

I sighed and looked down at the phone. How much time did Trina need? Had she listened to any of my messages? I poured my heart out as much as I could, and meant every word I said. Had anything I said affected her? And if so, how? Damn, this was frustrating. All for Sharon's pussy, I thought. I was putting myself through hell just for that.

I clicked off the television that I hadn't been watching for the past two hours. I was standing for no reason in particular other than the fact that I was tired of sitting on my ass. I looked at the time; it was almost four o'clock. Ahmad should be home, I thought. I was surprised I hadn't heard from him since I had come out of the hospital. Mike, I didn't expect to hear from with all of the drama he had going on with Mya, but Ahmad . . . Knowing him, he'd been caught up in schoolwork. I grabbed the phone and dialed his cell number. It was funny, but a few weeks earlier, Mike would have been the one I called, but the past couple of weeks had really changed my mindset. Now I looked at the value of what I had from the perspective that Ahmad used to preach to us about.

His cell rang several times and just when I thought his voice mail was going to click on, he answered. "Hello?"

"Yo, what's up, man?"

"Max?"

"Yeah it's me," I said, easing down to the couch again. "Damn, a brother gets shot and his boys forget all about him. 'Sup with that? I haven't heard from you or Mike since I was in the hospital."

Ahmad sighed heavily into the phone. "My bad, man. I've just had a lot of shit going on. How're you feeling, man?"

"I'm doing alright. I'm staying at my cousin's place right now. I'm getting stronger each day. My wounds are healing. Other than not hearing from Trina, I guess I can't complain too much."

"You haven't spoken to her?"

"Nah. Not since I saw her at the hospital."

"Damn, sorry to hear that."

"Yeah. She says she needs some time to figure shit out. I don't want to give it to her, but she's not returning any of my calls, so I guess I have no choice. Anyway, enough about that. You said you had a lot of shit going on. What's up?"

Ahmad gave another sigh. "Drama. Nothing but drama."

"Drama? I thought you handled your issues with your principal?"

"I did."

"So, what's up? What other drama you having? You and Shay alright?" Ahmad didn't say anything. It didn't take a genius to know that's where the drama was coming from. "What's going on with you guys?" I heard another sigh then silence. There was no doubt from his reluctance to speak that things were bad. "Talk to me, man. What's going on?"

"Man, shit's just all fucked up right now. My relationship with my wife, my friendship with Mike and Mya. Man..."

As his voice trailed off, I said, "Hold up, hold up. What the hell's going on? What happened with you and Shay? And what's this about things being fucked up with Mike?"

"Shay moved out today."

"What? What the hell happened?"

"She accused me of sleeping with Mya."

I didn't say anything right away. Had he really just said what I thought he'd said? "Run that by me again."

"Shay accused me of cheating on her with Mya. She took Nicole and left."

"Mya? Mike's Mya?"

"Yeah."

"Mike, as in our boy?"

"Yeah," Ahmad said almost inaudibly.

"Hold up! What do you mean she accused you of sleeping with Mya? Ahmad . . . did you and Mya fuck?" I couldn't believe I was hearing what I was hearing. *Sleeping with Mya? What the fuck?* Had he really done that? Had he really betrayed Mike like that? I didn't want to believe it. I couldn't believe it. No way, no how had Ahmad broken the sacred rule of friendship among men: Under no circumstance did you ever mess with, flirt with, or sleep with your boy's girl, wife, trick on the side, or ex. Never. Messing with a female your boy messes with or messed with is the ultimate, unforgivable act. I just couldn't believe Ahmad would cross that line. "What's going on, Ahmad?" I asked. "Please tell me you didn't do that."

A few seconds of silence passed before Ahmad answered me. "No, I didn't sleep with Mya."

"So, what's up with Shay's accusations?"

"Man, I didn't fuck Mya," Ahmad said.

"I know, man. You told me that already."

"I didn't . . . but I wanted to."

I didn't respond right away. I just sat, unmoving, digesting what he'd just admitted to me. I squeezed my eyes tightly and clenched my jaws. "Ahmad, I think you need to come over here and explain what the fuck's going on."

* * * * * *

I sat silently and stared at Ahmad with nothing but straight disappointment and disbelief coming from my eyes. He'd just given me the low down on all the drama he'd been going through; from him and Shay not having sex to Mya reaching out to him for comfort; from ending up at a hotel with her to being kicked out of his own house; from being beaten up by Mike to Shay mailing his shit to the school and demanding a divorce. His life had been nothing short of a real life soap opera.

I hadn't said a word the whole time he'd spoken. I just sat and listened as he explained how things had gotten out of hand, thinking over and over that he'd betrayed Mike. It's true that Mya put up with a lot of shit from Mike that she didn't deserve, but still, that was their business, their marriage, and Mya was Mike's wife. And Mike was our boy. Nothing should have ever happened between them. Ever.

"I don't even know what to say, man," I told him honestly.

Ahmad shrugged his shoulders and frowned. "There's not much you can say. I fucked up. I know, and now I'm paying for it."

"You think you and Shay are done for good?"

"I don't know."

"Jesus, Ahmad. This is some serious shit. I know the last thing you need is for someone to be on your case, but, man, this shit is fucked up. Mike's your boy. It don't matter that he's not a saint. He's still your boy. You should have never crossed the line and fucked with Mya."

"I know, man," Ahmad said, his voice filled with regret.

But I wasn't finished. "I gotta give Mike some credit, man. We're boys, but I probably would have shot your ass if you betrayed me like that." Ahmad looked up at me. I returned his surprised stare with a dead serious one of my own, because I was serious. I would have kicked his ass like Mike did, and I definitely would have shot him, boys or not. But he didn't fuck with Trina, so I didn't have to worry about that, and even though he could have, he didn't fuck Mya. "I guess you haven't spoken to Mike since you two had it out, huh?"

Ahmad shook his head. "Nah. Man, I really regret this shit. I've known Mike too long. This should have never happened."

I sighed. "Alright, look, I don't know what good it's gonna do, but I'm gonna give Mike a call and see where his head is at."

"Thanks, man."

"Don't thank me, bruh. For real, I don't know if there's any way to save y'all's friendship."

Ahmad frowned. "Yeah, I know."

I stared at Ahmad for a couple of seconds then puffed my cheeks out like Dizzy Gillespie and blew out air slowly. "Look, man. Why don't you go and try to make things right with Shay? I'll deal with Mike. Hopefully he ain't out on the streets looking for you."

Ahmad nodded and leaned forward, intertwining his fingers and resting his elbows on his knees. "Yo, I know what I did was wrong, and I know I've probably ruined my friendship with Mike for good, but I hope that you and I are still cool."

I looked at Ahmad for a sec and then said very seriously, "You crossed a line that should have never been crossed man," I stressed once again.

"I know," Ahmad answered.

"What were you thinking?"

Ahmad shrugged. "I was just trying to be a good friend."

"If Mike heard you say that, you know what he'd say, right?"

Ahmad sighed. "With a friend like me, who needs enemies?"

I frowned. "Go and try to save your marriage, man."

"Are we cool?" Ahmad asked.

I gave a subtle nod. "Yeah, man. We're cool."

"Thanks," Ahmad said, standing up. "I'll catch you later. And I hope things change with Trina."

I stood up slowly. "So do I, bruh."

After Ahmad left, I went back into the living room and called Mike's cell. I didn't get him so I left a message asking him to call me back. So much had changed for all of us. Mike and Mya were on their way to a likely divorce; Mike and Ahmad would probably never be boys again. This, of course, had a direct effect on the bond the three of us had. Shay and Ahmad were on eggshells, and Trina and I were in a state of limbo. I sighed again and sank back into the couch. This was not how things were supposed to be.

Mike

I opened my eyes when the sound of rushing water disturbed my sleep. Mya. She was back. *Thank God*, I thought. I'd been missing her like crazy since I walked away from her at the hotel. Yeah, she had cut me deeply and pissed me off to no end when she talked about wanting to fuck Ahmad, but I couldn't deny the fact that I loved her like crazy. I know I didn't show that by running around on her every chance I got, but it was true. She meant the world to me. Now that she was back, even though it wasn't gonna be easy, I planned on showing her how much she meant. I was surprised that she didn't wake me up when she came in. Was that a good or bad sign? Oh, well. She was back and that's what mattered.

I sat up in the bed, my head throbbing from another night of drowning my sorrows. I looked toward the bathroom and smiled. This would be the last time my head would hurt; my woman was back. I got out of bed slowly, made my way to the bathroom and pushed the door open. Steam whispered past me. She was in the shower. I smiled again, slipped out of my boxers, and moved to the tub, my manhood rising at the thought of making things up to my wife in a big way.

Unfortunately, that never happened.

When I pulled the shower curtain aside, I got the shock of my life. Standing in the shower with water running down their backs were two marble-white, oversized, identical blond women who could have easily made Sandra Bernhard look sexy. My dick shrunk within seconds. "Who the fuck are you, and what the fuck are you doing in my fucking bathroom?"

The girls looked from me to my now pruned dick, then to each other, laughing. I quickly backed away, reached for my boxers, and put them back on. I stepped to the tub as they turned off the water. "Who the fuck are you two?" I asked, opening the curtain again. I made sure to keep my eyes focused on their zit-covered faces; I'd already seen enough of their rolls.

The females giggled again and the slightly larger one spoke to her sister. "I told you he wouldn't remember."

"Remember what?" I yelled.

"Buying us drinks at the bar and then bringing us here to play doctor," the other sister answered.

As both women laughed, I shook my head. "No way! No fucking way did I sleep with you two whales."

The larger female gave me a nasty look and said, "You did and you liked it."

"Give it to me, big momma! Give it to Daddy!" the other sister sang.

As both sisters erupted with laughter, I shook my head again. There was no way. "I'm a fucking cop!" I yelled. "If you don't get your disgustingly fat asses out of my tub out of my fucking house I will shoot you for making ugly look good."

Without hesitation, the sisters stepped out of the tub. My blood pressure rose a notch or two higher as water dripped from their bodies to the floor.

"You're a real asshole!" the larger sister yelled. Before I knew what was happening, she spit in my face and stormed past me. I wiped the saliva away, but I didn't react. I just wanted them gone.

"You have two seconds to grab your extra large shit and leave!"

"Asshole!" the sister yelled again, grabbing her clothing from the floor. Giving them just enough time to slip on their bras and underwear, I quickly ushered them downstairs and out the back door. As I slammed the door shut behind them, they both yelled, "Asshole!"

I listened to them dress and curse me out in the backyard, and when they finally left, I leaned my forehead against the door and sighed. *Jesus Christ*, I thought. I couldn't believe what just happened. Shit. I didn't want to believe it. I thought long and hard about the previous night as my head ached. I remembered doing what I'd done every night since I left Mya at the hotel; I was on patrol, driving around aimlessly, not caring about any crime that could have been happening, and focused instead on Mya, Ahmad, and Raquel's claim that I got her pregnant. Once my shift was over, I went to the bar to drink myself silly once again. By this time, the bartender didn't need my address on a piece of paper. I didn't remember much after that. I was at the bar destroying my liver. Music was on and so was the muted television above the bar, set to ESPN.

Overweight twins. Where did they come in?

Think.

People were talking around me. Some might have even been talking to me. Maybe I talked to them.

Twins?

I remember glass shattering and then giggling. I think I looked toward the end of the bar to see who had dropped the glass. Overweight twins? No. Just two blondes.

Sitting.

Laughing.

Identical and looking good.

Shit.

I slammed my palm against the door a few times. This was by far the lowest I'd ever sunk. "Jesus." I pushed away from the door and to add insult to injury, slipped on a small puddle of water one of the twins left behind. I fell to the ground and stayed there for a few minutes. I'd finally hit rock bottom. *How's that for symbolism*? I chuckled a few times at the irony then the chuckling turned into an outright uproar. I was pathetic. My situation was pathetic. And for some reason, that was the funniest shit to me.

I laughed for a while, wiping tears from the corners of my eyes. I was a joke. For all of my talk and thinking that I was the man with my extramarital escapades, I was nothing but a joke, and I deserved everything I was getting.

I stood up and looked around at the kitchen. It was a wreck. Dishes were piled in the sink, overflowing onto the counter beside various cartons of take out food. For the first time, I noticed that there was a foul odor in the air. I rubbed my bald head and sighed. It was time for some serious clean up, but I didn't mean just the house. I'd hit bottom, and with nowhere to go but up, it was time to climb my way back up. No more drinking, no more meaningless fucking. My life had to change. Was there a chance of getting Mya back? I didn't know, but I was damn sure gonna try.

First things first; I had to see what the deal was with Raquel. I was almost positive that she was trying to trap me, but I had to be sure, so I'd take her to the doctor my damn self and see if she was pregnant for real. If she was, I'd have no choice but to wait until she had the baby to see if I was the father. I wasn't trying to have a baby with her, but if the baby turned out to be mine, I'd step up to the plate. My only concern was that if I somehow managed to get Mya back then found out I was a father, what would happen to Mya and me? How would she handle it? That was the ultimate question. Of course at this point, there was no point in wondering about that.

I dropped my chin to my chest and stared down at the ground. One step at a time, I reminded myself. I moved to the sink to get cracking on the heap that was there but then I thought about the twins again. "Fuck this," I said, throwing the sponge down. I turned and headed upstairs. I had to throw away the bed sheets and disinfect the bathroom before I did anything else.

It took all day, but I'd finally gotten the house cleaned. I sat on the couch, freshly showered, and grabbed the phone. Now that I'd taken care of the house, I had to move on to the next step. I had to call Raquel. This would be the first time I'd spoken to her since she'd called me talking about being pregnant. I wasn't in the mood for it, but I knew there'd be stress regardless. I fished in my wallet and removed the phone number she'd given me. I was just about to dial when the phone rang. I looked at the caller ID and saw Max's number appear. Damn, with everything that had been happening, I hadn't even called to check up on him. I hit the talk button. "Yo, what's up Max?" I asked, feeling guilty.

"Hey, what's going on, Mike? I haven't heard from you in a while, man. You forget about me?"

"Nah, man. I've just had a lot of shit going on. My bad. How you feeling?"

"I'm alive, dude, and that's what matters."

"I hear that."

"Anyway, the real question, man, is how are you?"

"What do you mean?"

There was silence for a couple of seconds then Max said, "I talked to Ahmad, man."

Just the mention of Ahmad's name caused me to grind my teeth. "Oh yeah?" I said, my blood pressure rising.

"Yeah. He came over and we talked."

I scowled. "What about?"

"He told me what happened with him and Mya, and he told me what went down with you and him."

I didn't say anything right away as I thought about the way I'd hit Ahmad after he'd 'fessed up to kissing Mya. "Fuck that nigga," I said, grabbing the remote from the cushion and throwing it across the room. "He's lucky I didn't shoot his bitch ass. That motherfucker was supposed to be my boy, Max."

"I know, man," Max said.

"Then how the fuck could he betray me like that?" I slammed my fist down on the coffee table in rage.

"Yo, calm down, Mike."

"Calm down?" I stood up and paced angrily about my living room, my hands itching to strike out at something. "That shit's easy for you to say, man. It wasn't your wife that he kissed and damn near had sex with. Put yourself in my shoes first and then talk to me about calming the fuck down!" I balled my fist and punched the wall, creating a nice sized hole. "Boys, man. We were fucking boys. You don't do that shit." I punched the wall again, making the hole a little bigger.

"I know it's fucked up man. Believe me, if I was in your position, I'd be pissed off and wanting to kill the nigga too. But I'm asking you, as hard as it is, to calm down and listen to what I have to say."

"Would you be able to calm down, Max?" I waited eagerly for his answer.

"No man, I wouldn't," he replied.

"Aw'ight then."

"Yeah, but I'd hope you would do your best to get me to do just that and listen to some sound advice you would have for me."

I chuckled. "Sound advice, huh?"

"Yeah, man."

I sighed and sat down on the couch. "The only advice I could use would be the best way to dispose of Ahmad's body."

"Come on, man. You don't mean that."

"Don't mean it? Max, you have no idea how serious I am."

"Mike, bruh, you're pissed off and that's understandable, but don't be irrational."

"Irrational?"

"Yeah. Man, you won't like this, but if it wouldn't have been Ahmad, it would have been someone else."

"You're right, Max. I don't like that."

"It's the truth, bruh. Face it. You treated Mya like shit for a lot of years. I mean, you gave her what she needed, but you were never the man that she needed you to be. I know you're probably pissed that I'm saying that, but believe me, if anyone can say this shit to you, it's me because I did the same shit with Trina. Mike, you broke Mya down emotionally and she reached out to Ahmad, a friend who's always been there for her. Yes, he was wrong. Dead wrong. But Mike, he didn't fuck her. He stopped when another nigga wouldn't have. And whether you like it or not, you have to give him some credit for that.

"None of us are perfect, bruh. I know you're pissed, and things may never be the same, but maybe you should think things through before you just let the friendship go. You can't lay all of the blame on him, man. You gotta be willing to take some yourself. You and Ahmad have a lot of history, man. Shit, we all do. It might be rough, but I think it's a friendship worth keeping."

"You done?" I asked as Max got quiet.

"Were you listening to me?"

"I heard," I said.

"So, what do you think?"

"I think you need to be in my shoes first and then speak to me."

Max sighed. "Come on, man, don't be bull-headed about this."

"Fuck you, Max!" I yelled. "How the fuck are you gonna tell me to not be bull-headed? The nigga had his tongue in my wife's mouth!"

"It takes two though, man."

"Ahmad should have never been the one! I don't give a fuck if he stopped." There were a few moments of silence on the phone after my outburst. My heart was beating heavily as pictures of Ahmad and Mya lying together ran through my mind. I knew that what Max said was true—another brother would have taken Mya for the ride she wanted, but still...It might have taken two, but Ahmad should have never been in the running in the first place.

I shook my head to make the pictures go away and sighed. I didn't mean to blow up on Max like that. I knew he was only trying to help, but he just didn't have any idea how bad I was hurting. Mya's betrayal was one thing, but Ahmad's was worse. Women come and go, but you're always supposed to be able to rely on your boys. "Look, man, I'm sorry about blowing up. This is not an easy pill for me to swallow."

"I know, man. I'm just saying think about things before you make your decisions. Ahmad wasn't the only one in the room, but he was the only one who stopped."

I frowned. "Yeah, I got you. Listen, I'm gonna get off this phone and cool down."

"Aw'ight, man. Take it easy, and come and check on a brotha when you can."

"Yeah, I'll do that."

I hung up the phone, slouched down in the couch and closed my eyes. This was some real frustrating shit.

Mya.

Ahmad.

Raquel.

Shit. I still had to deal with that issue.

I groaned and grabbed the phone again. As much as I didn't want to, I dialed her number.

"'Bout time you called me back," Raquel said, when she answered the line. I cursed to myself silently. I was so frustrated after my talk with Max that I'd forgotten to call from my cell phone. Now Raquel had my home phone number. Damn.

"Get dressed," I said.

"Excuse me?"

"Get dressed," I said again. "I'm coming over to pick you up in twenty minutes."

Raquel sucked her teeth loudly. "First of all, I ain't going nowhere with your ass, and second of all, even if I was, just where the hell would you be taking me?"

"I want proof, Raquel. You say you're pregnant, then I wanna see the fucking test results. Get dressed, because whether you like it or not, you're going with me to the walk-in clinic to have a pregnancy test done."

Raquel sucked her teeth again. "I ain't going nowhere."

I strangled the phone as I fought to keep my composure. "Raquel," I said, my voice tight. "Twenty fucking minutes. Be dressed and outside or else I will kick your door down and drag you out by your hair."

"Come near my apartment and I will call the police on your ass," she threatened.

I chuckled. "Raquel, I am the police. Remember?" Twenty minutes." I hung up as she started to say something, and tossed the phone to the side. "Goddammit!" I yelled. I stood up and went upstairs to change, praying that something good would happen for me and I would find out that Raquel was lying.

Trina

I felt it. For the very first time I felt it. There wasn't much force behind it, but I felt it. My baby kicked. I smiled and placed a hand on my slightly swollen stomach. My child. Max's child too. I sighed. I was missing Max like crazy. Surprisingly, he hadn't called me for the past couple of weeks. I know that's what I demanded because I needed the time, but with each day that passed by without a call from him, I found myself hoping that the next time the phone rang, it would be him. It never was. And now I felt the baby—our baby— kick.

I rubbed my stomach. *Max should be here*, I thought. I reached for the phone. I was still hurt by what he'd done, but the anger wasn't there anymore. Well, it wasn't as strong. I hit the talk button. He'd given me the time I needed and now it was time to see if I could move on with him. I knew the only way I would be able to determine that would be for him to come back home.

"Trina?" Max said as he answered.

I hesitated for a brief moment. "Yeah, it's me," I said softly.

"Is everything okay? Are you and the baby okay?"

I smiled. "Yes. We're both fine."

Max let out a sigh of relief. "Good."

"So how have you been feeling, Max?"

"I'm good," Max answered, his voice deepening a bit. "Not one hundred percent, but I'm getting there."

"Are you comfortable there by your cousin?"

"I'm as comfortable as I can be. Nothing like being home, of course."

"Of course," I replied. We were both silent for a second or two.

"So, umm . . . how have you been?" Max asked, breaking the silence. "Work and everything going alright?"

"Work's fine, and I've been good. Better than good, actually. Especially today."

"Why? What happened today?"

"I felt the baby kick."

Another couple of seconds passed then in a soft, slightly deflated tone, Max said, "Really?"

My smile grew wider. "Yes."

"Wow."

I opened my mouth to say something more, but paused. I was about to say the most difficult thing I'd had to say since finding out that he'd been sleeping with Sharon. As unwanted images popped into my mind, I wondered if I was doing the right thing. I took a slow, deep breath and released it, forcing the painful images to escape with my air. It was time to move forward—or at least it was time to try. "Max," I said finally.

"Yeah?"

"I've made a decision."

"You have?"

"Yes."

Max breathed heavily into the phone. "What is it?"

"I . . . I want you to come home."

"You do?"

"Yes."

"Baby, I've missed you," Max said.

As teardrops leaked from my eyes, I said, "I've missed you too."

"Trina, I'm sorry. Sorry for everything."

"I know, Max."

"I just want to make you happy. You and our baby."

"This won't be easy for me, Max. I won't get over what you did overnight. It's going to take time. A long time."

"I know, baby."

"Don't expect things to be the same as they were before. I've changed."

"Baby, I'm not the same."

"You're going to have to sleep in the spare bedroom until I'm ready."

"Baby, I'll sleep anywhere as long as I'm closer to you."

"I might not be ready for a while."

"Take all the time you need. I won't be going anywhere."

"Come home, Max."

"I am. I love you."

I wiped my tears away. "I love you too." I hung up the phone and buried my head in the arm of my sofa and cried. Max was coming home.

Mike

Damn. Raquel was pregnant. Nothing was going in my favor. Raquel didn't hesitate to throw it in my face once the results came back, either. "I told you I was pregnant. I told you I wasn't lying. I hope you're saving up that money because this is your baby, and your ass is gonna pay!"

I swear it took all my strength not to go off and hit her right in her fucking mouth. Shit, maybe if other people hadn't been around I would have, just to shut her the hell up.

At least I didn't have to deal with her big mouth when I left her ass stranded at the hospital and headed home. I was so damn irritated, frustrated, and pissed off. I wanted to go to the bar and drink until I passed out, but just before turning the car in that direction, I remembered the twins and changed my mind. I went home where I lay in darkness with only the stereo to keep me company.

As real R&B music from 96.3 WHUR's Quiet Storm played, I stretched out on my couch and thought about Mya. I know I said it before, but I was truly miserable without her. I had everything I could have ever wanted in a woman and I fucked that up. Damn.

I hit the talk button on the phone I'd been holding. I didn't know why I was about to try, but I dialed Mya's cell phone number. As expected, she didn't answer. I thought about leaving a message but changed my mind. What good would it have really done, anyway? I hung up the phone and sighed as Faith Evans' song "Soon As I Get Home" played. This was one of Mya's favorite songs. Damn.

I thought about Max's brutally honest words when he said that I'd treated Mya like shit for a lot of years, and I'd never been the man she needed me to be. I broke her down emotionally and she reached out to the one person would listen—Ahmad. It sucks that he was right.

I slammed my hand down on the sofa in frustration. I drove my wife into the arms of another man. I realized for the first time that I was a fool for ever thinking that wouldn't have happened eventually. Even though I scoffed at Ahmad's advice to change my ways before I lost Mya, I think in the back of my mind I knew he was right. Maybe once or twice I actually entertained the notion of being a faithful husband, but every time I did, some fine ass would appear and any thoughts of change would go away.

I chuckled as Mint Condition's song "What Kind Of Man Would I Be?" played. As far as Mint Condition were concerned, I wasn't much of a man. I grabbed the phone and started to dial Mya's cell again, but hung up before I hit the last button. I put the phone down and listened to the song.

Normally, during a frustrating moment in my life, I'd call either Max or Ahmad to talk and get some advice, but I couldn't do that this time. Max had said all he needed to say, and calling Ahmad was out of the question. "Traitor," I said out loud. As I said that, though, more of my conversation with Max popped into my head.

It takes two, he'd said. *Mya didn't stop, but Ahmad did.*

Ahmad had stopped. Someone else wouldn't have. Damn it. I had no choice but to accept that fact, and that pissed me off even more, because the reality was that it took a hell of a man to turn down ass that was being handed to him on a silver platter.

Why, though? Because he loved Shay like Mya said, or because he was my boy and couldn't take it to that level? Why stop? He could have hit it and I would have never known. So why didn't he do it? And why was that question bothering the hell out of me? Was it because I didn't know, if put in his position, whether I would have been man enough to turn it down? Was I a hypocrite?

Think about the friendship, Max had said. Ahmad and I had a lot of history between us. *Think about the friendship.*

I grumbled out loud and sat upright on the couch, grabbing the phone again. "Fuck you, Ahmad," I whispered. Then I dialed his cell.

Ahmad

Ring.

I was sitting at the kitchen with a multitude of students' papers spread out in front of me when I heard my cell phone ring. I was supposed to be grading test papers and reading reports—basically trying to catch up on all of the shit I hadn't been doing because I'd been too stressed. Instead of doing that, I was sitting at the table, staring at the clock on the wall, watching the minute hand make its way around. That's how my nights had been since Shay took Nicole and went to stay with her parents. I'd called there a couple of times to try to convince her to come back home so we could deal with our issues, but she never came to the phone.

"I'm sorry, Ahmad, but she doesn't want to talk to you." I heard Shay's voice in the background, then my mother-in-law said to her, "Ahmad is his name, child. I will not call him that."

Click.

That's pretty much how most of the calls had gone. I spoke to her father once and he gave me some comforting words.

"Give her some time to cool down, Ahmad. She's pissed and she has a right to be, but I know my daughter. She loves you. She's a lot like her mother, so she's going to put you through some hell for a while, but trust me. She'll come around and come to the phone eventually. She may not say what you want to hear, but she'll come, and that will be the beginning of the road back to happiness."

"Sounds like you've been through this before," I said.

"Ahmad, I've been with my wife for forty years. I've been through it all. And trust me, it'll never end."

"I got you," I said.

"Just make sure, Ahmad, that when that road begins, you're ready to walk it no matter how bumpy, cracked, or hot it is."

Ring.

I looked over at my phone then at the time. It was almost one in the morning. The only person who'd be calling me would be Shay. Maybe this was the beginning of the road my father-in-law had been talking about. I got up and went to the counter where my phone sat and looked at the caller ID. My heart pumped faster when I saw not Shay's parents' number but Mike's. I hadn't spoken to him since I confessed what had happened between Mya and me. With the way he pounced on me, and the rage in his voice when he told me to leave, I didn't think I'd ever be speaking to him again. Maybe Max had spoken to him. I grabbed the phone. For a split second I thought about letting it go to voice mail, but then I hit the talk button. "Hello?"

Silence was my answer. I waited for several seconds before I said, "Mike, I know you're there, man." I didn't say anything else. I just stood still in the middle of the kitchen and listened to him breathe heavily on the other end.

Finally, after a few minutes, Mike said, "Why didn't you fuck Mya?"

I knitted my brow. His question caught me off guard. "What?"

"Why didn't you fuck her? You had the chance. She was down. I would have never known. Why didn't you fuck her?"

"I couldn't do that to Shay, and I couldn't do that to you."

"You throwing my name in there for good measure?" Mike asked.

I frowned and leaned against the counter. "Nah, man. You were—you are my boy. I couldn't do that to you, to our friendship. Shit, I'd done enough."

"Why'd you ever let things get that far, Ahmad? Why'd you ever cross that line?"

I sighed. I could hear the pain in his voice. "I never meant to, man. I was . . . I was just trying to be a good friend. I was lending an ear when it was needed. Nothing was ever supposed to happen between us. Our situations were so different, yet the same. I guess we both needed some attention, so we gravitated toward one another. Believe me, man, I never meant for anything, however small it was, to happen."

"Do you love her?"

I didn't answer his question right away. Did I love her? That was the million-dollar question, wasn't it? At one point I'd told Mya that I thought I was falling in love with her. I think at the time I might have meant it, but as my world with Shay began to collapse I saw that my feelings for Mya were not love, but rather loneliness and lust. The more Shay and I fell apart, the more I saw that she was truly the only woman I loved. My disconnection from her made me feel things for Mya that weren't real. "Yeah, I love her, man," I said finally. "I've known her since high school and I've always cared about her, but I'm not in love with her. I'm in love with my wife."

Neither one of us spoke for a few seconds after my answer. I didn't know what he thought of what I'd said, but I was being straightforward and honest. I loved Mya. I always had and always would, but I knew deep in my heart that she and I weren't meant for each other. Shay was my better half. She was my soul mate.

"You're a better man than me, Ahmad," Mike said in a low, subdued tone.

"What do you mean?"

"I would have fucked her," he said flatly.

I closed my eyes a fraction. "Huh?"

"If Shay had wanted to sleep with me . . . I would have done it, and you would have never known. I hate that you ever crossed the line like you did, but . . ." Mike paused while I digested what he was admitting to me. "You're a better man than me."

Click.

I stood unable to move, with the phone in my hand. He would have fucked her and I would have never known. Damn. That was a hell of a thing to admit. I moved back to the table and sat down, feeling a slight ease from the weight on my shoulders. Mike wouldn't have stopped. Maybe there was some hope for our friendship after all. Only time would tell.

Speaking of time, it would be another two weeks before Shay surprised me and finally gave in and took one of my phone calls. I'd gotten to see Nicole in between that time, but that was only because my in-laws made Shay let them bring her to me. "She's your daughter," they said when they came by. "Your issues with Shay shouldn't affect your relationship with Nicole." I'd thanked them and spent the day playing with her, enjoying her laughter. When Shay's parents came to take her back, I almost refused to give her to them. *She's my daughter*, I'd told myself. I had a right to be with her. Then I thought about everything I'd put Shay through, the things I'd done, and decided that I'd done enough. I kissed my little girl goodbye and told her I'd see her soon. Shay's parents assured me that I would, and that eased my sadness a little.

I know a lot of guys in my position might not have given Nicole up. A lot of them would have fought tooth and nail and practically given their life before letting their daughter go. Believe me, I wanted to. Like I said, I almost didn't let her go, but as I considered Shay's feelings, I also thought about the effect my actions would have had on Nicole. She had already gone from hearing arguing around her, to me being kicked out and absent from home to being taken out of her own familiar surroundings and once again without me as a presence. I knew she was only eight months old and wouldn't remember any of the details years later, but I still didn't want to expose her to any more drama. So, as tough as it was, I decided to wait and hope that this storm between Shay and me would die out. Finally, two weeks later, that happened. When the call came, I was so caught off guard by it, that it took me a couple of long seconds to respond.

"It's been a while," I finally said.

"I wasn't ready to talk to you before, especially after what you did."

I sighed. "Shay, for the thousandth time, you know I didn't mean for that to happen. It was an accident."

"You've never put your hands on me before," Shay said.

"Shay, it wasn't like that. And you were the one who'd lost control."

"No, *you* were the one who was out of control, Ahmad. You lost control a long time ago."

I was about to respond, but I closed my mouth, clenched my jaws and held my tongue. I wasn't in the mood to argue again, and I knew if I said what I wanted to say, the call would have ended with Shay hanging up on me. Tense silence took over. I sat and listened to Shay breathe and thought about my father-in-law's advice about staying on the road no matter how bad it would be. I took a few deep breaths to calm down and then opened my mouth. "Look, Shay . . . " I started, but I was never able to finish.

"I want us to go to counseling," Shay said, cutting me off.

That shocked me. "Huh?"

"Counseling, Ahmad. If we're going to try and work this out, then we have to go."

"Shay, we don't need counseling. Just bring Nicole and come home, and let's talk things over."

"Counseling or nothing, Ahmad."

"Shay..."

"Counseling or nothing," she said again.

I couldn't believe she was actually giving me an ultimatum. Was she really willing to let everything go if I didn't agree to it? "What do you mean by nothing?" I asked. I needed to know just how serious she was. How far she was willing to go with all of this. "Are you saying that if I don't say yes to counseling that we're through?"

"Ahmad, if you're serious about salvaging this marriage, then you will make the right decision."

"Which is what—to discuss our private issues with a total stranger?" I shook my head.

"I got the name of a highly recommended marriage counselor in Silver Spring. I called and made an appointment for us for tomorrow afternoon at three o'clock."

"Tomorrow? Don't you think you should have discussed this with me first?"

"I didn't think that saving our marriage needed any discussion."

"We can work this out on our own, Shay. We don't need to pay money to a stranger, for them to know our business."

"This is the only way, Ahmad."

"No it isn't," I countered.

"Yes, it is. Tomorrow at three. I'll be there. If I don't hear from you before then, I'll assume that you want me to contact a divorce lawyer."

"Shay," I tried again. "We can..." Before I could say anything else, the line went dead. I slammed the phone down and bowed my head. I couldn't believe it. A marriage counselor. There was nothing wrong with one for other people, but we didn't need one. All we needed to do was sit down and talk things out. That's all it was going to take. Communication. "Damn it," I whispered. Never in a million years did I think that I'd be in this position.

A counselor or my marriage. I know that anything said to a counselor is supposed to be confidential, and that counselors are prohibited from discussing a patient's issue with anyone else, but I was no fool. I didn't care how good the counselor was; they were human and imperfect, and that meant that at some point they discussed their patients with a colleague, a spouse, or a friend. This meant that the chances of your business going from the colleague, spouse, or friend's mouth, to someone else's ears were high. Once that happened—forget it—women were talking about you in the salons or at church, and the brothers were talking about your shit in the barbershops. That's exactly what I didn't want.

I cursed out loud again and slammed my hand down on the table. My temples throbbed from the frustration that, sooner or later, my drama with Shay could become the thing to gossip about. A counselor or my marriage. I thought about Shay and Nicole and how I missed having them in my life, and my shoulders dropped as I conceded defeat.

I picked up the phone and dialed Shay's parents' number. When her mother answered, I said, "Tell Shay I need the directions."

Mike

I had just finished lighting the last candle in the middle of the dining table when the doorbell rang. I put the lighter down and took a moment to look at the romantic picture I'd created. China dinnerware that hadn't been used in over a year was laid out, along with a sterling silverware set that had been given to Mya and me at our wedding but we'd used only once. In the middle of the table sat two candles, now lit and filling the air with the scent of vanilla—Mya's favorite. A bucket of ice with White Zinfandel chilling inside sat in the corner of the table, with two crystal wineglasses beside it. Adding to the ambience, Mya's favorite artist, Najee, was blowing his saxophone softly in the background.

Pleased with the scene, I turned off the light, leaving the dining area with only a candlelit glow. I walked to the front door. As I put my hand on the knob, I took a slow, nervous breath. I didn't know what was going to happen, but at least I'd gotten Mya to agree to come over and talk.

My conversation with Ahmad had really opened my eyes in a major way. I would have slept with Shay. There was no doubt about it. And my admitting that to Ahmad and, more importantly, myself, was what prompted me to keep calling Mya until, one day, she finally took my call.

I had expected the conversation to be a heated one, but to my surprise it was far from that. Mya and I made small talk for a few minutes, talking primarily about work and world events. We were both unhappy that U.S. soldiers were dying over in Iraq, and we weren't feeling Arnold Schwarzenegger's run for the governorship of

California. It was nothing personal for me. I just thought he should stick to acting. Anyway, after the small talk, Mya and I fell into an uneasy silence. The time had come for us to deal with the shit I'd caused.

"Mya, I don't want to lose you," I said, making the first move. She didn't respond to my comment and after a few seconds, I said, "Did you hear me?"

Another second or two passed before she responded. "I heard you." That was it.

"Well?"

"Well what?"

"What do you think about what I said?"

All the pleasantry gone in her voice, Mya snapped, "You should have thought of that a long time ago."

"Mya, baby . . . I've done a lot of thinking, a lot of soul searching since you left. I was a fool, Mya. I have been for a long time. Too long."

Mya huffed into the phone. "Mike, I really don't want to hear this. Damn it, I don't know why the hell I answered your call."

"Because you missed me?" I said hopefully.

"No, I don't."

"Yes you do," I countered. I knew I was right, because I could hear it beneath the anger. "I miss you too." She didn't respond. I sighed. "Listen, I know you're pissed off at me. Shit, you have every right to be."

"You're an asshole, Mike," she cut in.

"I know, Mya. I am." I think my admission caught her by surprise because she didn't say anything. I kept pressing. "Like I said, I've done a lot of thinking lately, and there's so much that I've come to realize."

"Oh, really?" Mya asked in a tone filled with angry skepticism.

"Yes, really. Listen, I want to see you."

"I don't think that would be a good idea."

"Please. I just want to talk. There's a lot that I want—no, need to say to you, but I want to do it face to face. Please come over tomorrow night."

"Mike . . . "

"Please, Mya. I just want to talk."

She was quiet for a little while, and that silence had me feeling uneasy about what her answer was going to be. I was about to beg her again when she said, "Okay. What time?"

I smiled and mouthed a silent *thank you*. "Is seven-thirty good?"

"Fine."

Click.

I hadn't expected her to hang up on me like that, and I'll be honest, it kind of bothered me. But I got over it quickly. She'd agreed to come over and that's what mattered.

I opened the door and smiled at Mya, who stood on the other side looking better than I ever remember. "You look great," I said. Mya stared at me but didn't say anything. I cleared my throat and stepped to the side for her to come in. It was obvious that this was going to be a humbling evening, an evening that hopefully wouldn't be over too quickly. I'd done everything that I could think of to try and weaken the barrier that I knew she was going to have up. I'd slaved in the kitchen and prepared her favorite meal—baked macaroni pie, baked chicken, green beans, and a garden fresh salad. I also got her favorite desert—cheesecake straight from the Cheesecake Factory at the harbor.

The food, the candlelight, the wine and the music wasn't all I'd done. I'd also dressed for the evening. While Mya was looking every bit the fine woman that she was in her strapless black gown and black pumps, I made sure to dress just the way she liked. I had on my white linen top and khaki pants straight from

Nordstrom's, and my sandy brown sandals courtesy of Kenneth Cole. Mya always loved the island look on me.

"I'm glad you came," I said, watching her ample behind switch as she walked past me. I got a whiff of her perfume and licked my lips. I was definitely looking forward to a long evening, but then the train wreck came.

Mya turned around and faced me. "I can't stay long," she said as I closed the door.

"You can't?"

"No. I have plans."

"Plans? With who?"

"That is none of your business."

"What do you mean it's none of my business? You're my damn wife." I knew the moment I said it that it was the wrong thing to say.

Mya gave me an *I know you didn't* look. "You know what? I'm leaving." She made a move to walk past me, but I put my hands up.

"Wait, Mya. Look, I didn't mean to come off like that, okay? It's just that you agreed to come over and talk. I even made dinner."

Mya folded her arms across her chest. "I did agree to come and talk, but I never said I'd stay here long."

"But I have a lot to say, and I'm sure you do too."

"No, I don't."

"You don't?"

"No. Like you, I've done a lot of thinking too, especially after I got off the phone with you. Before yesterday I swore that the next time I saw you I was going to call you every foul name in the book, just to let you know how much I hate you for the way you've treated me. You broke my heart by getting another woman pregnant.

"But after I hung up the phone yesterday, I did something I hadn't done in a long time. I laughed. You sounded so pathetic, Mike. Talking about your soul-searching and your sudden desire to not lose me. Pathetic."

I stood stunned and hurt by the callousness in her voice. This was not what I was expecting the night to be like. I knew there was probably going to be some yelling, but not this.

"You are a real piece of shit, Mike. Why I stayed with you so long, I don't know. I punished myself for no damn reason."

"Mya—"

"Shut up, Mike. Shut up and let me finish. I told you I made plans, and I intend on keeping them. The only reason I came over here is to tell you that I'm through with you. I'm not wasting my time with your bullshit anymore. I'm divorcing your ass and I wanted to tell you that to your face. I hope you and your dick are happy, because that's all you ever gave a damn about."

With nothing else to say, Mya stormed past me and opened the front door. Her words had bitten me so badly that I didn't even make an attempt to stop her.

"I'll be sending a mover for my things in a few days," she said just before walking through the door. The final nail in the coffin was when she said, "Goodbye, Mike. Goodbye and good riddance." She slammed the door behind her, leaving me alone with the Sade CD now playing her classic hit, "Smooth Operator."

I didn't know what to do. I couldn't believe that had just happened. I couldn't believe she'd come down on me like that. A divorce. Damn. If she hadn't been there to tell me that in person I don't think I would believed her. A divorce. Her eyes were so serious and unflinching. We were through. There was no denying it.

I locked the front door and went into the dining room to sit down at the table. *A divorce*, I thought again. I reached for a champagne glass and the White Zinfandel. As I filled my glass, my CD player switched from the Sade CD to one of my all-time favorite songs,

"True" by Spandau Ballet. I swallowed the glassful of wine in one gulp then refilled it. When I finished the second glass, I got up and went into the kitchen. I'd really gone all out with the dinner. It was smelling damn good.

I sighed and shrugged my shoulders. *I tried*, I thought. It was now time to move on. I threw the food away, ordered a pizza, and ate that by candlelight.

Mya

Leaving Mike was probably one of the hardest things I'd ever had to do. It had taken all of my strength to get in my car and drive away from the house. I wanted to turn around so many times and go back to him. Once or twice I almost did, but when I thought about doing it, tempted by how good he'd looked and smelled and how much effort he'd put into winning my heart, I remembered him talking about how much soul-searching he'd done. That kept my foot pressing down on the gas pedal. Soul searching? Why couldn't he have done that before? Why did he have to wait so long to tell me that he didn't want to lose me?

Bastard.

Leaving him was the best decision I'd made in a long time. Speaking of decisions, I regretted everything that happened between Ahmad and me. I'd be lying if I said that I didn't miss his smile, his eyes, his kiss, his touch—just his ability to make me feel safe. Because I did. I missed just being around him. I wanted to call him to see how he was doing. I wanted to tell him what decision I'd come to about Mike. I just wanted to talk to him, to hear him, but I couldn't.

In my loneliness and need to feel loved, I ruined a series of beautiful friendships—Ahmad and myself, which truly hurts, Ahmad and Mike, and also my friendship with Shay. I didn't know if Ahmad ever told her what happened between us, but I knew that Shay was no fool, and I was pretty certain that she didn't want to have anything to do with me. I know if I was in her position, I'd hate me too.

I never intentionally set out to disrespect her or her marriage. Things just happened. Even though it takes two, and some of the blame fell on Ahmad's shoulders, I still had to admit the fact that I should have never allowed anything to happen. My own husband was running around on me, so I knew what it felt like to have my heart broken. Once something happened, I should have been the one to stop things, not Ahmad. But I didn't, and now things would never be the same.

I didn't bother to wipe the tears away as they fell from my eyes. I parked my car in front of my cousin's house and shut off the engine. I didn't move for a long while. I just sat and let my tears cascade down my cheeks, falling from my chin to my dress. I'd been lying when I told Mike I had plans. I just said that and wore what I wore to help him understand what he'd lost. I wanted him to see me at my best when I told him goodbye. That was the image I wanted stuck in his mind. For Mike, everything was tits and ass. When I walked out of that house, I stuck my chest out and switched my ass so hard that I know in the back of his shallow mind he was asking himself how he could have let that fine pussy get away. It sounds crass to say that, but I realized that all I ever truly was to him was just some pussy.

When my eyes could cry no more, I opened the door and got out of the car. Even though my cousin said I didn't have to move, I'd be moving from her house to my own apartment in a couple of days. I just needed to be alone in my own space, to do my own thing. Besides, even though she wouldn't admit it, I knew I was cramping her style. I walked to the front door and slid the key in the lock. I looked up at the night sky and stared at the stars glittering in the darkness. When I picked the brightest one, I closed my eyes and made a wish. Then I stepped inside to move on.

Six Months Later

Shay

Six months had passed since Ahmad and I started going to counseling, and I was happy to say that although things weren't perfect, they were getting better—slowly. I have to admit I was skeptical about the counseling helping us get past our issues. I only suggested it to Ahmad because my mother insisted I give it a try. I never knew it, but my parents had gone to a marriage counselor years ago after my father had an affair. My father slept with his secretary, and it devastated my mother. So much so that she suffered severe bouts of depression for months. I never knew that my parents had been having problems of any kind because the one thing they did, which is something that Ahmad and I are now making a conscious effort to do with Nicole, was to never argue in front of me.

I went through life thinking that my parents never had anything more than a disagreement here, a disagreement there, never anything too serious. It was almost as though they had a perfect marriage because they never raised their voices at each other, and they never called each other out of their names. During that entire time they had been on the verge of divorce, my father slept on the floor in the bedroom. They kept their issues behind closed doors and put up a façade that had everybody fooled.

How my mother dealt with raising me and minding the home while keeping a smile on my face, I don't know. I couldn't stand to be around Ahmad, and all he'd done was kiss Mya. He admitted that during one of the counseling sessions. One of the hardest things I'd ever had to do was sit silent while he confessed what happened and why. He had been lonely and feeling neglected, and Mya was there when I hadn't been.

My intent was to go off on him, but when he finished talking I couldn't speak. When the counselor asked me to describe how I was feeling, I just shook my head, walked out with tears running down my face, got in my mother's car, drove back to my parents' house and cried the rest of the night while my mother took care of Nicole. Ahmad called me, but I didn't take the call. I just didn't want to talk to him. He kissed her, and as badly as I wanted to hate him, I knew that I couldn't because I was partly to blame. I didn't speak to Ahmad until our next session with the counselor.

Although it was hard, I explained how much it hurt me to know what Ahmad had done, and then I did something even harder and explained why I had pushed him away for as long as I had. I told him and the counselor all about my insecurities with my weight gain, how I couldn't stand the sight of myself, and because of that, I didn't think Ahmad could stand the sight of me either. I also talked about my fear of getting pregnant again. Although I love my daughter with all my heart, the discomfort of pregnancy and the pain of delivery left such a bitter pill in my mouth that I just didn't want Ahmad's dick anywhere near me.

The counselor suggested that I could have been suffering from a form of post-partum depression, which not only affected my self-esteem, but also my desire to have sex. He said there were medications I could take for it that would help to keep my spirits high and help my libido, but I hate popping pills, so I decided to take charge and take matters into my own hands. Although I was learning to accept my post-pregnancy body, I knew I would truly feel better once I was in better shape.

The first thing I did was start a diet and exercise regiment. I went back to my girl Regina, who used to do my hair before I became pregnant, and had my shoulder-length damaged hair cut and styled like Toni Braxton when she first came out on the scene. With my new hairstyle and the slow but steady pounds I was dropping, my self-esteem increased dramatically, and so did the attention from men. That was just fine with me. Oh, I didn't want any of them, but a sistah still likes to know she's wanted.

Getting everything out into the open had been a very painful but necessary eye-opener for me. I realized that divorcing Ahmad would have truly been a mistake because aside from the issues we'd discussed, we were really a damn good couple. We had our differences just like everyone else, but other than that, our union was blessed.

I took my mother out to dinner to thank her for her insistence on the marriage counselor. She'd helped save my marriage. My mother smiled and told me to do the same for Nicole when her time came. I nodded at what she was telling me: Men will be men. As women, all we can do is love them and demand respect.

After the dinner with my mother, I decided to move back home. Ahmad couldn't stop smiling when I showed up at the front door. Because I wasn't ready, I asked him to sleep in the living room for a while. We were back under the same roof, but I still had to work out the trust issues. I didn't think he'd ever hurt me like that again, but you never know. Surprisingly, he just said yes and then enveloped Nicole and me in his arms.

So, that's how we'd been living—rebuilding together but sleeping apart. At some point that was going to have to change. I mean let's face it, the sex had been overdue, but we couldn't move to the next step until I was ready. I didn't know when that would be until I woke up wet and horny one morning. Before I could enjoy the feel of Ahmad inside me, though, there was one thing I needed to do.

"We need to talk. In person."

There was silence at first, and then, after a long sigh, I heard, "Where?"

"I'm in the mood for Mexican," I said. "Meet me at Don Pablo's in an hour."

She was silent again, then finally answered, "Okay."

An hour later I was sitting in a booth in Don Pablo's with my hands folded in front of me on the table, staring at Mya, who was having a hard time looking me in the eye.

I didn't say anything to her for a long time. I just glared at her and struggled to keep my hands from flying off the table to reach out for her neck. Believe me, I wanted to choke the hell out of that bitch. Our waitress came and dropped off a couple of glasses of water and was about to ask us if we wanted to order, but I cut my eyes at her. Seconds later, she was gone, giving Mya and me the privacy she was smart enough to know we needed.

I took a sip of water and cleared my throat. "So," I said, putting the glass down. "Do you want to go first, or should I?"

Mya looked at me then quickly looked away and shrugged. "Doesn't matter," she said.

Pitiful, I thought. *Bitch was woman enough to move in on my husband, but didn't have the guts to speak.* I nodded. "You know I want to kick your ass, don't you?" I asked bluntly. She didn't say anything. "Look at me, Mya," I demanded. I kept my voice low, but there was enough bite for her to know that I wasn't playing with her.

When she looked up, I continued.

"The only reason I haven't reached across this table and laid into you is because I'm a grown ass woman, which is more than I can say for your sorry ass."

Mya sighed, but didn't dare pull her eyes away from mine. "Shay, look—"

"Oh hell no!" I said, my voice louder than before. "Bitch, I gave you a chance to speak and you didn't want it, so just sit there and listen carefully to everything that I have to say. I want to beat your ass so bad my hands are itching. We were friends, Mya. I let you in my home. How dare you disrespect me like that? Tramp!"

I paused and bore into her with my eyes. I know people around us had heard me because I could feel their stares on us, but I didn't care.

"Did you really think you could steal my husband? You ain't shit but a skinny bitch with perky breasts, Mya. Now, you may have gotten some of Ahmad's attention with that skinny ass and your damsel in distress act, but did you really think he saw anything more than that in you?" I sucked my teeth. "Please. You're a girl, Mya, an immature-ass girl who tried to seduce her husband's best friend. That's what girls do. A woman doesn't do shit like that. Ahmad may be a fool, but he's not stupid. He knows the difference between a girl and a woman, and as much as you tried to cloud his mind with your calls and your tears and your promises to be a better woman for him—"

Mya's eyes grew wide as I said that. I raised an eyebrow and curled my lips. "Oh yes, he told me. He told me everything you said and everything that happened between you two. *Everything*. You see, he loves me, and despite everything you tried, he knew he had a woman at home. A real woman who truly cares about him."

"I do care about him," Mya said.

I twisted my mouth into a sneer. "Oh, please. If you gave a damn about Ahmad, you would have never tried to get him in bed. Why, Mya? Why did you disrespect me when I did nothing but be your friend? Why did you disrespect your friendship with Ahmad?"

With tears falling from her eyes, Mya said, "I didn't mean . . . I never meant to disrespect you. I never meant for anything to happen between Ahmad and me. I just . . . I just . . . ."

"You just what?"

Mya shook her head and wiped tears away with the back of her hand. "Forget it, Shay. You wouldn't understand. You don't know what it was like for me. You don't know what it was like to live with a man like Mike. You have no idea what it was like to be disrespected day in and day out."

"You're damn right I don't!" I yelled. "And you know what? I never would have, because I would have never put up with a trifling ass dog like Mike. Never. I'm a woman, Mya, a woman who demands respect. And that just proves my point that you are a girl, because only a girl would allow a man to run around on her whenever the hell he wanted to while she stayed at home waiting for him."

As I said that, someone yelled out, "I know that's right" from the crowd of diners, who'd all become quiet to listen in. I kept my eyes fixed on Mya while she sobbed and choked on her tears. I shook my head and frowned. If I hadn't been so pissed I might have passed her a napkin to wipe her tears away, but I was more than pissed. I kept my ass still and let her cry.

The restaurant manager came by the table to ask if everything was okay, and when I told him yes, he suggested as politely as he could that Mya and I take our discussion outside. I shook my head and grabbed my purse. "No need for that," I said, my eyes on Mya. "Our discussion is over." I stood up and looked down at her. For a brief moment, my anger faded and allowed a feeling of pity to come over me. Although she'd been wrong for doing what she did, no woman deserved to be treated the way Mike had treated her. Despite her mistakes, Mya was essentially a good woman. But she should have never fucked with my man.

"Mya, I was civil and grown today, but if you try to contact Ahmad in any way, shape or form, I promise the next time we meet, I will more than make up for the beat down I'd love to give you right now." Nothing else needed to be said. I smiled at the manager, looked down at Mya one last time, then walked out of the restaurant. Before the doors closed behind me, I think I heard clapping.

Satisfied that I'd gotten all of the monkeys off of my back, I went home to my husband and daughter. That night, when Nicole fell asleep, I made love to my husband.

Trina

I gently placed Max, Jr. in his bassinet, covered him, kissed his forehead, and touched his soft cheek. My boy. I smiled as I watched him sleeping soundlessly. He was so beautiful, so precious and tiny. It was almost unbelievable that delivering him had been so hard. I almost passed out from the pain. No matter how hard I pushed, Max Jr. refused to come out. He was so insistent about staying in the womb that the doctor had to push down on my belly to get him to come down. But like his father in the hospital, Max, Jr. was a fighter.

Like I said, I almost passed out from the exhaustion and strain from bearing down. More than a couple of times, against my will, my eyes closed and everyone and everything around me started to disappear. Thankfully, Max, who'd been at my side, wiping my forehead with a damp cloth, had been able to keep me from slipping into deep slumber. Finally, after twelve hours of labor and after the doctor had to use a suction to pull him out, Max, Jr. was born.

I kissed him on his forehead and smiled again and then stood and stared down at Max, who was asleep in the bed. Being shot and beaten close to death had been a tragic and frightening experience, but it was one that made him a changed man. Max was not the man I knew before all of the shit with Sharon happened. That Max was an underachieving, lazy, non-romantic, insensitive ass. I made a lot of excuses for him. Especially to my sister, who'd told me time and time again to leave his ass and find a real man. Well, thanks to Sharon, I did leave his ass, and I did find a real man. The Max who came back home was just that. He was as attentive as he used to be when we first started dating. For the first time, my needs, both during and after the pregnancy, came before his.

Like I said, everything about him had changed, even his appearance. The cornrows he used to wear were gone, and he now sported a low, close to bald fade. He'd switched from the baggy, young boy clothing to a more classic style. "I'm a grown-up," had been his response when I commented about his change in style one night. "It's time for me to look like one, and act like one too."

And that he did.

Max was determined to become a success in the music industry. So much so that he changed the direction of all of the artists he had, and really pushed towards getting them signed. Eventually, his determination and vision paid off. He got not one, but two acts signed to major labels, and he was now working with a third group who were destined to become the next NSYNC. Yeah, they were white, but the boys could blow for real.

I blew my husband a kiss and left the room. I was exhausted. Max, Jr. was an angel, but he was also definitely a handful. In between changing his diapers, breastfeeding him every two hours and making sure Max and I weren't malnourished, I barely had time to nap. Even though Max helped as much as he could, sweet dreams for myself didn't come too often. I planned to take advantage of his sleeping, and get some myself, but before I could, I had something to do.

I sat down in the living room with the phone in my hand and took a deep breath. This was not going to be an easy call. After a few seconds of meditated silence, I was ready. I hit the talk button, pressed *67 to block my call, then dialed.

"Who this?"

"It's Trina," I said, not recognizing the voice on the other end.

"Trina? Who—oh, hold on a minute." I heard the person announce my presence on the phone. Seconds later Sharon picked up the phone. "Trina? Where the hell are you? Don't you know I been tryin' to see my grandson?"

My hands started to shake with anger. My sister told me Sharon had been trying to get a hold of me. Since Max and I had reconciled, we'd moved and gotten a new phone number. She also told me that my brother had been shot and killed in a drug deal done wrong. It's sad to say, but I never shed a tear over his death.

"Sharon," I said softly, "the only reason I'm calling you is to tell you to stop wasting your time trying to contact me."

"What the fuck is that supposed to mean?" Sharon barked out. "I want to see my grandson."

I gritted my teeth. I had been trying to stay above her level and remain civilized, but it was impossible. I had too much anger built up inside. "Your grandson? Bitch, you know damn well you don't really give a shit about him. All you want is to parade him around to your ghetto friends. I want you to listen and listen good, Sharon. You will never, *ever* see my son. As long as I'm living and breathing, he will not even know your trifling ass exists. I hope you're not going around telling people you have a grandson because if you are, you need to go and change that quick. He is as dead to you as your trifling ass son."

I paused to let my bitter words sink in. Surprisingly, Sharon didn't respond. While Max and I had been apart, I thought long and hard about how to get Sharon back for all she'd done. Had I not been pregnant, I would have beaten her ass. I spent days just thinking of a way to get my revenge on her, but I was never able to come up with anything. Other than sex and getting drunk and high, there was nothing Sharon seemed to care about. But when my sister called and told me about Sharon's excitement and effort to find me after Max, Jr. had been born, I realized right then and there how I could hurt her for all she'd done.

"Are you listening to me, bitch?" I continued. "You have no grandchild."

"Trina," Sharon said, trying to mask a voice filled with pain. "Don't be like that. That's my grandson. He's my blood."

I couldn't help but laugh at her pitiful words. "Bitch, I hate your ass. I swear if I could, I'd drip my body and my son's body dry to get rid of all of this blood we have inside of us. I'd replace it with someone else's so that you could never say that again. You are a poor excuse for a woman, a mother, and a human being. Go to hell, Sharon. That's where your dirty ass belongs."

I pulled the phone away to hang up, but before I did, there was one last thing I had to say. I put it back to my ear and with a wicked smile, said, "Oh, and thank you for almost having Max killed. He's a better man, and a better fuck than ever before. Bitch."

I hung up the phone and exhaled. Now I could go and get some sleep. And I was serious about Max. He was laying it down in the bedroom better than ever. Forget sleep, I thought, getting up from the couch. I was going to bed to get some.

Epilogue—Ahmad

Life is a trip.

A year ago, life for Mike, Max and me was completely different. Mike was married to Mya and at the same time tapping whatever ass came his way, Max was sexing his ghetto-ass mother-in-law, and I was living like a born-again virgin against my will. And then the bottom fell out from all of us. Now here we were, our lives and friendships completely turned around.

We were at Clyde's in Columbia, chilling at the bar, not really saying much of anything. With our drinks in hand, we stared aimlessly up at the television hanging in the corner, watching ESPN highlights that we didn't really give a damn about. It was weird, the three of us being there together. We hadn't hung out since our lives did 180-degree turns.

Max and I had spoken occasionally, updating each other on what had been going on. That didn't happen too often, though, because he and Trina had their hands full with Max, Jr. Having been through the infant stage with Nicole, I knew that the only thing he and Trina would want to do when they had down time was sit and relax. I usually just waited for him to call me.

I was really happy and proud of the changes Max had made in his life. Family and career had finally become number one for him, and we now had more in common than ever before.

As for his relationship with Mike, he'd told me that with his change in attitude and lifestyle, their friendship had changed dramatically. After having lost Mya and fathering a child to a woman that he absolutely couldn't stand, Mike hadn't changed a bit. According to Max, he was still up to his old tricks. That didn't surprise me at all. He might be considered strong by most standards, but when it came to women, he'd always been weak. I guess the old saying truly applies to him—once a dog, always a dog.

This was the first time Mike and I were anywhere together since our one-sided fight, and I hadn't spoken to him since he called me and admitted that I was a better man than he was. I didn't see it that way, though. I may not have slept with Mya, but my reason for not doing so was more out of respect and love for Shay than it was for Mike. Had I been single, things would have been different, and therefore I would have been no better than Mike.

Every now and then Mike and I exchanged glances, but we didn't speak. Not to each other, anyway.

"Damn, did you see the hit that he laid on that guy?" Max said, commenting on a sports highlight.

I nodded and took a sip of my usual bitch drink, an Amaretto Sour. "Yeah. That was pretty massive."

Mike didn't say anything.

We got quiet again. After a few minutes, out of nowhere, Mike slammed his beer down and said, "Max, I don't know why I gave in to you and agreed to come here. This is a waste of my time. I'm outta here." He got up to leave, but Max grabbed his arm.

"Hold up, man. Don't leave."

Mike pulled his arm away and fixed his eyes on me. "I don't want to be here, Max."

I sighed. I knew coming was going to be a bad idea. I should have said no when I had the chance. "Look, why don't I just leave?" I got up from my stool.

"Yeah, why don't you do that?" Mike agreed.

"Why don't you chill the hell out, Mike?" I snapped. "I'm really tired of you and your fucking victim act."

"Bitch, the only victim here's gonna be your ass."

"Bring it, Mike," I said, clenching my fists at my sides. If things were gonna come to blows between us, this time I was gonna make sure and get my hits in.

Before things could get to that, Max stood between us and held us back. "Fellas, fellas. Come on, let's not do this."

"Fuck that," Mike said, trying to get past him. "I wanna see if that nigga will still talk shit after his mouth is busted."

"And what's that gonna do, Mike? Show that you can kick his ass?"

"Hell yeah," Mike said, his eyes on me.

I flared my nostrils. "I wasn't ready for you before, Mike, but I am now. Kicking my ass ain't gonna be so easy."

"Let's go then!" Mike tried again to barrel past Max, but Max held fast.

"Ahmad, nigga, will you shut the fuck up and go wait outside?" Max looked at me with serious eyes. Obviously, this reunion hadn't been going the way he'd planned.

I looked at Mike then at Max again, then opened my fists and with a frown, walked outside. As I walked out, the manager was asking Max if there was a problem. I sighed as the doors closed behind me. Yeah, there was a big problem.

I'd been sitting on the bench outside the restaurant for almost forty-five minutes. I really don't know why the hell I stayed that long. Maybe somewhere in the subconscious part of my mind I stayed because I really wanted to talk to Mike again and see if saving our friendship was going to be a possibility. Or maybe I really just wanted a crack at kicking his ass. I don't know. Whatever my reason, I stayed until Mike walked out of Clyde's—without Max—and looked over at me. I stood up quickly and balled my fists as he came toward me.

"I didn't come to fight," he said, stopping just two feet in front of me.

I watched him skeptically and then looked down at his hands. They were unclenched. "What'd you come out here for then? And where's Max?"

Mike sighed and looked to the restaurant. I looked too and saw Max through the glass, sitting by the bar, staring at us. "I came to talk, man," Mike said, facing me again.

"Talk, huh?" My hands were still balled.

"Yeah, man. Talk."

I closed my eyes a bit, and passed my tongue over the front of my top teeth. "Why the change? I thought you wanted to kick my ass."

Mike clenched his fists momentarily and then unclenched them. "I do."

"So, why the change?"

Mike turned and looked out at the man-made Columbia lake. "Because it would be wrong," he said solemnly.

I looked at him but didn't say anything. I turned toward the lake.

"It's tough for me to stand here next to you and not beat you down, Ahmad," Mike said evenly. I knew he had more to say, so I didn't respond. "I mean, it's taking everything for me not to do that." He turned and faced me. "Shit, man, we were boys. I know I wasn't always the best to Mya, but how could you do me like that?"

I shrugged. "I don't know, Mike. Believe me, if I could take back everything that happened, I'd do it in a heartbeat. I hate that I damaged our friendship, our bond, the way I did."

Silence overtook the conversation again. Mike finally said, "Do you remember what I said to you on the phone the last time we spoke?"

I nodded. "Yeah."

"What do you think of that?"

I thought about his question for a moment and then said, "I guess neither one of us is perfect."

Mike nodded. "I guess not."

"So, what's next, man?"

Mike sighed. "I don't know. You cut me deep, Ahmad. Real deep. But I would have cut you deeper."

"But you didn't," I said.

"No, I didn't. But you stopped."

"And you wouldn't have," I said.

We stood in silence, both accepting each other's faults along with our own. I didn't know how long it was gonna take, but I think we both knew that our friendship would survive.

"Have you spoken to Mya?" Mike asked.

I shook my head. "No. Not since I left her at the hotel."

"She should have divorced me a long time ago, you know?"

"I know."

Mike chuckled. "I love pussy, man."

I looked at him and shook my head as I laughed. "You're funny, man."

Mike laughed along with me. "I don't think I'll ever change."

"No chance in hell," I said. We both exploded with laughter.

"Hey, what's so funny?"

We turned to see Max walking toward us.

"You, you pigeon-toed bastard," Mike said.

I looked at Max's walk and laughed even louder. "He's right."

"Fuck both of you," Max said, smiling. The three of us laughed together.

"So, are we cool?" Max asked, his face getting serious.

Mike and I looked at each other. That was the million-dollar question, wasn't it?

I put out my hand and waited for the answer.

Mike stared at me for a few seconds then nodded. He took my hand. "We're cool."

"Aw'ight then," Max said, clapping us on our backs. "Now, can we please get back inside and get our grub on?"

We all laughed and then headed to the doors. Before walking inside, I tapped Mike on his shoulder. "Mike, hold up a sec."

He stopped walking and turned around. "'Sup?"

"Before we go in, I gotta ask you something."

"Shoot."

"If we would have fought, how do you know you would have kicked my ass?"

Mike sucked his teeth. "Nigga, please. You remember what happened last time, don't you?"

"Man, you caught me off guard."

"Okay. I'll give you that," Mike said. "You wanna settle that before we go in?"

I thought about it for a moment. "I would, but I'm hungry."

"Whatever, man."

We laughed and stepped back inside Clyde's, our friendship intact and probably stronger than before.

Reading Group Questions

1) Mike and Mya had been together since high school. Why do you think they lasted as long as they did?

2) What was it about Sharon that made Max cheat on Trina? What would have been your reaction to finding out that your husband was involved intimately with your mother?

3) Shay dealt with deep and very serious body image issues that took their toll on her marriage. Do you feel these issues pushed Ahmad into Mya's arms, or would it have eventually happened anyway?

4) Do you think Mya and Ahmad were truly falling in love with one another?

5) Ahmad crossed the line of friendship by being involved with Mya. Do you feel that Mike was justified for his anger and resentment toward Ahmad, or had he gotten his just desserts?

6) Why do you think Sharon went after Max? Did she truly hate her daughter? If so, why?

7) If put in Mya's or Ahmad's position, would you have stopped?

8) Ahmad and Mike's friendship survived the strain of betrayal. Why? Put in a similar position, would your friendship have survived?

9) Who was the strongest character and who was the weakest? Why?

10) Did Max deserve a second chance with Trina after what he'd done?

11) Did Mike ever truly love Mya?

12) What kind of father do you think Mike will be? Is it possible for a man to be a dog like Mike and still be a good father?

13) The book examines the themes of friendship and marriage, and sometimes being faithful to one makes it hard to be faithful to the other. What's more important, being faithful to your spouse or faithful to your friends?

14) Ahmad never admitted to doing anything more than kissing Mya. Why do you think he chose to stop his confession there? Would Shay have had an even harder time forgiving him if she knew how close he had really come to sleeping with Mya? What are the boundaries for cheating? Is everything forgivable as long as there is no penetration?

The following is sample chapter of
Dwayne S. Joseph's up coming novel,
Never Say Never.

Reesa

"That's it. I'm through with his ass!"

I threw the covers off of me, got out of bed and went to the living room and turned on the TV. I was pissed, and sleep wasn't an option. I banged on my remote control as I switched channels, not really looking for anything to watch, just switching to release my anger and frustration. I meant what I yelled a couple of minutes before. I was through with his ass. Simon. My man, or maybe I should say my headache for the past two years. He was the reason I was losing sleep—yet again.

I cursed out loud and threw the remote over to the couch across from me, leaving the channel on an infomercial for some butt and thigh machine that my fat ass would never use. Okay, it wasn't fat. Just healthy. Damn it, why couldn't Simon just come home like a good boyfriend was supposed to? It was damn near four in the morning! I knew he was out doing his thing, but damn, did it have to be at this time of the night? I mean shit, couldn't he wheel and deal during the daytime? Of course he couldn't. I don't even know why I was asking.

I squeezed my eyes shut tightly and tugged on my braids. The stress I was going through was my own fault. I knew what I was getting into when I first got together with Simon. He was one of those good-looking brothers with a body straight out of *Muscle and Fitness* magazine, who hadn't earned an honest day's pay in his life. You know the type of man I'm talking about, ladies. Simon had wheeled and dealed, schemed, and hustled any and every way he could to put cash in his pocket. He'd been a car dealer, drug dealer, pimp, male escort, thug for hire, bouncer, chef, stick-up kid—the list goes on and on. Basically, you name it, he'd done it. I could tell by the way he strolled the first night we'd met that he didn't live nine to five like the rest of us.

Usually, I wouldn't have given a brother like Simon the time of day. I mean, let's face it; he was a playboy and I was a future financial planner. But ladies, I won't lie to you. I hadn't had an orgasm in four months, so when Simon stepped to me that night, it was damn hard to ignore his LL-like lips, his reach-out-and-squeeze-me pecs, and his abundance in the crotch area. Like I said, I knew the minute he approached me that he wasn't the type of man I'd marry, but I had drinks in my system and I was horny. Before I could even stop myself, Simon and I were leaving the club and heading back to my apartment to get our multiple-orgasmic freak on. It was only supposed to be a one-time sexual romp with Simon. I mean, come on; we were like oil and water. We just didn't mix.

Until we hit my bed.

I swear I have never had a man work me over the way Simon worked me. Brother had me singing opera beneath my sheets. He obviously must have been just as impressed with me, because he called me up the next night looking for more. Of course I obliged. Night after night, Simon and I would hook up and work off our calories. Normally, after we were done freaking Simon would go home, but one night after we did our do, he held me in his arms and didn't leave. We'd been together ever since.

I wish I could say that my relationship with Simon had been nothing but roses, but obviously, since I was up at four a.m., pissed and ready to kick his ass out for the umpteenth time, it hadn't. Simon had brought so much drama into my world it was ridiculous. If I wasn't dealing with his son's mother, Cecilia, who couldn't stand me, then I was dealing with the stack of bills that were all in my name. The phone, the credit cards, *his* cell phone, the car payment, and the rent—all under Reesa Sheree Nichols. Since I was the only one with a real job and credit to worry about, I was the one who had to worry about making sure the bills got paid. Oh, don't get me wrong, Simon helped with the bills when he could, but you probably already know that didn't happen too often.

"Damn it, I'm through with his ass," I said again.

How many times had I said that? Too many. But this time I meant it. I deserved better. I deserved more. I'm a woman—an attractive, caring, giving, successful, independent, intelligent black woman who should have a man of equal stature to lie next to at night. But damn it, why did I have to be thirty-three years old? You're probably wondering what's wrong with being thirty-three years old. Well, I can tell you the answer to that with one word. Children. See, I'd always planned to have about three kids by this age because I wanted to be like my mother: a young, fit, forty-something-year-old woman with grown-ass kids. But instead of having kids in my twenties like I wanted, I went from one unsatisfying relationship to the next, and then for about three years I hit a drought and couldn't find a good man to save my life.

Now here I was at thirty-three with no little rugrats to call my own, and my cut-off age of thirty-five fast approaching. Yes, I said cut-off. I always said that I wouldn't have kids past my mid-thirties, and I intended to stick to that. I wasn't like these new-age women who want to have kids in their forties and fifties. Oh, nooo. Not me. Not my body. Thirty-five or it's none at all.

And there lay my problem.

Simon was far from being any kind of real man, but he was still a man with working sperm, and I won't lie . . . For all of his faults, I'll admit, I did have feelings for him. But here was the problem: If I left him, what the hell was I going to do? Start over? Spend another who knows how many days, months or years searching for Mr. Right? And what's to say that I'd find Mr. Right anyway? Shit, with each day that went by, my hips got wider, the pouch below my belly got larger, and my breasts got saggier. In other words, the odds of a man finding me attractive and wanting to settle down with me were decreasing, so for all of my talk about Simon, wasn't he the best chance I had for reaching my goal by thirty-five? Did I really want to take the chance of being alone and lonely? I don't think so.

I grabbed the remote control and shut off the television. Standing still in the darkness, I said to myself, "I'm through with his ass." Then I went back to bed.